REGINA SHEN: RESILIENCE

LANCE ERLICK

Finlee Augare Books (Chicago)

This is a work of fiction. All of the characters, organizations, and events portrayed herein are either products of the author's imagination or are used fictitiously, and any similarities to actual persons, organizations, or events are entirely coincidental. Also, though locations used in this work exist, for dramatic effect details have been altered. Accordingly, they should be considered fictitious.

Edited by Leah Carson and Laurie Laliberte
Cover Design by Donna Harriman Murillo

Finlee Augare Books, Chicago, IL
ISBN: 978-0-9914643-5-7 (print)
ISBN: 978-0-9914643-6-4 (e-book)
Library of Congress Control Number: 2015903554

Printed in the United States of America

To those who find themselves in impossible situations

ONE

Richmond Swamps, June ACM 296

A gray Department of Antiquities patrol boat motored across our path. I paddled into a cattail-covered cove, kept a wary eye for alligators, and waited for the gray-uniformed agents to leave. In the morning heat, sweat trickled down my neck and soaked my green canvas top, causing me to itch. I ignored the irritation and swarms of black flies.

"Regina, we should go home," Colleen whispered from the front of my log-boat.

"We'll be fine, sis," I said to keep her calm. "School is safe." I hoped.

While there was ebb and flow to life in the swamps, three patrol sightings so far this week were unusual, and it was only Thursday. Something was up.

The Antiquities boat finally headed up the channel. We crossed and tied the mooring rope to reeds below our school. I made sure the log-boat was secure and hidden from view, in case the patrol returned. Then I led Colleen up the rocky incline beside stilts that kept the wood-frame buildings above water.

Colleen and I hurried to our respective classes. There was no one in the clearing between the buildings, on the stairs, or at the tiny balconies by classroom entrances. I ran up the steps, pushed open the rickety wood door, and dropped my wet, muddy boots beside others on a stone slab inside.

School was the best part of my day. I didn't have to watch my twelve-year-old sister, since she was secure in her own classroom. Mo-Mere, our nickname for our teacher, Marisa Seville, brought the dozen girls in her class warm soup of beans, turtle, and spuds.

My favorite part: she let me touch real books—brittle paper ones, yellowed, edges worn, with stories that tickled my mind, stories the World Federation had purged from the Mesh-cloud. Mo-Mere's books made the six-days-a-week slog through miles of swamp in a hollowed-out log worthwhile.

"Regina," Mo-Mere placed her weathered face next to mine and whispered in a warm voice with a tough edge. "You might be my best student, but that doesn't excuse tardiness." She pinched my cheeks to let me know she meant both comments.

She was too kind. Though I was fifteen, doing seventeen-year-old work, I took too much of Mo-Mere's time. She was like a second mom to me. In fact, the other girls gossiped that she was my donor mother, providing half her DNA to Mom to conceive me in the local fertility clinic. Mom refused to talk to me of such matters.

Mo-Mere nudged me toward the four rows of four small tables facing the front of the room. "Take your seat. I was telling the class I received a report of a Category-5 hurricane bearing down on us tomorrow night."

I shrugged. This would be the second big storm of the year.

A new student sat in the first row, in front of Mo-Mere's rough-cut maple desk. I took the vacant seat next to her, where no one else wanted to sit, so I could learn without all the distractions of the older girls whispering. Mostly they gossiped about how I had a little girl's body. My hips hadn't filled out, and I refused to stuff my bra like two girls did.

We all wore the same faded green canvas trousers and pullovers. Raw canvas came in one color, dull green, and most of us Marginals had nothing to barter for expensive dyes. Mo-Mere said if I studied hard, she might get me into the university on the other side of the Great Barrier Wall, in the Federation proper. "You could become a Professional and have a real future."

Yet life outside the Richmond Swamps seemed unimaginable. This was the only world I knew, unless you counted the literary world of banned books by ancients such as Charles Dickens, Isaac Asimov, and David Brin.

Compared to the river and swamp channels, the classroom felt small, boxy, and musty, though I didn't mind if it meant I could read.

"Let's pray to the Blessed Mary," Mo-Mere said, as part of our Federation-required morning ritual.

Tapping my foot, I mumbled along with the other students, paying no attention to words as distant as the world beyond the Great Wall, a massive concrete structure that separated us from the Federation. They accepted only one religion, though it seemed to me they'd picked the wrong one: devotion to Mary Devereaux and the other Grand Old Dames.

Our teacher pointed a gnarled wooden stick at the board on the right side of the room. "Let's recite our Twelve Commandments."

I mouthed by rote, recalling phrases with what Mo-Mere called my photographic memory. "Thou shalt not kill," "Thou shalt not steal," "Thou shalt not leave the Marginal swamps without Federation permission." Blah, blah, blah.

"Everyone should live as a Marginal swamp rat for a year," Mo-Mere said, "before complaining about their life." She made this sound like a badge of honor, a way to build character and help us survive in our drenched world. She'd said this on my first week and repeated it whenever a new student arrived.

"Who can tell Beth how the Community Movement and Federation began?" Mo-Mere's intense eyes looked from student to student. When no one volunteered, her sharp eyes drilled into me until I nodded.

She expected me to give the official answer for the new student, another chance to stand out so the older girls could ridicule me. It didn't matter. They wouldn't be friends with the "little girl" no matter what I did.

While I longed to be out, making preparations for the storm, my heart raced to recall official histories. I wanted Mo-Mere to like me so she'd let me read precious books she hid from other students. "You're the luckiest of the lucky," she'd told me. She only accepted students whose mothers could barter food, clothing, or other necessaries. Those whose moms couldn't pay had to drop out.

"Three centuries ago," I said, "our atmosphere warmed, glaciers melted, and oceans rose, destroying croplands. The Great Collapse threatened to destroy civilization. The Community Movement rose up to establish the World Federation. They restored peace in order to save us." The last was a big lie. They restored peace so they could be in charge and remake the world in their image. To do so, they purged all knowledge and books from Before the Community Movement (BCM).

I didn't add how GODs ran the Community Movement and its World Federation. Their notorious Department of Antiquities controlled all electronic information on the Mesh, eliminating anyone and any information that threatened their control. Even those were just words to me. I'd never seen the Federation, GODs, or the Community Movement, although Antiquities patrols made their presence known.

I stopped my foot from thumping on the creaky wood floor.

Girls behind me snickered. *"Restoorr."* They were making fun of my Federation accent, which Mom and Mo-Mere insisted I learn. It made me sound like Beth and some of the other newcomers.

Mo-Mere's face hardened. "That's enough." She looked around the classroom then at me. "Very good, Regina. With waters rising, the Federation built the Great Barrier Wall to our west to hold back the seas and protect as much cropland as they could." She gave the same introduction to each new student. Listening to it again had me squirming in my seat.

"Why are we on the wet side of the Wall?" I blurted out, since Marginals had helped build the Wall centuries ago.

Mo-Mere scowled at such an obvious question. "Why don't you answer for Beth's benefit?"

I shifted my bony rump on the wood seat, hung my head for disappointing her, and gave the official answer. "Marginals were cast out of the good lands after they rebelled." Except my ancestors had been in the Federation at that time.

"And?" Mo-Mere prompted.

"We must work hard to prove our worth to the Federation." I looked up. "But every year, the waters swamp more of our lands. Soon, we won't have anywhere to live."

"That's why you must work for a chance to go to their university."

"But—"

"Regina Shen! That's enough. See me after class."

While pretending to frown in shame, inside I smiled at the chance to spend more time with Mo-Mere. Looking around, I realized I'd dug a bigger grave for myself with the other girls. I wanted to learn, even if they didn't.

Mo-Mere stood in front of her desk, towering over me. "This storm could be the worst in my lifetime." She let that sink in.

Worst was relative. Each storm took homes and land, and made us scramble, but they were all bad. She seemed more worried this time.

"Since the storm isn't expected until tomorrow night, school will be open in the morning, unless your moms want you home. Don't take unnecessary risks. If you do come, bring examples of how you've prepared. In order to survive, we must share with other students and neighbors."

She looked around the small room to be sure we were listening. "Find the highest shelter you can with protection against storm surges. Make sure you have emergency supplies, including medicines. Think about how the storm will affect your gardens and how you'll hunt for food. Be careful what you scrounge to eat. Remember the pictures I showed you of poisonous seafood."

* * *

Inspector Joanne Demarco watched the growing storm system onscreen from the helm of her Department of Antiquities patrol boat in the middle of the Richmond Swamps. Waves broke along the port side. *The hurricane will make landfall tomorrow night,* she thought. A big storm would send tens of thousands of Marginals scrambling for the Barrier Walls created to hold out them as well as the seas. *They'll offer themselves into servitude for a chance to live.*

She remembered those days as a child. She swore never to let anything return her to the life of a swamp rat. Yet here she was, doing the Federation's dirty work. A promotion might improve that.

An alarm pierced the calm, the sort that would send you jumping for lifeboats. Demarco cursed under her breath, forced a smile, and locked the cabin door. She took a deep breath and activated her Mesh-reader.

North American Governor Gina Wilmette's ancient face filled the screen with a wide canvas of wrinkles and tufts of skin. Like all Grand Old Dames, the governor was more than 300 years old. Meds, treatments, and replacement parts had helped, though she still looked like the fossils Demarco seized while clamping down on local salvage efforts.

"How's my favorite Antiquities agent?" the governor said in a politically cheery voice.

I'm probably the only Antiquities agent you know. "There's a storm brewing," Demarco said, sending an image of the massive swirl on her weather screen to the governor. It was the biggest she could recall, as if three storms had merged into one.

"There always is," the governor said, the mask of surgeries and makeup dulling any facial expression. "The reason I called is … are you aware fertility clinics are failing everywhere?"

"I was not, Your Majesty." Though Demarco had heard rumors.

"We'll need more than flimsy Barrier Walls to protect us from this. The Antarctic governor pretends she has matters under control, but they're failing. Failing! The Federation made a huge mistake putting all our eggs in her basket, but she convinced the premier that Antarctica was the safest place on the planet."

While the governor let off steam, Demarco contrasted the calm of the swamp around her to what this new storm would do. At least the southern continent didn't have Marginals to deal with. Their glass-domed cities were impenetrable, though maybe that was a lie perpetrated by Antarctica's Department of Antiquities. As North America's chief inspector, Demarco had manipulated enough reports on behalf of Governor Wilmette to know how.

She returned her thoughts to the governor's comments. Though birth rates had dropped worldwide, Demarco never suspected a conspiracy, certainly not one involving the rivalry between Wilmette and the Antarctic governor. "Do we know the cause?"

"My medical experts tell me more defects enter the process with each generation. EggFusion Fertilization now fails to provide live births. If we can't solve this, we're a generation away from extinction."

The inspector mulled over the news. She had no children by choice, mostly the job, but the possibility of never having kids raised the stakes. This was the first time the governor discussed this issue so candidly. Demarco wondered why Wilmette was telling her now. Then it came.

"I need you to track down rumors of Marginal DNA offering better potential. They certainly replicate like mosquitoes."

The chief inspector rarely interested herself in affairs beyond North America, but this was big. It was time to toady up to her boss and set expectations. "I'll take this on personally, Your Majesty, but so far we've found no evidence."

"Look harder." The skin on the governor's face pulled in various directions, as if all the surgery in the world couldn't fix her. "You know what it means if we find a solution, even if it does come from our Marginal swamp rats."

"I understand the urgency, Your Majesty. I'm on it." A win could put the governor of North America in line as successor to the current Federation Premier, another GOD whose health was ... less than robust. Yet what did that mean for Demarco? Well, failure meant return to the shrinking swamps as an outcast, or worse.

Demarco cleared her throat. "I sent you an image of the storm."

"I see it."

"Our meteorological group reports the super-cell will hit the east coast tomorrow night. Rains will be heavy with damaging winds. We expect flooding on our side of the Wall."

"Your recommendation?" the governor asked.

"Open the dams. Push river and lake water beyond the Barrier."

"Will that stabilize our water levels?"

"It'll help. It'll also thin out the Marginal population." Demarco lowered her voice. "Meaning fewer candidates for—"

"I know what it means. Have all your resources to put tracking devices on Marginals and draw blood samples. When the storm comes, have patrols and bounty hunters round up all the girls. We'll sort them later, use what we can, and throw back the rest."

Like throwing back undersized sea bass, Demarco thought. "We'll tag as many as we can. Then I'll oversee the roundup. What about the dams?"

"Open them. I don't need mayors complaining we let them down. Then find me girls with productive DNA."

TWO

Detention for me meant Colleen had to stay at school until I was ready to take her home.

"I'm hungry," Colleen whined, when I came to tell her. She brushed her dark-chocolate hair to look more adorable and more worthy of me giving in, which meant stop getting detention. "I want to go home." Her pleading eyes tore at me.

"Mom won't be there," I said. "She's diving salvage to barter for new boots." This was a stretch. I had no idea what Mom did while we were away.

Colleen stared at her toes poking through. "Why do you have to get detention every day?"

"I'll make it up to you later."

I scooted her into her classroom and headed down the rickety wood steps of her schoolhouse and across the grassy clearing. The sky to the east took on a charcoal gray appearance while the sun broiled in the afternoon sky. I hurried up the steps and into my own classroom.

At the back, Mo-Mere lived in a one-room apartment, with a bed, a small clothes chest, and her kitchen nook. Stilts kept the buildings above surge waters. So far. But each storm brought the channel closer.

Her apartment gave off a hint of welcoming fragrances from her potpourri, a collection of hybrid herbs she bred and grew in a garden across the clearing. The floral scent masked the odor of rot and decay from ever-humid wood and fumes from hot tar on the roof. The calming scents contrasted with sharp, lush swamp odors each time I stepped outside.

Mo-Mere stood over a wood-burning stove in the corner brewing an herbal tea. "What am I to do with you?" She turned to face me. "Your mother wants you in school. Eleventh grade is as high as we go and you're beyond that." She raised my chin until I looked at her. "I'm not scolding. I've never had such a precocious child. But that doesn't give you permission to speak your mind in class or in public. Watch what you say around others."

I stared at the worn wood floor in need of new varnish before it rotted through. Fixing Mo-Mere's place was a welcome form of detention. Making myself useful opened up reading opportunities. I looked up. "What's the value of education unless I can express my thoughts? You taught me that."

"Regina, I taught you to think for yourself. It's your responsibility to know when not to speak your mind."

"What's the point of learning if I can't speak out against injustice?"

Mo-Mere's eyes bored into me. "You know the answer."

Out of frustration, I picked up a Chinese cipher puzzle she set out when we were alone, a tribute to my mother's heritage. It had taken me longer than other brainteasers to crack and still challenged me with traps. I liked its deceptive simplicity, and it never got me into trouble.

"Well?" Mo-Mere prompted.

I looked at her and remembered she was challenging me to answer. "We can't be sure those cast out of the Federation, like Beth, aren't spies."

"It's not just her. There's no telling who might turn you in to Antiquities for speaking out against the Federation."

"How can speaking the truth be wrong?" I asked.

"There's truth and there's integrity." She poured the tea. "For example, if you met the ugliest girl in the world, would you tell her?"

"Only if I wanted a fight."

Mo-Mere laughed. "There you have it." She put two cups of tea on the table with some hard biscuits.

I sat on a wood-stump stool, cradled the hot tea, and stared at a biscuit she'd put out. Eating her food brought guilt. She had so little. Yet I was hungry and she was willing. I ate because I assumed Mom bartered for this.

Mo-Mere picked up my right foot and examined my toes. "Your feet are still damp. You need to get them and your boots dry every day to avoid swamp rot. You need a new pair of boots."

I studied my feet. They felt as they usually did, tough and feverish. Cool water made them feel better. "You don't like me asking questions."

"Questions are fine, just not in class. Federation spies look for hints of rebellion." She fanned her arm out toward the river. "Don't make the same mistake as those who came before you. Learn your studies and someday I'll try to get you into a university on the other side of the Wall."

"How? The Federation won't issue us IDs."

"Leave that to me. For now, focus on making it through this storm."

* * *

Looking around the classroom and Mo-Mere's apartment, you'd never guess she owned any print books. For class, she'd scrounged up a dozen old-style electronic Mesh-readers with big screens and huge keyboards. I hoped she hadn't bartered too much for them. Run off the school's solar panels, the devices gave us access to the Mesh-cloud and Federation-approved texts while we were at school.

The Mesh included official Community Movement history as well as texts on foods, medicines, and skills to help us survive in the swamps and accept our lot at the bottom of the caste system. It was hardly worth eleven years of schooling, but I kept coming back because Mo-Mere supplemented Mesh-learning with her own experiences.

She pushed the stove aside, raised a trap door, and pulled up a plastic-wrapped package. I wondered what she would surprise me with today. I wanted more of her stories, our real history that she didn't share in class. Instead of giving me answers, she often produced another book, as if that might answer my questions. Either that or she was telling me I wasn't ready for the answers.

"Why does the Federation hate us so much? I mean, there hasn't been a rebellion in over 200 years."

"Their spies grab anyone they think might lead a rebellion. Beyond the Wall, citizens feel that things aren't so bad as long as the Department of Antiquities doesn't reclassify them as Marginals and dump them along the coastal swamps."

"Is that what happened to you?"

"A long time ago," Mo-Mere said. She toweled off the package that kept her books dry and unwrapped it.

"What was it like over there?"

"People complained about food and clothing shortages, though it was nothing like here. They say the one thing worse than growing up a Marginal is to know a better life and have the Federation throw you into the swamps. I came about the same time as your mother."

"She refuses to talk about the past." I sipped the tea, relishing its bittersweet flavor. Mom never had tea, but herbal tea was one of Mo-Mere's guilty pleasures. It probably cost her dearly in barter. "Why did they cast you and Mom out?"

"That's a story for another time," Mo-Mere said. She drank her tea.

"Please tell me."

Mo-Mere sighed and rolled her eyes upward, as if reading memories off the weathered wood-beams. "I taught at their university. I asked a few too many questions."

"And they didn't like that?"

"Elites never do. It was harder for your mom. I expected them to cast me out, but the move shocked her."

"Why was she thrown out?"

"You'll have to ask her."

"All she'll say is if I ever get out of the swamps to never do anything that would bring me back." I cradled my tea like one of Mo-Mere's books. "But this is my home."

"You could be one of the lucky ones. Don't waste what chances you get."

I shrugged. All I knew was around me: swamps, water, gators, and snakes. I couldn't imagine leaving. "I've heard there are worse places than the seaside swamps, like deserts spreading on every continent."

"Bad is bad. Promise you'll make good use of your life. Don't let your brain go to waste."

I wanted to remove my brain and hand it to her, since she prized it so much. She could wrap it in plastic like her precious books. "Why can't we cross the Wall and mingle as we do here?"

"Ah, my precocious one. Our Barrier Wall is hundreds of feet high, up to a thousand feet thick around rivers. It spans from the Panama Canal to the Arctic. Another Wall covers the Pacific coast. There's no way into the Federation without permission. They have all sorts of surveillance along the Wall in natural light, infrared, and motion sensors. It would be impossible to dig under it. If you followed the rivers, you'd drown or the Wall turbines would chop you up. Patrols catch those who try to climb over."

"They want us to drown like rats, then."

Mo-Mere placed a book with a leather cover on the table. "Why don't we try this: *A Tale of Two Cities*? It's about a time of hardships and spies. You can't let anyone know. The Federation banned this at the highest levels."

"Why do they forbid all knowledge from before the Great Collapse? What do the Community Movement and Federation fear so much?"

"They fear ideas that could spur rebellion, my dear. And don't forget the Department of Antiquities, their quasi-religious arm. They make sure citizens can't find books, artifacts, or other evidence of the past. That's why we must be very careful with our treasures."

"How can the Federation wipe out history and literature when people like you can remember and pass that knowledge on?" I asked.

"You know the answer, my dear."

I shrugged at her use of the Socratic Method on me, making me search for my own answers. "The Federation controls the Mesh and bans all writing that's not online. With their centralized data, when the Department of Antiquities changes history, they change it everywhere. But—"

"That's correct," Mo-Mere said. "And what happens to anyone the Antiquities patrols catch?"

"They execute Marginals or send us into slave labor. They throw citizen offenders over the Wall to drown."

"And the swamps are a savage world for them. Most die."

"But you and Mom survived," I said.

"Someday, perhaps, you'll help to make this a better world."

That made me smile. Her greatest wish was that I fulfill some prophecy of hers. But how could I when a huge Barrier Wall separated us from the powerful Federation? *Well, everyone needs a dream.*

* * *

I opened the delicate cover to yellowed pages, crisp and brittle to my touch. I held these fragile pages in reverence for the knowledge few except me could read. I spoke aloud to hear the opening words in my ears. "It was the best of times."

While Mo-Mere wrapped the other books, I read to myself. After she'd placed the package beneath the stove, I stopped and looked up. "What does it mean '... *his* hands cut off...' and '... because *he* had not ...'?"

"You've run across those terms before."

"I know, but what does it *really* mean?"

"Ah, I wondered when you'd get around to asking. Have you not wondered how beavers and rats and alligators create their young without our fertility clinics?"

My face burned while I held my gaze on the wise old woman. I wanted to ask the question that nagged at me, about my birth, but I feared the answer.

Mo-Mere sat across from me, her eyes drifting up to the timbered wall behind me. "A male connects with a female and they make babies without the need of a fertility clinic." She smiled. "We used to refer to males as *he* or *him.*"

"Why haven't I met any?"

She sighed, seemed to consider making me answer, and looked at me. "The Great Collapse brought chaos. Gangs of men roamed the world, causing much pain to the women around them. The Community Movement arose to put a stop to those assaults. When they won, they decided we didn't need men. They had EggFusion Fertilization labs where they could take skin cells from one woman, coax them into stem cells, and use those to fertilize another woman's egg to create a child between them. Relying on that procedure, they eliminated males."

I shifted my rear on the tree stump. "Do we still have males?"

She shook her head. "Not in a long while. There's gossip they're hiding here in the swamps, but look around. Where would you hide without the Department of Antiquities finding out?"

"So, for 300 years there have been no males and the Department is worried we'll find one."

Mo-Mere laughed. "They worry about every little thing. It's their job to fret so Grand Old Dames, and the Elites who serve them, can sleep at night."

"Didn't males fight back?"

"After decades of warring among themselves, they'd become so weak they were exiled into the swamps as outcasts. Then they were hunted down and killed off."

"Sounds brutal," I said.

"The Federation also uses EFF for domesticated animals like cows, pigs, dogs, and cats. That removes any reminders of maleness, so people won't ask uncomfortable questions."

"Like me?"

She patted my hand.

"What about the women? Didn't they rebel against having their fathers, brothers, and sons taken away?"

"In the beginning they did."

"I take it they lost," I said.

"After males were expelled, EFF gave the government complete power over breeding. Women within the Federation could only have children if they obeyed. Those who rebelled were thrown over the Wall to fend for themselves."

"Have you ever met a man?"

"Where would I? Read up. I have to go for storm supplies. I'll be back in an hour."

I was torn between reading and joining her to visit the barter houses and see what might be available for exchange.

She must have read my mind. "It's too dangerous for you to come. A storm brings unsavory characters interested in taking advantage. Besides, you need to expand your mind in order to survive in the Federation."

"They won't want me to know this book."

Mo-Mere smiled. "The purpose of reading isn't to memorize, though you do that very well. It's to widen your perspective, sharpen critical thinking, and to expand your heart. Don't just memorize, though if you commit this to memory and copy it later, the world will be grateful."

"I know."

"And don't get so wrapped up that you lose track of time or surroundings. Keep your ears sharp in case we get company. If for any reason I'm not back in two hours, put the book in the cabinet over the sink basin and take your sister straight home. I don't want you out after dark."

THREE

I absorbed the words a page at a time. Holding the brittle paper, I paused to let the story sift into memory like spud sugar dissolving in tea. I eased over a new leaf in anticipation of more.

In the story, a wide channel like our Barrier Wall separated prosperous England from desperate France. Except our Richmond Swamps had become a giant penal colony. Reading the story made me feel free, unshackled by the Federation, the Department of Antiquities, or the problems of the world beyond the Wall. I tried to imagine myself in love with two men, men who would do anything to protect me. On reflection, I couldn't imagine how they could protect me here in the swamps with the Department of Antiquities hunting them. Maybe I would have to protect them. Either way, it stirred my blood.

I scanned the last page of the book into memory and sat back. Mo-Mere rushed into the apartment. "It's late. You should have left already." She took the book and placed it in her cupboard.

Stretching, I said, "I sure hope I can do something noble."

"That wasn't the point of the book." Mo-Mere pushed me toward her door. "Not the only point, at least. Don't you dare sacrifice yourself. We'll talk later. Get your boots on and hurry home. Don't forget Colleen."

I hung my head in shame. Last month, I'd been so caught up in a story I'd read that I'd started home before Colleen screamed to alert me I'd forgotten to pick her up, again. She was so mad she made me do all the paddling.

Pulling on my boots, I recalled the text of Dickens' book to convert it to long-term memory. "Did I do something wrong, Mo-Mere?"

"No." She sighed. "I'd let you stay, but your mother would worry. I have no way to let her know."

"She wouldn't mind. She's always busy, even on Sundays."

"Regina, you know better. Besides, patrols are out like black flies. I don't know what they're looking for, but I don't like it. Get going. Don't stop for any salvage side trips. This is no time to barter for another goat. Promise you'll go straight home."

I hadn't seen Mo-Mere this angry and scared before.

Colleen was napping in her wood-frame classroom. When I woke her, she looked stunned. "Are we home? Did you forget me again?" She looked around and shook her head. "You got another detention. Why do I have to be punished?"

I tugged on her torn boots. *I should do some salvage to get her a new pair.* "I'm sorry. We need to hurry."

With the sun fading behind trees on the west side of the island, we headed down the steps. I led the way beside the log stilts that held up the schoolhouse. We reached my hollowed-out log-boat beneath the window to Mo-Mere's classroom.

"Why can't you be like the other girls?" Colleen asked when we reached the shore.

I shrugged and untied the mooring rope. *We can't change our nature.*

Two gray-coated Antiquities agents entered the clearing in front of the school. They were the bogeybeasts we had nightmares about. Yet this was the first time I'd seen them at the school. *Mo-Mere's black flies.*

I helped Colleen into the boat and tossed the rope inside. I shooed a couple of rats that tried to hitch a ride and gave Colleen our Antiquities signal. She huddled low, clutching her turquoise necklace, a gift from Mom. I pushed the boat and slid into the back. Colleen pointed to an alligator surfacing among the cattails and tucked in her arms, making herself small.

I couldn't blame her. Last week she'd stumbled upon one of her classmates. Well, what was left of her after a gator caught her skipping class. She'd sneaked around the east side of the island, far from the schoolrooms, and found a hidden cove in which to soak her feet. Her legs were gone. Mo-Mere couldn't save her. Colleen still bore the terror.

When the gray-coats weren't looking, I paddled out onto the muddy channel. Water extended in all directions, dotted with drenched trees, cattails, rush, and other swamp grasses. Small islands rose above the murky waters. Bigger islands to the west belonged to the "better class" of Marginals: the ones who succeeded at bartering salvage goods from sunken Richmond, and bounty hunters who collected girls to sell to Federation farms and mines.

The Department of Antiquities not only squashed any history the Community Movement didn't like and anything that smacked of rebellion, but they also hated scavengers who raided island settlements, and diving salvagers like Mom and me. That included most Marginals who struggled to survive in these swamps. I understood why Antiquities would destroy my family and Mo-Mere if they learned about the books we'd salvaged, but what did they have to fear from dishes and steel pots?

Seeing Antiquities agents at school made me cautious. I steered close to shore, watching for alligators, snakes, and the spare coyote that somehow survived out here. They all made a decent feast, if they didn't eat you first. I'd read that before the Great Collapse, gators had been a shy species, less than a dozen feet long, avoiding humans unless disturbed. To punish us, the Federation introduced crocodile DNA to create larger, more aggressive gators.

I paddled across a channel and hugged the shore of the next island.

"Got you, you little swamp rat," said a terse voice behind me.

Something pinched my neck. My sister stifled a scream and turned to jump overboard. The broad snout of an alligator poked above the water. Colleen dropped back into the log-boat and curled into a ball.

I couldn't move my arms or legs. The paddle fell from my grip and landed at my feet. I couldn't feel anything below my neck. I stared at the charcoal sky, which grew darker by the minute. I'd heard of bounty hunters using nerve block when they captured girls, but I never expected to feel it myself.

Someone pulled our boat through the cattails along the shore. She had a clump of ebony hair surrounding a coarse, pockmarked face, and wore the Department of Antiquities emblem on her gray uniform. In fact, she had the insignia of the chief inspector.

Intense eyes burned into me. "You can't escape our patrols. We see and hear everything." The Antiquities woman grabbed Colleen's left arm, lifted her, and brandished a needle. "This won't hurt."

Colleen cried out.

"Leave her alone," I said. "She hasn't done anything."

"New regulations." The coarse-faced one pinched my sister's arm and jabbed a huge needle into the puckered skin.

Colleen slumped like a dead squirrel, her head cocked to the side. She whimpered.

I tried to muster my strength to help her, but my muscles failed to respond. "Let her go."

Coarse-face dropped Colleen into the boat and turned to me. "A rebel fighter, eh?"

"No, ma'am."

"Then what's the fuss?" She grabbed my left arm, pinched my skin, and stuck me with her needle.

The jab brought no pain, yet I felt violated. "What are you giving us?"

"A tracking implant, so we can find you later. The nerve block will fade. Then you can be on your way." She drew blood, slapped a bandage over the open sores, and dropped me into my boat.

I fell backward and saw two other gray uniforms. One held a tranquilizer rifle; that must have been what first pinched me.

Coarse-face drew blood from Colleen and put a bandage on her oozing arm. Then the chief inspector joined the other women in an Antiquities speedboat.

"I can't understand where all these girls come from," one of the gray-coats said. "You'd think they'd stop breeding."

Coarse-face rolled her eyes and shook her head. "They should have all died out by now. Come on. Maybe the gators will do the job."

"I can't move," I yelled. "At least shoo them away."

* * *

I lay beneath angry black clouds, wanting to kick myself for falling into a patrol trap, but my legs wouldn't move. They must have used infrared to track us. My mistake was believing the shore too shallow for patrol boats. These agents had a smaller speedboat some patrols attached to their larger boats. I didn't feel blessed for the privilege of the chief inspector's attention.

The gray-coats sped away. I craned my neck to see if any dangerous predators awaited their next meal. "Colleen, you okay?" I barely saw her slumped in front.

"No."

I'd failed her. Mo-Mere had warned me and I couldn't protect Colleen. Rats boarded the boat and scurried down the sides toward her. The gator to my right swam closer.

"Regina!"

"I see them." I grunted, trying to jerk my body awake. My head banged against the log-boat. My arms quivered and fell. My left arm stung where that devil had injected me. *Good. The nerve block must be wearing off.* The bandage from the implant bulged over my wound.

Dark clouds swirled above us, moving west. They threatened to blot out the plum sunset with the beginnings of the storm. Rain fell, a drizzle at first, then heavier. I lay face up with water splashing my eyes, nose, and mouth.

"Regina, they're biting."

"Jump as if something scared you."

She grunted and rocked the log. "It's not helping."

"Don't make another sound." I spotted an alligator nosing the side of the log. All it had to do was bump us just right and we'd spill over, paralyzed.

Clenching my fists, I lifted a leg. It dropped like limp noodles. I did it again. This time, my right arm shot halfway up before it collapsed. One of the rats fell off the log. The gator's long snout shot up. Bone crunched in the gator's jaws.

I kept still, holding my breath. I recalled that the fastest way to cleanse toxins was to get my blood circulating.

Thinking about Antiquities agents did the trick. My heart raced. I tightened my muscles. "Grrr."

"Regina, the rats."

"Raaa!" My arms and legs twitched in the air. I was a turtle on its back. Rats scurried away. The alligator rocked our log. Another rat dropped off, distracting the gator. "Raaa!" My arms and legs moved together. Feeling returned to my toes and fingers.

The alligator snapped, trying to grab my leg. Its lunge scooted our boat into the channel. The gator followed.

"Raaa!" I aimed for a rat and knocked it off. We floated free of the cattails. With my right hand I grabbed a paddle and dropped it. I grabbed again, swung at a rat near Colleen, and knocked one off.

Another rat bit the end of the paddle and hung on. I smacked it against the log. The rat let go and scurried toward Colleen.

"Regina!"

Two gators approached from the right, their eyes above the muddy water. I let go of the paddle and pushed myself into a sitting position. My head slumped back like a stone. I shoved a rat from my end of the boat and shooed the ones near Colleen.

The rancid breath of a gator blew in from behind me. Straining to grip the paddle in both hands, I got in a few strokes. That sent us in a wide arc. I switched sides. If it had been only one gator, I might have pulled the crossbow from beneath my seat, but I didn't want to waste arrows. I couldn't afford to lose the bow overboard.

Colleen stirred. "Get these rats off."

"You can move your arms now. When one bites, grab it behind the neck and snap. It'll make for a good dinner tonight."

"Can't you?"

I switched sides and paddled. "Would you rather be a gator's dinner?"

One of the rats bit her leg. She grabbed it and snapped the neck. She threw the body into the middle of the boat and grabbed another by her left shoulder.

"Good girl. Mom will be proud."

"This is your fault, for detention."

Pile on the guilt.

When I'd put enough distance between the gators and us, I helped Colleen with the remaining rats until we had four carcasses. She crawled up into my arms and wept. She hadn't cried until then, brave girl.

I stroked her stringy hair and held her tight, letting her have a good cry while I watched for water snakes.

Colleen dried her eyes and looked up at me. "Don't ever leave me. Promise."

"I promise."

She returned to the front of the boat and helped me paddle toward home. I was tempted to dive for salvage among the sunken homes of Richmond, though each dive got harder. Over the centuries, salvagers like me had stripped sunken homes of valuable metals, stone, and glass. Gypsum wallboard had turned to mush. Nails rusted. Antiquities patrols set traps to keep us away.

Most times I came up empty, but one day I found a treasure

trove: more specially-coated stainless cookware than I could carry in Mom's skiff. I picked the best for her and bartered the rest for a goat to provide milk for Colleen and me. Mom acted upset that I'd taken this risk, but at least Colleen had good teeth and bones.

The rains came harder. Roiling black clouds took over the sky. Colleen feared the dark, and the oncoming storm could trap us. I paddled harder.

FOUR

Rain covered us like a soggy blanket. Night terror crept into Colleen's eyes.

Nighttime was the worst. Nocturnal predators came out. Some, like the owls, didn't frighten me, but somehow coyotes made it from island to island like the rats. When they couldn't find birds or smaller mammals, they turned on humans, particularly at night. There were snakes: poisonous cottonmouths, and pythons with powerful muscles that could choke. And they hid well. Hungry gators lurked nearby. One had even wandered into the clearing by our cabin. When she wouldn't leave, we made a good dinner of her, similar to chicken but with tougher meat.

We finally reached the cove of our own tiny island. No smoke came from the chimney, which meant Mom's cooking fire wasn't burning. No lights shined from our cabin. That sent shivers up my spine.

We'd have to tie up the log-boat in the dark and feel our way home, hoping to avoid the many traps we used to snare food and keep out raiders and scavengers. I'd snagged small gators with them, and a coyote. I'd also found a trap with blood, flesh, and shreds of green canvas: scavengers.

In the dark, I pulled my crossbow from beneath my seat and peeled off the plastic sheathing. Then I freed my quiver of short arrows. I'd been lucky to salvage synthetic material from a submerged home that I then spent hours twisting and reverse-twisting into the strongest bow string I'd ever seen. With it, I'd hit rats, squirrels, and alligators at a distance Mom said was impossible. The submerged homeowner must have been a great hunter.

I pulled the boat up behind the reeds.

"Where's Mom?" Colleen asked.

"She's probably out bartering," I whispered. "Be quiet and keep your ears sharp."

In the soggy darkness, I couldn't see Mom's boat. I slung the quiver of arrows over my shoulder and attached the bow. I grabbed the rats by the tails and tucked Colleen's hand to my elbow. Using a stick to test for traps, we moved through tall grass. With no stars in the stormy sky to guide us, we reached the pebbly trail that led up to the leaky log hut we called home.

Colleen clutched my arm; her dread coursed through me. Inching forward, I tested each step with the stick. Something snapped shut with a metallic clank. I froze and listened.

Hearing nothing else through the wind and rain, I lifted the stick, now heavy and awkward, its tip in the jaws of a trap. I waved the stick before me and pushed forward, testing the ground twice before moving. When we reached the clearing, lightning illuminated our single-room log cabin. It wasn't hard to find if you kept heading uphill. Colleen squeezed my arm.

A gun clicked.

I reached for my bow to notch an arrow, though a bow was a poor weapon against a gun in the dark, particularly if we faced scavengers with infrared and night vision.

"Mom?" Colleen trembled.

A faint light flickered to my right. "You scared me," Mom said. "I thought you were scavengers." She moved closer. "Where's the cooking fire?" she snapped. "You should have been home hours ago."

"She got detention again," Colleen volunteered and ran to Mom.

"I pay for classes so you can learn, not so you can bother Madam Seville. Find some dry wood and get the fire going." She slung the shotgun over her shoulder.

In the flicker of the light beam, I saw bags under Mom's eyes. I handed her the rats and looked around before she took Colleen and the light inside.

I ran to the side of the cabin, picked up an armful of driftwood I'd cut that morning, and carried it inside. An oil-rag lamp cast faint shadows on the walls. It was too dark to read, but Mom had no books, not even a Mesh-reader with government-approved texts.

"You're lucky patrol agents didn't take you away," Mom said after hearing the tale from Colleen. "From now on, come straight home after school. No more salvage. And make sure those patrols don't follow you. There's work to be done around here."

"Why would patrols take us?" Colleen asked.

"I don't know." Mom glared at me not to say more. "I just don't want to lose you two monkeys." She hugged Colleen.

Mom had me skin the rats. Then she fried them up in a skillet with wild spuds and greens that survived in our garden: a feast, more than we often had on Sundays. Leftovers would make for a good stew.

"Do you have school tomorrow?" she asked.

I nodded.

"Make sure you don't get detention. Is that clear? A terrible storm is brewing. I want you and Colleen home the instant class is over. Don't fail me."

Getting home in an instant would have been impossible without one of the Federation's sky-jumpers, which we could only watch from the ground. I didn't say so. Mom was in enough of a sour mood.

We sat around our tree-stump table. Mom propped her shotgun next to her in case we got visitors. Colleen and I waited until Mom nodded that we could eat. We rarely said prayers. Mom said Community Movement GODs were false gods, and praying to anyone else risked arrest and days without food in a Marginal prison cage.

I looked into her sunken eyes. "Thanks, Mom, for giving us a good home."

She looked up and smiled, which did little to soften her sadness. "Thank you for providing dinner."

That sounded like a Marginal barter exchange, which saddened me. I often wondered what her life might have been without us. Was I keeping her from doing better? She took no joy in having children, me at least. Yet this weight of guilt didn't originate with her. It came from reading stories from other times and places.

Unlike Mo-Mere, who used every moment to teach, Mom didn't let us talk over dinner. She hadn't in a very long time. Like Federation Elites, she didn't like me asking questions. When I'd asked about her past and my donor mother, she distracted me with chores. Six months ago, we stopped talking altogether, except when we couldn't avoid it.

I wanted to ask about her life across the Wall and how she'd survived when they cast her out. Her response, etched in her weary eyes, was usually to drop it. I didn't know how to bridge the growing rift between us.

After dinner, Mom put the leftovers in a stainless container I'd salvaged. While Colleen climbed onto her cot across from the kitchen and pretended to sleep, Mom locked the doors and windows, and filled canvas bags for the next day.

I hated storms. They meant leaving home to hunt for higher ground. The worst part was sitting around listening to the winds and rain pounding us, wondering if that storm would take our cabin. We'd been fortunate so far, but Mom's eyes looked weary, as if she knew something about this hurricane.

Her gloom heightened my need for answers; I might not get another chance. I ached to learn about my donor mother and why Colleen and I looked dissimilar, with different Hispanic features as well as Mom's Chinese ones. She'd told me our donor was a Hispanic woman who died of some mutating disease they couldn't cure. I had no memories of her. Mom even refused to tell me her name, as if shame worse than being Marginals had befallen our family.

I approached Mom. Before I could frame a question, she said, "Check the water tanks."

Deflated, I pulled on my boots.

"While you're out, pick some fruit. We'll need it."

In the dark rain, I went to the water tanks. Two years before, after a storm, wells all around took on brine and bacteria that killed neighbors. We could no longer pump from the well into our kitchen basin, so Mom and I built crank pumps to bring muddy water up from the channel into a holding tank. Next to that, we made a small boiling chamber over a wood stove to use when we could find dry wood. The evaporated water went through a compressor and a counter-flow heat exchanger that transferred heat from cleaned water to incoming channel water. As a result, we had fresh water for the kitchen basin and for taking quick, cool showers. The system worked most of the time if I maintained it. Lucky Marginals refurbished solar heaters salvaged from now-sunken Richmond. We weren't that fortunate.

To save firewood, I used the foot pump to fill the river tank. Then I put sheltered wood into the cast-iron burner so we would have fresh water in the morning. On my way into the cabin I remembered the fruit. Mo-Mere said if you didn't eat citrus, you got scurvy. One of the students she took on last year had the bleeding gums and sores. Mo-Mere nursed the girl back, but she dropped out of school when her mom couldn't pay.

To avoid such ailments, we had an orange tree on the northeast side of the clearing for maximum sunlight, and an apple tree with a little more afternoon shade.

Rain streamed down my cheeks. I wiped my eyes and found the orange tree by light seeping through the cabin's drapes. I listened for scavengers or gators, and strained to see if snakes nested in the tree.

Taking a deep breath, I rolled up my canvas shirt and reached up. My hand brushed through leaves and settled on an orange, firm and ripe. Something slithered onto my arm. I brushed it away and grabbed the orange.

I waved my hand through the leaves until I found a second orange, but it was too small. A third didn't feel ripe. After finding two ripe ones close together, I plucked them and wrapped them in my drenched canvas top. I found another and decided four would be enough for four days.

Nearby was the apple tree. I only found two apples low enough to pick, and they were probably green. I picked them anyhow. A snake dropped onto my shoulders and curled around me. Holding the fruit with my left hand, I headed for the cabin and grabbed hold of snake muscle as thick as my thumb. By cabin light, I saw I had the head, and thankfully it wasn't a python or a cottonmouth. The snake's body coiled around my arm and neck.

I placed the fruit on the porch, pulled a knife from my belt, and sliced through the snake's head. Its body tightened around me. The head hung by a strand of muscle and then came loose. I threw it into the clearing, dropped the knife next to the fruit, and uncoiled the ropelike creature from my neck. After attaching the knife to my belt and gathering up the apples and oranges in my soaked top, I grabbed the snake and entered the cabin. I placed my spoils on the tree stump table.

Mom nodded at the snake and kissed my forehead. "You're a good girl. That'll give us something for tomorrow. Never let your guard down. Not for a moment. I'm not angry. I'm worried … for both of you. Today the patrols got too close. Don't ever let them take you."

"I know, Mom."

Guilt was worse than the rare times she yelled at me.

I pulled off my boots, stacked them by the door, and dried off with terrycloth. Then I changed my canvas clothes and crawled onto my cot in the corner next to Colleen. She was snoring.

My fingers dug beneath the head of my bed, into a crack between wall and floor, feeling for a medallion. It looked like ancient coins before the Great Collapse and yet not like any I'd seen in Mo-Mere's books.

By the flicker of Mom's oil lamp, I studied the intricate designs I recognized as symbols for water, air, earth, and fire, with a fifth symbol I couldn't identify. When I'd found it among Mom's things and asked her about it, she'd thrown the flat metal disk into the channel and told me to forget I'd ever seen it. Since metal was so prized, her actions only made it that much more precious to me.

Of course I'd salvaged it and hid it away. Now I returned the mysterious coin to its hiding place and removed the bandage from my left arm. The swelling had gone down. It felt like a wasp sting with an ugly red spot in the middle. I wanted to dig out the tracking chip, but I'd heard that brought the severe penalty of swamp prison, where you had to fight off snakes and rats impatient for you to die.

FIVE

In the morning, dark, angry clouds pushed in from the north, bringing cooler air. Colleen and I were soaked by the time we reached school.

"Sorry, dear," Mo-Mere said from the school doorway. "I cancelled classes so students could help their families prepare."

"But it's Friday."

"They're calling this the storm of the century."

Because we lived farthest from school, we were the last to know. "That's what they said last year," I told her. I tugged at my wet, muddy boots.

Mo-Mere lifted my chin. "I'd love to let you dry out and read, but you need to go home and prepare. This could be the big one legends warned about."

"I thought that was Federation propaganda."

"Take Colleen home before the channel becomes impassible."

I hung my head. "Patrols grabbed us on the way home yesterday."

Mo-Mere sighed and rolled up the loose ragged canvas of my sleeve to examine my arm. She disappeared into her apartment, leaving me in her classroom watching muddy puddles grow larger outside.

She returned with ointment and a fresh bandage. "This should help it heal. The Department of Antiquities likes to keep track of Marginals. I'm surprised it took this long to tag you." Her face turned gloomy, like the sky.

"Why would the Department care what happens to us? I mean, we're outside the Federation."

"For the most part they don't, but they worry when we salvage sunken cities."

"The cities have been picked clean," I said.

"Not all, and even if they have, the Federation can't be sure. They're afraid we'll find something to lift us out of poverty."

"That *would* make this less of a prison."

She laughed. "They're petrified we'll find something to challenge their authority."

"It doesn't explain sticking this chip into me." I pointed to my arm.

"No, my clever one, it doesn't. For some reason, they've taken a keen interest in tagging all our girls."

"Is that why they came to school yesterday? Is that why you cancelled?"

Mo-Mere nodded. "Hurry home. Stay clear of patrols. Nothing good comes from dealing with them. Get to the highest ground and grab hold of anything that won't float you out to sea. Good luck."

"Where will you go?"

"Don't worry about me. Just take care of Colleen and your mom." She pushed a small package of crackers into my hand and kissed my forehead.

I hugged Mo-Mere as if even then, I knew this storm would change everything. I stared at her face, imprinting it on my memory.

Outside, Colleen stood in the rain; her dark hair drooped around her face. "Tell me you didn't get detention."

"Not today, you drowned rat."

She ran up the rickety wooden steps and pretended to hit me. Instead, she took my hand. I waved to Mo-Mere and lingered until she went inside. I looked at six other classroom/apartments on stilts clustered around a growing muddy pond. Then I led Colleen to our log-boat.

Waters rose as I paddled out into the channel. The rush and cattails didn't hide as much of the horizon as they had the day before. The shoreline on either side grew farther away. The current was stronger, making it hard to move upstream.

"Come on, Colleen. If you help, we'll get home sooner."

She grumbled but took the front paddle.

At least the alligators made themselves scarce. Snakes slithered by on frothy waters. One washed into the boat. Its markings were those Mo-Mere had shown us as a baby python. When it got bigger, it could choke the life out of you. I looked for its mother.

Water rose within our boat but the log would float. I kept moving. The snake slithered out. Broken branches floated by along with mud-caked log bundles, some tarred to keep out weather. Another bundle headed toward us.

"Starboard," I yelled.

We paddled hard off the port side, sending us in an arc. The bundle of logs smacked the back of our boat, pushing us close to rocks.

"Port," I yelled. We paddled the other side.

The boat bounced against rocks and spun around, facing out to sea.

"Turn and head the other way," I said. The nice thing about my log-boat was that either end could be the bow.

The center of the channel grew frothy, the current strong. We had to stay close to shore, risking rocks, debris, and whatever else lurked in the shallows.

Through the curtain of thick rain, I spotted a patrol boat skulking in the seaward channels. It kept its distance from floating debris. Already this storm felt like the King James Bible, threatening a flood that was growing faster than any I'd seen before. It was as if a dam had burst.

I pulled close to an island and crossed the channel, using the land and trees as a shield from the patrol. Out in the middle, the channel pushed us downstream. We had to paddle hard to get to the other side and retrace our way upstream. My arms ached, but we couldn't let up.

Behind me, red-faced Colleen splashed at the water, barely countering my strokes to keep us straight. I found a cove away from the main current where I turned the boat around so I could watch her and what lay ahead.

"Can we rest?" she asked.

"Wouldn't you rather get home?"

She nodded and put her paddle into the water. "Home."

I didn't mention the patrol.

* * *

It seemed to take forever, but we avoided the patrol and made it home. Mom stood in the cove preparing her rectangular flat-bottomed skiff. Her hair draped around her cheeks like a wet rag.

"I was coming to get you," she said. "Grab your things. We have to move upstream. Waters are rising too fast, and this is just the beginning."

Rain fell hard as hail, pounding my head and back. Mom had loaded the skiff with the stainless container of leftovers, along with bundles I took to be food and our bedding wrapped in reclaimed plastic. I helped her secure the last packages to the frame.

Packets filled every space. Mom must have figured we'd never return. *No time to dwell.*

With all the supplies, the skiff rode low in the water. Waves washed over the side. I looked up the hill for a glimpse of the cabin, trying to think of what else I could rescue.

"Let's go," Mom said.

With sadness, I spotted a scrap of floral cloth clinging to the tallest tree of our island. Last year, Mom had said she'd punish me the rest of my life for wasting the precious material. She'd bartered for cloth to make Colleen a canvas dress. In a fanciful mood, I'd attached the cloth to a kite frame with an arrow as the main stem. Using my crossbow, I launched the kite above the trees. It caught the breeze and soared like a crow until a strong wind blew it into the tree. I'd tugged the fishing line to get the kite down until it shattered. The arrow and line broke free, leaving the cloth wrapped around upper limbs too fragile to climb. The high-test fishing line hadn't broken.

I climbed in next to Colleen and handed her a bucket. "We need to bail or we'll sink." I tied the cord from the bucket around her wrist so it wouldn't fly away.

Mom pushed the skiff away from the cove, and sat facing me.

"Where to?" I asked, tying my bucket to my seat.

When we were out in the channel, she rowed upstream. Muscles in her arms rippled with each stroke. "A friend, Vera Morton agreed to take us in. They have another ten feet on us."

I sensed her saying a prayer, as all families did during storms that the waters didn't take more than we could afford to lose, which wasn't much. While she rowed, I pointed away from rocks and debris, and helped Colleen bail. We barely kept up with the sheets of rain filling the boat.

When the current pushed Mom too close to shore, I wiped rain from my face and pointed upstream. A wave washed over the side of the skiff. I kept scooping out water. Mom's face grew weary. Her strokes slowed until I feared we weren't keeping up with the angry current.

"I can row," I said.

"Keep bailing."

The sky grew dark as twilight. With winds coming from the northeast and no rudder, it was hard for Mom to keep us on the right path. Easterly gusts churned the waters. This was the dangerous time, when a wall of water could capsize us, sending our boat crashing against trees and rocks. I'd seen that in the last big storm, causing a wreck with no survivors.

Lightning flashed. Rain pelted us from the northeast. I took a spare oar and leaned over the side.

"Navigate," Mom said. "And bail."

"The current's too strong," I yelled over the howling wind. "We won't make it."

"Don't talk like that." Her voice strained. I could almost feel Mom reaching out to grab me and Colleen. "I won't have my daughters defeated," she said. "Do you hear? No matter what happens to me, survive this. I have *not* sacrificed for you two to give up."

Colleen bailed faster. "I'm not giving up, Mom. I promise. I won't."

Yet she was growing tired. We all were.

The winds picked up out of the east. Rain pounded harder, coming horizontally. Yet we were fighting current from the west. That gave me an idea.

I tied the skiff's stern mooring rope around my waist, pulled a sheet from one of Mom's bundles, and tied two ends to my feet. Holding up the other two corners, I stood and let my body and the sheet act as a sail. Rain slapped my face. My mouth and nose filled with water. I gagged and coughed. We caught the wind, moved away from a nearby shore, then up the channel.

My legs strained to keep standing. Cramps gripped my calf muscles. My arms fought to hold the sheet out for maximum sail. Shaking, I held that position until I couldn't get a breath. I dropped into my seat, checked my compass, and helped Colleen bail.

Legs burned, arms ached. I stood again and fought the wind. I coughed, took a deep breath with too much water, and coughed again. At least the rain cleansed the air. My giggly classmates would say that was unnatural. Yet these cleansings sharpened my senses to the crowded aromas of the swamps, odors that could warn of danger. That reverie gave me strength to push through pain and fatigue.

I took a break to help Colleen bail and stood again, struggling to maintain my balance against the pull of nature. Lightning struck nearby. A tree sparked. The pungent odor of ozone filled my sinuses. Rains doused the fire before the tree could light up the sky. Shorn branches tumbled into the rising waters.

Wind howled in my ears, a deafening cry announcing that this was the end. This flood would cleanse the world of Marginal swamp rats and wash us out to sea for our sins against the Community Movement. That was what the Federation taught us. We were the cursed ones, the damned. *Well, damn them.*

Mom didn't scold me. She didn't yell at me to stop and bail. I smiled and pushed through the pain.

SIX

I was still standing, shaking, and struggling to breathe when the skiff came to an abrupt stop. The rope saved me from falling backward toward the bow. I dropped the soaked sheet, collapsed onto my seat, and looked around. Clouds had turned charcoal black, closing in around us. We were in a cove, away from the river's rising current, a new inlet that hadn't existed before this storm.

Mom tied the front of the skiff to a tree trunk and returned to help me up. "You did great, dear. I'm so proud of you." She held me in her arms with rain cascading over us. "You saved us. You did."

When she let go, I slumped into my seat. Rain splattered Colleen's ashen face, matting her chocolate hair against her cheeks. Mom lifted her out of the skiff and led her up the rocky hill. I climbed out, untied two plastic-covered bundles from the skiff's rail, and struggled to carry them uphill. Rain-slick rocks slowed my climb. Rivulets of water raced toward the shore. I tripped, dropped my load, and braced to protect my head.

Covered in mud, I reached the top of the hill. A log cabin stood at the highest point, next to two other homes across a small clearing. I trudged forward under the weight of the bundles. My rubbery legs threatened to collapse. A big woman burst out of the nearest cabin. A porch light shining on her face showed frizzy brown hair and mysterious dark eyes. She aimed a flashlight toward me.

"You must be Regina. Bless you. You're a very brave girl. Go inside and get dry. Oh, and call me Aunt Vera."

With her cape over her head, she hurried down to the skiff. I went in and dropped my bundles by the door. A young version of Vera greeted me. "Give me your boots and clothes, and we'll dry them by the fireplace."

They had an actual stone fireplace, where Mom and Colleen sat in their underwear. I added my clothes to the pile and joined them. The girl who'd greeted me approached with a younger girl who looked to be her sister. They both had dark, tanned skin, tar-black hair, and elongated faces.

"I'm Jasmine," the older girl said, "and this is Aimee." She acted as if she knew me, though I didn't recall seeing either of them before.

"What was it like out there?" Aimee asked with too much enthusiasm.

"You don't want to go out."

"Your mom said you acted like a human sail. That sounds exciting."

"The wind was too strong. If our skiff hadn't been so heavy, we might have flipped." I didn't want her getting any ideas.

"Come on, you little worm," Jasmine told her sister. "Let's get dinner ready."

I dropped next to Mom, who held Colleen. They both looked okay, though exhausted. *Try fighting the wind.*

Aunt Vera made several trips while I stayed rooted to the spot, wondering how our home would fare. We'd sustained water damage and erosion last year. Mo-Mere said it was only a matter of time. Marginal life was all about eating away of the land, corrosion of our bodies, wasting away of the population, and a wearing down of our spirits, if we let it.

After locking the door, Aunt Vera hung up her wet clothes and set out six plates on a long table that wouldn't have fit in our home.

Mom and Colleen stood behind empty seats, Mom the farthest from the kitchen. I joined them and stood across from Jasmine. "Thanks for helping us," I said to be polite. I wondered how much Mom had bartered for this.

Vera smiled and sat closest to the kitchen. "We need to stick together and help each other during tough times. This has to be the worst storm I've seen." She passed out plates heaped with catfish and spuds.

Mom nodded. "That wind is coming right up the channel."

"We should expect storm surges," Vera said. "Last time it almost washed our boats out to sea. Then what would we do? Eat hearty. We mustn't waste good food."

"We should take extra precautions," Mom said. "Could you watch my girls? I need to check upstream."

"Your family's always welcome. It'll be nice to have company."

It sounded as if they'd planned this and chose that moment to announce it to Colleen and me. "Mom, please don't go without us." Something told me this was different than other times she'd left me with Colleen.

"You should be safe until I return. Now eat. And mind Aunt Vera as you would me."

Not having eaten since dinner last night, I dug into the catfish first, for the protein. I had the notion of having seen Vera long ago, maybe while bartering. I couldn't be sure.

"Make sure to pack everything tonight," Vera said. "It pays to be prepared."

"My stuff's already packed," Jasmine said with pride.

"So is mine," Aimee said.

I rolled my eyes. What kiss-ups.

"Mom, family should stick together at times like this." I talked around a mouthful of fish, better seasoned than anything we had at home. "You know how tough the rowing was."

"I need to make inquiries. Without bundles and passengers, rowing will be easier."

"The Federation forbids us going near the Wall."

Mom patted my hand. "Don't worry, dear. Eat up. You need your strength."

"When are you leaving?" I asked.

"In the morning. Stop fussing. Not another word."

As at home, we ate in silence. I got the impression Vera's family talked over meals, because she gave her daughters a stern look. They stared at their plates while they ate. It had to be Mom, afraid we might say something that would condemn us. Already, I felt the void of her leaving.

After dinner, Mom gave me a long hug. It was like saying good-bye to Mo-Mere. Mom's eyes looked too dark, the shadows beneath them growing as if they might swallow her vision.

"Get some sleep," she said. "We'll talk later."

* * *

Despite the storm's heavy winds and rain, Inspector Demarco took the sky-jumper to Charleston. *When the governor of North America summons, you come if you have any hope of rising above your birth station.* At times like this, Demarco cursed her ambition. It had taken constant vigilance to erase markers of her low Marginal birth from her accent, clothes, and mannerisms so she could pass as a Professional. She took pride in her transformation.

Of course, the Mesh held evidence of her birth for the uppity-ups to peruse. At least Demarco had become useful to the governor. Now she needed to pay homage, hoping that if the governor became the new premier, it would mean advancement for the chief inspector as well.

Governor Wilmette's mansion stood on a mountaintop in Charleston with a view on three sides of the most beautiful countryside in North America. Charleston was drier than the coasts and greener than the desert heartland and parched west. Farms prospered, making this the most valuable real estate in North America, and the governor had a choice piece of it.

Her nervous, frail assistant bowed to greet Demarco in the marble foyer. She was a frightened Working Stiff under the thumb of a Grand Old Dame, feeling the wear of trying to keep up with her master's whims. At least the inspector didn't have to see the governor on a daily basis.

The Working Stiff's subservient manner gave the inspector a splash of pride. Demarco had come a long way from her humble beginnings. She held that smile while she followed the assistant down an oak-lined marble corridor and into a huge office with teak shelves filled with artifacts the chief inspector had confiscated from salvagers.

After the assistant closed the door, the inspector bowed out of respect to the 300-and-some-year-old Grand Old Dame seated behind an ugly, oversized, mahogany desk with as many ripples from wear as the governor. She was a goddess to the people since she, like other GODs, had lived through the Great Collapse and helped the Community Movement restore order and peace.

This relic from the beginnings of modern times looked well for such an advanced age, a tribute to the most advanced and expensive stem cell treatments and body part replacements. Yet Demarco had no wish to be this old. She placed a ten-inch-tall golden statue of an ancient ruin on a coaster on the polished desk. "I hope this meets with the governor's approval."

Governor Wilmette picked up the gold trinket and plopped it on a teak shelf behind her without looking at it. It was part of the cache of pricey barter items she would need in her bid to upstage the Antarctic governor, another Grand Old Dame, in her bid to become the next World Federation Premier. The inspector's ambition was to follow the governor and receive a coveted post in the Federation capital in Antarctica. Otherwise, why toady up to the shriveled relic and give up all of these souvenirs?

The governor offered Demarco an upholstered seat and sat in her plush high-back behind her desk. "I see your hunt for artifacts goes well."

"All in your service, Your Majesty." Demarco bowed her head and remained standing.

"Please sit," the governor said. "I asked to see you in person to impress upon you the importance of our fertility crisis. The Antarctic governor tells lies yet she still has the premier's ear. We need to turn the tables. We need to find the rumored Marginal DNA and foster our own fertility research to break this deadlock."

"We've found no evidence there's any truth behind the rumor, Your Majesty."

Governor Wilmette waved her hand dismissively. "I know all that. Yet it mystifies me that Marginals breed and multiply despite shrinking lands, miserable hardships, and the worst fertility clinics in the world. Meanwhile, our clinics are failing. Grand Old Dames like me are too old. Blessed Mary knows we don't need more of my offspring." She glared at Demarco as if expecting the inspector to disagree.

When the inspector couldn't bring herself to say the world needed more GOD progeny, since she was sure it didn't, the governor continued, "Elite DNA has become almost infertile. Professional DNA is not far behind. Even Working Stiffs aren't reproducing."

"What do your scientists say?"

The governor shook her head. "That Antarctic bitch denies we have a problem. 'Only a glitch,' to use her words. Our clinics have speculated about environmental causes, but then how in the world could Marginals be fertile while they barely cling to life?"

"If not environmental, then genetic," Demarco said, trying to move this along so she could get back to work.

"That's my guess. Perhaps genetic mutations caused by climate change, which would still be an environmental issue. My researchers say it has to do with diminished telomeres preventing cells from dividing and replenishing. We also have problems with malfunctioning micro-RNA or enzymes or endogenetics."

Demarco had the impression Governor Wilmette had no clue, but she wouldn't commit career or actual suicide by saying so. More likely, the governor didn't care about the details, only results.

"Our DNA isn't allowing viable fetuses to develop," Wilmette said. "With each generation, the problem grows exponentially worse. The second generation is half as fertile as the first. The third is half again as the second. Best I can tell this all began about a hundred years ago. In three generations, we've lost ninety percent of our fertility as a species. How in hell has the Antarctic governor kept this quiet?"

The answer, Demarco didn't say, *is that Antiquities controls all information on the Mesh through cloud databases. No one sees what we don't want seen.* Evidently, her counterpart in Antarctica had purged fertility records, though Governor Wilmette was old enough to remember.

The governor looked up. "Explain to me how Marginal DNA has remained more vital." With eyes that looked glazed over, she stared past Demarco. "You'd think with poor nutrition they couldn't have children."

"We run their clinics for one purpose, Your Majesty: to perform experiments we can't do on Federation citizens."

"Yet they reproduce like cockroaches." Governor Wilmette stomped her foot as if squishing one. "They should have died out to ease their drain on our resources." She turned her eyes on the inspector. "You know they had the gall to demand we feed them after the last storm."

Demarco nodded. She'd been on the front lines reporting that news to the governor. "Every year, our department takes thousands of young Marginal girls to work on farms, in mines, or in homes as maids and childcare providers. Our inspections of their fertility clinics show they're down to one percent or less, except for those who cooperate with us. Those lucky souls get diversity strains, so we can test new combinations. Yet the supply never dries up."

"It's all those criminals we dump over the Wall," the governor said.

"Rarely children, Your Majesty. The demand for laborers has been too great."

"Then you see how vital it is to find unique Marginal DNA. Figure out how they're doing this."

Demarco held her frustration in check while she kept her head bowed and her eyes on the governor. "We've tested tens of thousands of Marginals. Children of those dumped over the Wall show the same signs of DNA telomere impairment as our children do, and they're an increasing portion of the Marginal population. Old-timers are dying off. We have yet to find a single blood sample that doesn't reflect damage. Can't we find a way to repair the telomeres?"

"Evidently not." Governor Wilmette stood and paced. In ancient pictures, she was a tall, striking woman. Now she was big all around. She moved with surprising agility for her age, no doubt due to artificial hips, knees, feet, and countless heart transplants. "In the early days of the Community Movement, we held the surviving males on stud farms. Did you know that?"

Demarco shook her head. She didn't dwell on ancient rumors; in fact, she'd worked hard to eradicate them. Seeing Wilmette in motion, she wondered if any part of the governor was original equipment, including the brain. Early memories sure were.

"It worked for a while," the governor said. Whatever she'd done to her brain, her mind was still razor sharp, enhanced in some ways.

Don't let age fool you, Demarco reminded herself.

"They were like their bee counterparts," the governor said, "there to service the queens, and nothing more. Then they rebelled. Security patrols had to kill most. The others lost their will to live. They died off or killed each other: mercy killing, they called it. Pathetic." She faced the inspector, wagging her finger. "If we can't find another solution to the fertility crisis, find a way to bring them back. I don't fancy males running around loose, but stud farms might be okay. We'll just have to figure out how to maintain them so they don't become suicidal."

The inspector cringed at yet another impossible request she couldn't refuse. She lowered her voice. "With all due respect, Your Majesty. How would you propose we do that when there's no male DNA left?" Legend had it her own Department of Antiquities had, in its early days, raided DNA vaults to eradicate all evidence.

"Damn it. I don't care." The governor glared at Demarco. "Your job is to find solutions, not to stand in my way."

"I wouldn't presume."

"Either find me a Marginal without telomere damage or get me male DNA samples. I don't care." Governor Wilmette returned to her seat, exhausted by the exchange.

"Yes, Your Majesty. We're wrapping up blood tests on the last of the Richmond swamp rats." With no known DNA vaults left, only a miracle would resurrect men, and Demarco didn't believe in miracles.

"Help me free ourselves from bondage to that Antarctic sow." The governor sounded pleading. Her eyes narrowed like tiny black lasers. "You know what that could mean, don't you?"

Demarco nodded. "Premier Wilmette." She waited for the governor to add how that would benefit Demarco. An awkward silence followed.

The chief inspector's Mesh-reader buzzed. She pulled it out.

Governor Wilmette grimaced, which highlighted wrinkles she'd paid dearly to soften. "Put that damned thing away."

"News, Your Majesty. Blood samples on two girls we tagged look promising: Regina and Colleen Shen. Their DNA doesn't show the telomere defects we've found in all the other samples."

"Really!" Wilmette stood and leaned on her desk.

"We need to run more tests."

"Bring them to me. When can you get them to my lab?"

"We're tracking their implants," Demarco said. "The moment I get back, I'll see to it."

"See to it personally."

"They're only fifteen and twelve."

"Bring them, bring them," the governor said. "Let me worry about their ages."

Demarco had reservations about bringing these young girls in just yet. The data was premature, and this wasn't the first time the governor had sent her speeding up the wrong channel. Her other concern: she could only count on the grace of a Grand Old Dame as long as she remained useful. Before Demarco provided the key to Wilmette becoming the next premier, she wanted more assurances than how good fortunes might trickle down.

If the governor didn't promote her to a post in Antarctica, the new governor of North America might not have use for the Marginal inspector, and all the artifacts she'd skimmed would count for nothing. After all, the Federation barred Marginals from possessing them.

There was a fine line between receiving the governor's wrath for failing and losing usefulness after the governor got what she wanted. Then again, if Demarco didn't deliver, the governor would find someone else who would.

SEVEN

Colleen and I lay on cots in the corner of the big room opposite the kitchen. Aunt Vera sent her daughters into their bedroom and extinguished the oil-rag lamp, plunging us into darkness. "Don't want the winds blowing it over and setting the house on fire," she said.

She took Mom into the other bedroom. I heard them whispering, but couldn't make out what they said, only that they both sounded worried. Colleen, who didn't like the dark even on a calm night, moved her cot next to mine. Still it took her a long time to fall asleep.

The storm battered the house all night, letting up for a moment, then howling louder than before. Damp air wormed its way through cracks in the tarred log walls and around windows, pushing its clamminess along the east side of the great hall.

The storm was still raging when I woke early, feeling as if I hadn't slept. I got ready to do chores before school.

It took a moment to realize weren't at home. There would be no school on account of the storm. My thin sheet was soaked, as was Colleen's and the floor around us. Across the room, Mom's bedding was gone.

I slid off my cot onto the wet wood floor and crossed the room looking for where she might have gone to stay dry. "Mom," I whispered. Her backpack was gone.

Winds rattled windows and the cabin's frame. Spray hit my face through cracks in the wall. I stuffed bits of rag, but it was hopeless.

Puddles pooled across the floor. I knocked on Aunt Vera's door.

"What is it, child?" She opened the door, wearing the same green canvas from the night before.

"Mom's gone."

Closing her eyes, Vera nodded. "She didn't want to disturb you. She went upriver to scout higher ground. I promised to look after you."

"She left us." My stomach twitched. She'd never gone during a storm before. I tensed my muscles to keep from sobbing.

Aunt Vera held me. "It'll be okay. I'm sure she'll be back soon."

I pushed away, ran to the front door, and opened it to a scene of horror. Waves broke against the base of the porch as if the house had become its own island. When they retreated, they dragged part of the vegetable garden with them. Rain pelted my face.

"Water's up to the steps," I said.

Aunt Vera joined me in the doorway and gasped. "Gather your things. We have to go."

"We can't," I said. "We have to wait for Mom."

"No time." Aunt Vera hurried into her daughters' room.

Colleen stirred. "Where's Mom?"

"I don't know," Aunt Vera said, returning with bags. *A lie.* Mom must have said something last night.

Aunt Vera gathered bags by the front door while I helped Colleen with hers.

Jasmine came in, rubbing her eyes. "Why do I only get two bags?"

"Only what you can carry," Vera said. "Quick."

Aimee carried her bag to the door, dropped it in a puddle, and joined Colleen. "That's a pretty necklace. Are the stones real?" Mom had given Colleen the long turquoise string of beads for her last birthday. Colleen hadn't taken it off, even to shower.

I pulled Mom's bundles toward the door. "Why are the waters rising so fast?"

"Federation must be pumping water our way. No more questions."

Loud pounding at the door sounded above the din of the wind and rain. A leather-faced woman, with her hair tied under a waterproof hat, barged in. She must have been from one of the other cabins.

45

"Boat's ready," she said. "We leave in five. Can I help carry?"

Vera pointed to bags her girls had placed by the door. "Regina, this is Aunt Yvonne. She has a motorboat we'll take upriver to meet your mom. Let's go. Quick, quick."

Jasmine and Aimee each wore a backpack. I pulled on mine, helped Colleen with hers, and grabbed two of Mom's plastic-wrapped bundles. Aimee grinned with excitement, not a lick of fear in her. Jasmine looked scared for both of them. I couldn't believe we had to flee our refuge.

Colleen squeezed the turquoise necklace dangling lose around her neck. "Is Mom coming back?" Her face hardened as she tried to act brave.

"We'll meet her along the way." I forced a smile and led her toward the open door. Waves lapped the stairs leading up to the wooden porch. Waters were rising much faster than last time. All our things back home would be soaked, ruined. Our poor goat remained tethered to a tree behind our house. We should have brought her, but there wasn't room in the skiff. We almost hadn't made it ourselves. Now we would have no milk and nothing to barter except our backpacks and Mom's wrapped bundles.

The moment we stepped outside, the winds blew me against the side of the cabin and knocked Colleen backward. The necklace flopped over her shoulder and caught on her chin. She grabbed it and dropped the bundle. I grabbed her package and steadied myself against the railing. Then I pulled myself and Colleen down the steps into calf-deep water. The boat bobbed behind the middle cabin with water behind it as far as I could see, as if this were the last stretch of land before the open seas. And I was looking upstream.

How could Mom abandon us during such a storm? Family is everything. I hoped she was okay and whatever caused her to leave was worth it. The year before, my friend Heather lost her mom during the worst of a storm. Afterward, I waited with her, but her mother didn't return. Later we heard she'd gone up north. She hadn't died. No, she'd abandoned Heather. With no one to pay fees, Heather had to drop out of school. She got by on salvage until bounty hunters took her.

I fought tightness in my gut and moved forward. Rain washed away any tears. Mom had dropped us like so much useless salvage, and we threw almost nothing away. Were we less useful than her precious salvage goods? Maybe it wasn't fair to accuse Mom so quickly, but I felt betrayed at how distant she'd become. For months she'd withdrawn, as if Colleen and I were too much burden. She worried constantly about not finding enough salvage to barter. Now she was gone.

Colleen stumbled. Yvonne carried her onto the boat. I sloshed through water that filled my thin boots. I lost my footing, gulped air, and went under.

I clutched my bundles, refusing to let go of our few remaining possessions. I wasn't sure what was in the packages, just that they were ours and it was my job to protect them.

Aunt Yvonne grabbed hold of me and helped me up. She handed the plastic-wrapped packages to Aunt Vera and helped me onto the boat.

The vessel was big. Colleen and I stood on the upper deck looking at the swirling seas. Aunt Vera took her girls to the covered lower deck. Another woman I took to be the mother of a third family nudged three girls Colleen's age and younger below. They bumped into each other trying to get below deck. Since fuel was scarce in the Richmond Swamps, these families must have bartered dearly to power this boat.

From the deck I bore witness to the end of the only world I knew. We weren't on Noah's ark, but it would have to do. Waves battered the boat against a rocky ledge that threatened to destroy us. Choppy water splashed over the sides. Winds pushed upriver, while the rains kept coming.

Aunt Yvonne untied ropes that moored the boat to a tree and looked up at the same instant I saw it: a big gray boat heading our way. The cruiser had the distinct markings of the Department of Antiquities, along with one of their quiet inboard motors. In the last storm they and their bounty hunter friends kidnapped dozens of girls to sell across the Barrier Wall as farm, mine, and factory slaves. When questioned afterward, agents claimed those girls had died in the storm. Yet I'd watched them being carted off.

Behind the patrol boat, a wall of water pushed its way up the channel.

Yvonne crawled aboard next to me and called to the woman at the helm: "Patrols! Surge! Head west."

I pulled Colleen toward the steps leading down. The boat rocked, sending her sprawling across the deck. I reached for her hand.

The wall of water hit the cluster of homes, splintering them like twigs. That could have been us. The cabins dulled the wave's appetite as the boat sped away. Then the water crashed around the back of the island and hit us from both sides. I held tight to the railing and reached for my sister. She slid down the deck toward the bow and then washed toward the stern, yelling all the way. I grabbed hold of her arm and pulled her to the railing. She let go of the necklace and clung to me. The necklace bounced over her head, arcing across the water.

"No!" she cried. "Mommy's necklace. I can't lose her."

I pressed Colleen's hands to the railing and reached for her precious keepsake. Waves flung the boat sideways. I lost my footing and tumbled over the railing, feet over head. I gulped air before hitting the water, and tumbled. I couldn't find up. My lungs burned. The waters tossed me like bubbles in a boiling pot. I finally surfaced, gasping for air. The boat pulled away.

At the railing, Yvonne held Colleen, who cried out, "Regina, don't leave me." Colleen reached out as if she could pluck me from the water. The current pulled me under. I swam back to the surface.

The wind picked up and swallowed all further traces of their voices. I swam to no avail. Then I treaded water, waiting for the boat to return. It didn't slow, didn't turn around. A wave crested. The patrol boat still headed our way.

I'm here. Come back.

With the patrol in pursuit, Vera's boat wasn't coming back. First Mom left, now Vera. I clenched my fists and realized I held something: Colleen's turquoise necklace. Somewhere in all that tumbling, I'd grabbed it and held on. I tucked it into my pocket and watched Vera's boat disappear beyond my reach.

I was on my own.

EIGHT

After the surge, the waters retreated, sucking everything out to sea. Soon they would threaten again. They always did while the winds raged up the channel. Staying put was a recipe for death. I wasn't ready to die. I couldn't. My job was to protect Colleen.

"Stop feeling sorry for yourself," Mo-Mere would say. *Focus.*

I turned toward the much smaller island where Aunt Vera and the others lived. The house in the middle was gone, down to a few support beams. The one on the right lacked a roof. Aunt Vera's home stood, though it leaned to the side.

The current pulled me alongside the island, toward the sea. I wasn't strong enough to swim in the ocean, and besides, farther out were sharks and vicious crocodiles.

I dove under the waves and swam hard westward, counting on the current to bring me closer to the island. I came up for air and tried again. I reached an eddy where the water couldn't decide which side of the island to take, and swam to shore, to what had been the back porch of the middle house. I dragged myself up onto the floorboards.

Another wave crashed over me. *Enough.*

Holding my breath, I clung to battered floorboards. Water tugged me upstream. I didn't let go. When the water retreated, it settled higher than before but left me above the surface. I gulped air. All this water brought a tremendous thirst, yet I'd watched girls drink unfiltered channel water and get ill. I didn't drink.

The retreating wave took part of the third cabin with it. I scrambled to my feet and sloshed through calf-deep water to Aunt Vera's home to look for anything salvageable that would help me survive. The front door was gone, the porch shattered. The cabin itself looked ready to collapse. I had to find something to eat and drink, and secure a boat. I looked for the kitchen.

Water crashed through the doorway, shattered a window, and sent me sliding toward the back of the cabin. I braced against the bedroom doorway while a torrent of winds and water shoved the cabin in several directions.

When that subsided, I waded to the kitchen cupboard. A few jugs of drinking water remained. I gulped one, fastened the top, and tucked the empty under my canvas shirt. I took a second jug, drank some, and attached it to my belt. Beside the sink basin, I found soggy biscuits. It wasn't Mo-Mere's turtle soup, but it would have to do as breakfast. I hoped my teacher had reached safety. She would know what to do.

Vera had taken most of the food. In the bedrooms, clothes sloshed in inches of water around soaked beds. I didn't have a boat or any way to carry them to safety.

The next wave hit and tugged my feet from under me. Walls swayed. I struggled to stay afloat, and then swam, holding on to whatever I could. When the waters pulled away, I clung to the front doorframe. The island looked smaller. I needed a boat, some way to move to other islands. Yvonne's craft was gone, so was Mom's skiff. All that remained were floating debris, and a coil of rope. Rope was a vital survival tool, so I wrapped some around my waist and knotted it.

Another wave headed toward the cabin. I pushed away from the front door, reached Vera's bedroom, and clung to the doorframe. The wave broke over the porch. The front wall disintegrated, leaving only the front doorframe.

The entire cabin tilted backward with a screeching groan. Waters retreated, pulling the bedroom doorframe and wall forward like brittle pages in a book. Wood splintered and creaked in pain. The bedroom wall gave way and slid toward the front of the cabin, dragging me with it. I grabbed hold of the front doorframe and held on, trying to keep my head above water.

With no support, the roof scraped down what was left of the side walls, hit the doorframe, and splintered wood around me.

Holding air in my lungs, I slid underwater, under the roof.

No matter how many storms I'd survived, nothing prepared me for the next. Each was different, with its own character. Some were quick, reminding us what it meant to be Marginal. Others lingered as if enjoying the misery they brought. Some were hungry, gobbling up land and possessions. Others were vicious, demanding human and animal sacrifices. Each extracted something special as a toll for survival.

Water tugged me and the cabin in several directions. I couldn't get out from under the roof. I found an air pocket and sucked in all I could. Retreating waves shifted the roof and pulled me beneath it, toward the open sea.

After the roof cleared the porch, I pushed myself to the edge, grabbed hold, and pulled my chin above water. I was holding on to a piece of cabin wall, a bundle of logs bound by rope and tar. The shattered remains of Vera's cabin floated alongside me. Little was left of the island except for a few trees and bushes that stubbornly clung to the remaining ground. They bowed in deference to the waves. All the bartering for materials, and months of labor to build, had vanished in one flood. There was nothing I could do. This seemed unreal. Vera's island was higher than ours. My home had no chance.

Waves bobbed me up and down. The waters retreated, revealing the bare foundations of three cabins. Behind them, the patrol broke off its pursuit of Aunt Yvonne's boat and navigated around clusters of branches and wreckage. It made no sense for a patrol boat to be so close to debris, taking risks during the worst of the storm. They usually left that for their bounty hunters.

Bits of cabin surrounded me, along with clothing and branches. My bundle of logs was twice my height in length, half that in width, and it floated. I had that, at least. The river moved too fast with too much debris to swim back to Vera's island. Besides, there wasn't a boat. Instead, I floated out to sea with little water or food, no fishing line, and little hope of finding any.

Another wave rolled up the channel, dragging the raft in the undertow before it. I clung tight to the upstream side of the logs and took a deep breath. The wave washed over me, jostling the raft. When I surfaced and looked forward, I didn't see any of the islands that once dotted the channels, just telltale treetops swaying in waves, hinting of lost homes.

Behind me, the patrol boat turned to head right toward me. *Toward me!*

What was going on? Was this the same Coarse-face who grabbed Colleen and jabbed needles into our arms? I couldn't outrun a patrol.

The rain pounded so hard I could barely see. My nose and mouth filled with spray coming at me sideways from the east. I felt as if I were drowning in spite of my raft.

Whenever waves crested, the patrol boat appeared closer. It had to be tracking me. Otherwise, why brave the debris and waves battering their boat? *Why me? Are you coming to rescue me? Did you see me fall overboard?*

No, they couldn't have seen me in the cabin. It had to be the chip that old Coarse-face jabbed into my arm. I hated that woman. Yet she could save me from dehydration, hunger, drowning, and sharks. She was my last hope. I waved my arms.

Mo-Mere's voice resonated in my head. "Avoid Antiquities patrols no matter what." Coarse-face hadn't been interested in our welfare when she'd left us paralyzed, surrounded by gators and rats. Mom said we were lucky patrols hadn't taken us. My head cleared. Patrols kidnapped girls to sell beyond the Wall. They wanted to make money off me. I wouldn't let that woman get her hands on me again.

I climbed into the water, draped my left arm over the corner of the raft, and clutched the end log. Keeping my head above the surface was hard. I loosened the loop of bandage from my upper arm and pushed it down my arm. I risked infection, but I couldn't let them catch me and send me away.

The swelling had gone down, but the puncture hole remained visible. From my belt, I tugged the utility knife I'd salvaged from a Richmond ruin, dug part of the blade into the raft to help open it, and cringed. Another wave was coming. Holding my breath, I clung to the log and my knife.

After the raft surfaced, I gasped for air and looked around. The patrol boat raced into the wave. Hand trembling, I pressed the point of the blade against my flesh. I didn't want to do this. I clung to the raft. When the water crested, the patrol boat had braved the wave and turned toward me. I bit back tears. *Mom, why did you leave?*

Clenching my teeth, I stabbed the blade into my upper arm. *Ahgh. Damn, damn, it hurts.* My breathing turned shallow. The stab was much worse than when Coarse-face injected the chip. She'd paralyzed me first with her tranquilizer gun. I pushed the knife point beneath the implanted chip and dug it out, letting it rest on my arm. Smaller than an apple seed, the chip seemed too tiny to cause all this trouble.

My arm throbbed. I closed the knife and fastened it to my belt. Water splashed the open wound. I grabbed the implant chip before it sank, rinsed off my blood, and clenched it between my teeth. I peeled a splinter from a raft log, dug a groove with my thumb, and forced the chip in. Then I set it afloat, pushing it away. *You won't catch me that easily.*

Grrr. My arm stung like a toothache. Blood oozed from my wound. I hadn't thought this through. The scent of blood would attract gators, sharks, and other critters.

I wanted to undo what I'd done. *Too late.*

To stop the bleeding, I pulled the bandage over the wound. Leaning back, I took a deep breath to steady my nerves. The wood chip with my tracking chip floated nearby, too close.

The patrol boat closed in. I pushed water toward the chip, but everything was floating toward the sea. Another wave washed over me. I scrambled to the surface, gasped for air, and hugged the raft. I no longer saw the splinter with my chip. The patrol boat slowed and inched closer. I needed somewhere to hide.

All I saw above water were treetops. This storm had flooded our home as prior storms had taken families farther east. I hoped the gators took refuge in calmer waters. I looked around and didn't see any, but then, they hung low in the water.

I was tempted to let the patrol boat catch me. They might feed me and fix my wounds. But I'd removed my tracking chip. That brought punishments worse than becoming a farm or factory slave. *You did it this time, Regina.*

The patrol boat motored closer. I slipped lower in the water between chunks of cabin wall and tucked my legs up. I pretended to be a gator with only my nose and eyes above water. When the patrol boat pulled next to my raft, I took a deep breath and ducked under water.

The image of the boat etched in my mind. Two gray-uniformed agents scanned with binoculars. Eleven girls in soaked green canvas stood chained to the railing. Two were giggly girls from my class. They didn't look so cheerful now.

A third Antiquities agent stood along the starboard side: the coarse-faced devil who had tagged me. I wondered if she could tell from my tracking device whether I was dead or alive, and whether the device was still in my arm. I stayed near the edge of the raft, listening.

"I don't see any live ones," one of the agents said.

"Keep looking." Coarse-face's voice carried a hint of Marginal twang. "This girl is of vital interest."

I couldn't imagine why. Had they overheard me speaking out at school?

The patrol boat puttered around my floating logs. I waited until my lungs were ready to burst before I surfaced. The boat bumped fragments of local lives, those of Aunt Vera and her friends.

Every minute we moved farther from safety and everything I knew. Who was I kidding? I couldn't survive on the ocean by myself. I should take my chances and let them pick me up. "Wait." My thin voice vanished on the wind. Panicked, I started to climb onto my raft so I could scream for them to return.

Wait, I said to myself.

My mind replayed images of the Marginal girls chained, like my goat, to the railing. They didn't look happy or saved. The giggly ones looked terrified. I thought of Robert Louis Stevenson's Kidnapped and refused to join them.

NINE

Demarco cursed her ineffective infrared sensors. The heat and storm were ghosting images. That would change when temperatures dropped. For now, she depended on her handheld tracking screen, homed in on Regina Shen's chip.

"More to starboard," Demarco called out to the captain.

If the governor hadn't insisted on the side trip to Charleston, Demarco could have grabbed both girls before they left that island. For that matter, if it hadn't been for the storm, she would have used the faster sea-skimmer, but it was prone to capsize in rough seas. As it was, she barely got there in time to see someone fall overboard and the island destroyed.

If she hadn't seen a girl slip into the water at the same time Regina's tracking chip fell overboard, Demarco would have pursued the fleeing boat. But something told her the older girl was the more interesting target. Breaking off the pursuit, she sent bounty hunters to intercept the motorboat that carried Colleen and went after Regina, though she hadn't yet decided how to play this whole scenario with the governor.

If she acquired the girls, she would have something to barter with, but Grand Old Dames like the governor didn't barter like Marginals. GODs took what they deemed theirs. Demarco needed a way to gain advantage. Having Regina Shen in custody would help.

The problem was that all the inspector had was the tracking chip with no infrared image around it. Aerial drones couldn't check the area in these winds. Meanwhile, the chip's signal floated downstream toward the sea. If the girl had any sense, she'd make herself visible before it was too late, but Marginals weren't the trusting sort. Demarco knew firsthand. *Suspicion keeps you alive out here.*

Ignoring incoming waves and clusters of logs and debris that could damage or destroy the graphene-fiberglass composite patrol boat, Demarco pressed the captain to pursue the signal. "Starboard, damn it."

"With all due respect, Chief Inspector, there's too much debris. If one of these waves dashes us."

"Enough!" Demarco said. "Stop sniveling. Governor's orders. You know what that means."

"We have too many girls already. We're riding too low in the water."

Demarco glanced at the girls chained to the rear port and starboard railings. That had been her before she'd made herself useful to a patrol captain, then to an Antiquities inspector, and finally to the governor. The first move involved betraying classmates at a school up north. The memory was a sting that never faded. Dumping these girls overboard to make room for Regina Shen might do them a favor.

"Inspector, we need to pull away." The captain pointed to another big wave and turned the patrol boat into it.

Pulled from her reverie, Demarco watched the wave crest over the bow. It rocked the boat like a toy and banged them into tree limbs. She cursed under her breath.

"We have to pull out," the captain said. "We're getting swamped."

"Negative." Demarco clutched her handheld tracker. "That's why you have extra bilge pumps. We stay until we find the girl. This mission is more important than our lives. Bring us ninety degrees to starboard. Over there."

The inspector scanned infrared over rafts that had been parts of homes, and then scanned the area around the chip's signal. There was no clear heat signature anywhere near it. If that was her, she might be dead. Then what would Demarco tell the governor? She couldn't think about that now. With even the slightest chance the Shen girl was alive, it was imperative to keep hunting.

The tracking scanner located the signal to within a foot. When they drew close, Demarco had one of her agents cast a net. "Scoop up whatever you can."

If necessary, she'd send crew onto smaller speedboats to drag the girl in, storm or not. Two of her agents pulled up the net. The scanner showed the chip rising. *Got you.*

The captain turned the boat into the next wave as the net flopped onto the bow deck. Demarco stared into the flat net with a few chunks of drenched wood. *Damn it.* "There's nothing there."

She tapped the side of her tracking scanner. Sure enough, it showed Regina Shen in the net. No one was there, unless the girl had turned into a ghost. That sent chills up the inspector's spine. *I don't care what Marginal mythology says, there's no such thing as ghosts.*

She dropped to her bony knees on the wet, hard deck and examined the pitiful catch. Three splinters of wood presented themselves. She separated them a foot apart and used the scanner, hoping beyond hope it would send her elsewhere. The tracker pointed to the one on the left. She picked it up. "More light."

Water washed over the side, drenching Demarco. She clutched the chunk of wood and steadied herself with the railing. This was so undignified, so Marginal. Yet she couldn't quit. One of her agents flashed a beam over the wood. Sure enough, a tiny sliver of metal the size of a rice grain reflected from its burrow deep inside the wood. *Damn you, Regina Shen.*

To be sure, she swung the chip, which registered movement on the tracking device. She stuffed the chunk of wood with the chip into a soaked jacket pocket, got to her feet, and glared over the side of the boat at frothy waters.

"The chip didn't come out by itself," she muttered through clenched teeth. "You think you're clever? I *will* find you."

"What was that, Inspector?"

Demarco pocketed the tracking device and panned her infrared scanner over the entire area. *Where did you go, you little swamp rat?*

The images on the screen were like ghosts, nothing material enough to be human. The Shen girl could have removed the chip at any time after she fell off the boat. Most likely she did it beforehand. *You're still on the boat, aren't you?*

"Head north," Demarco said. "Now."

The boat groaned when a clump of logs plowed into its side, bumping the craft sideways. More debris headed toward them.

* * *

Waves broke over me. Once again the hum of the patrol boat's motor grew closer. *Antiquities patrols aren't saviors,* I reminded myself. *They're the enemy. They kidnapped and hurt girls, sent them to the other side of the Barrier Wall as slaves.* As hard as life in the swamps had been, I couldn't imagine not seeing my family again.

I clung to the side of the raft farthest from the patrol boat and stayed as low as possible, my body aimed at the boat to present the smallest infrared image. It seemed to take forever before the boat pulled away. I dared not lift my head to look. Then I was all alone, drifting out to where sharks waited for me.

When I could no longer hear the boat, I crawled onto the raft and looked around. No boats. No land. Treetops undulated in the water. Rain pelted my face. Amid the deluge, I almost missed a familiar image: floral cloth clung to the upper limbs of a treetop maybe five feet above water. Kite cloth, dress material, my home.

There was something strange about looking at the tree from above, particularly when mostly submerged. I wondered if this was how survivors of Atlantis felt, if the myths of that deluge were true and anyone had survived. Maybe we knew so little about Atlanteans or where their land was located because they, too, had a Department of Antiquities that didn't want us to remember. Maybe it was to protect their treasures.

I tied off one end of my rope to a raft log, the other around my waist, and swam hard toward the tree. When I reached the upper branches, I removed the rope from my waist and tied it to the tree trunk.

I clung to the tree. Upstream, the patrol boat weaved between clusters of debris, still hunting. I took a deep breath and dived to what was left of my home.

There was little chance of finding much in the raging waters without help from my diving mask and breathing bladder, but I had to try. I'd never imagined salvaging my own home as I had what was left of the flooded ruins of Richmond. Sneaking off in Mom's skiff, I often anchored in tall grasses near deep waters. I would put on salvaged goggles and a breathing bladder I'd made from rubbery material, and dive to the ruins.

Like on many of my dives around Richmond, I returned to the surface after checking my home empty-handed. The raft pulled on the rope and the tree. The patrol boat zigzagged north, toward Aunt Vera's place. When they returned, which they would, the raft roped to my tree would give me away.

With no idea what I might find, I dove again. In flooded Richmond, generations before me had salvaged usable metal, stone, and other items that had survived the chaos and wars during the Great Collapse and subsequent floods. Paved streets between buildings overflowed with crab beds and seaweed. No names or signs remained to distinguish one flooded building shell from another. In contrast, I hoped to be the first to salvage my home.

What I needed more than anything was a boat, or even a log, which would be lighter and less visible to patrols. I grabbed the rope and followed it toward the raft. If I cut the bindings that held the raft together, I could separate a single log, and maybe make it to another island.

Before I reached the raft, the rope tugged me backward, digging into calluses on my hands. It tumbled me in the air and whipped me around, while the raft floated away. *Damn.* My knot hadn't held. To avoid being swept out to sea with nothing, I pulled myself hand-over-hand on the rope toward the tree, which had snapped upright.

I clung to tender treetop branches and caught my breath. *Now what?* The rains kept coming, but calm would bring no relief. I knew what I had to do, what I'd trained myself to do through hundreds of dives. I had to salvage.

I removed my water jugs, secured them to the tree, and pulled in the rope, which thankfully hadn't gone with the raft. I tied the loose end around my waist, took a deep breath, and dove beneath the branches. In the muddy waters I tried to locate our house. When my lungs burned, I surfaced, sucked in air, and dove again, using tree branches to pull me down. On my third attempt, I reached the spot where the house had been. Like Aunt Vera's home, our cabin had shattered and washed away.

On my next attempt, I scrounged around the foundation for anything useful. I was about to give up when my fingers caught something wedged into the cabin foundation. It was flat, cylindrical and metallic. With lungs screaming for relief, I worked it free. It had to be the bronze medallion Mom had thrown into the channel, the one she later confessed came from my donor mother.

Several more dives revealed none of our few possessions. The river-water tank had separated from its platform along with our clean water tank. The cabin's cast-iron burner was missing. Even our blessed goat had vanished, along with the metal stake that held her rope. Exhausted, I surfaced. I couldn't stay, yet I had to keep searching for survival tools. At least the patrol boat was no longer visible. No lights in any direction.

A growing ache swelled inside me. I should have surrendered to the patrol. All I had was rope and two water jugs, one empty. A wave washed over and threatened to tear me from my tree. I hugged the upper branches until it passed, and then took in air. Scooting higher, I looked around. To the west were half-submerged trees on flooded neighbor islands: Pulaski and Mendez. Nosy as neighbors could be, but good people. And ... *Oh, look! A ridge.*

I had to find a way to reach it, but how?

* * *

I dove again, to where I'd anchored my log-boat. It dangled like a buoy, with its hind end moored to a tree trunk. That gave me an idea. I surfaced for air and dove again. After I secured the rope around my waist, I untied the mooring and kicked to help the log-boat lift me to the surface.

After catching my breath, I used the other rope to pull me back to the tree. Then I tied my boat to the trunk, removed the other rope, and looked around. The rains slowed, the waters calmed, and the patrol boat was out of sight. *For now.*

My boat bobbed in the water, trailing downstream. I checked the compartment under the rear seat. My crossbow was still there with six steel-headed arrows, high-test fishing line, and a rod. I also found my goggles and breathing bladder, both soggy. That was more than nothing.

I untangled the torn bit of material from the top of the tree and stuffed it below my seat. After securing the empty water jug under my canvas top, I attached the half-empty one to my belt and sat in the log-boat, facing the open sea. The current was too strong to paddle upstream.

The winds died down. The rains stopped. Above me, a circle of clear sky poked through a blanket of black clouds: the eye of the storm. In none of the other storms had I witnessed such a wondrous sight: a dab of hope, as if the universe were talking to me.

I shook myself from the vision. This calm wouldn't last. I had to move or wait out the rest of the storm, while clinging to the top of my tree and waiting for the patrol boat to return. "Stay alive," Mo-Mere would say. "Stay free and make something useful of your life."

Sounds easy enough.

Heading west to higher ground had to be better than fighting the current upstream with only a paddle. With no time to waste, I secured one end of my high-test fishing line to the tail of a polymer composite arrow I'd salvaged from a former hunter. After making sure it would handle a sharp tug, I notched the arrow into my crossbow and cranked the bowstring tight. Then I took aim at a tree ninety yards to the west. I'd nailed more distant targets with this bow, but not while dragging fishing line.

I aimed, fired, and missed, a few feet downstream and too low. I drew in the line, notched the arrow, cranked tighter, and released. On my third attempt, I hit a tree trunk above the waterline. When I tugged, it pulled me and my boat westward, while the distant tree leaned in my direction. The arrow held, thanks to the serrated stainless head.

Downstream was calm. Upstream, I spotted lights.

Here goes. This one's for you, Mo-Mere.

I tied one of the boat's mooring ropes around my waist, unfastened the other from the tree, and said good-bye to my home. I doubted I'd ever find it again without the cloth. My boat swooped downstream in a wide arc below Pulaski's tree. The log bumped across choppy current and banged into floating branches and debris of lives I might have known: a pillow, empty water jugs, and bits of soggy bread. With my knees braced inside the boat, the fishing line tugged my arms. I prayed that it, and I, would hold up.

Adjusting my weight so the line wouldn't pull me out of my boat, I reeled myself toward the tree. The storm's calm was like the moments after a summer thunderstorm. But more damage threatened before this one finished with me. I got into a rhythm: lean back to pull my boat closer, and then spin the reel while I leaned forward, like rowing a boat.

My mind wandered to Mo-Mere. After such a violent storm surge, could her books have survived? I couldn't accept a world without printed books. I sobbed at the loss and then laughed at the absurdity. Here I worried about missing the chance to explore another read while holding on for dear life. My arms ached as badly as they did when I helped Mom get us to Aunt Vera's place. It was only a day before, yet it seemed a lifetime ago.

I wound the line, pulling the boat through a torrent of wreckage: logs, clothes, and plastic, everything in a Marginal's life that could float. An empty water tank drifted nearby. While I repeated the rowing rhythm, images flooded my mind. The floating debris was like the Persian army rushing toward me, something I'd read in Mo-Mere's collection.

Logs bumped the boat and spun me sideways. I braced my knees to keep pointed at the tree. I wanted to be brave like the Spartans, though as I recalled, they all died.

Every muscle in my arms and legs protested each turn of the reel. My mind flashed through Mo-Mere's histories. The Alamo. All killed. Masada. The same. Valiant resistance against irresistible forces. I had to fight with every last breath.

When I was close to the tree, I tied down the rod and reel with the log-boat's mooring rope. Then I unfastened rope from around my waist and lassoed the treetop. I pulled until I could tie a mooring line to the tree, and rested for a moment. Already, the clear circle of sky was moving away.

With my knife I dug out my precious steel arrowhead. I checked the fishing line's knot. Then I notched the arrow and took aim at a tree farther west. Clumps of trees beckoned beyond, with unfriendly neighbors. The Upper Marginals considered themselves better than the rest of us because they lived on higher ground, closer to the Wall. Yet they were only a few more storms surges away from what we had.

With the eye of the storm moving, I didn't have time to daydream. It took four attempts to hit the next tree and secure the line. After releasing the rope and swinging below Mendez's tree, I took a deep breath and began to reel myself in. Drawing in the line was like catching a monstrous fish. My arms were pulling out of their sockets. Thoughts of Mom cropped up, alone in this storm. Colleen with strangers. I reminded myself that when the winds picked up, shooting an arrow wouldn't work. While wreckage floated by, I spun the reel.

By the time I'd secured my arrow into the third tree, that of a family I didn't know, the winds picked up, this time coming from the south. Waves and wind fought over my boat, tossing us back and forth. While I clung to my reel, the line pulled with the weight of an elephant, though it was only the log-boat, me, and the current. Rain pelted the side of my face. The tree didn't seem to get any closer.

Praying the line didn't snap, I drew it in and cursed Mom. She'd abandoned Colleen and me. No matter what her excuse, she'd left. This anger had been building for months, stifled because Mom wouldn't let me talk to her. It was rage without outlet, since I depended on Mom for a home and the bartered fees she provided Mo-Mere as my teacher.

I shook it off and forced my weary arms to make one more turn on the reel, and another. My knees burned while I struggled to keep the current from twisting me sideways, which would increase the pull and snap the fishing line.

When I glanced east, I no longer saw the trees I'd used to get this far. If the line broke, there was no way back. Even my home tree vanished beneath incoming waves. A cluster of tree limbs floated by, far too close. I kept drawing in line.

The sky darkened. Boat lights poked through the rain. At first, it looked like an Antiquities patrol. I couldn't be sure. My legs cramped trying to hold the boat straight. My knees felt ready to snap. I'd lost friends to prior storms, including a teacher. There was no time to panic or feel sorry for myself. *Keep going.*

Once more I turned the reel, and again, until I couldn't do another and then forced myself. The boat to the east grew larger, closer, and grayer, though that could have been darkening clouds and the steamy blanket of rain. Was that a boat's throaty motor or the wind? I pulled myself closer to the clump of trees. Waters receded, revealing a rocky ledge. I couldn't look back. I knew what was coming, what always came after waters slipped away.

Don't panic. Prepare.

I secured the rope, tied the rod to the log-boat, and locked the reel. The empty water jug clung beneath my soaked canvas top. Holding tight to carved handholds, I lay down inside the boat, took the deepest breath, and considered getting my breathing bladder. *No time.*

Water crashed over the back of the log, covering me. The boat bobbed to the surface. Unable to breathe, I gripped the handles. The line slackened. The boat sped like a powerboat. The trees and island came up too fast. The line wouldn't hold if the wave threw us too far. The log-boat lifted, rose, and then fell. It hit something, bounced, and hit again.

TEN

With rains picking up, my log-boat floated amid a tangle of trees. The wave retreated, pulling the boat down through lower branches. I hung tight to the side handles and kept my head inside until the boat came to rest. Only then did I look around.

My boat and I were floating five yards inland from the tree with my arrow. I secured the mooring rope to the nearest tree and swam the short distance to recover my arrow.

A boat headed my way, but I still couldn't tell what type. I felt my left arm and remembered: the tracking chip was gone. If this was a patrol boat, were they hunting me or all girls fleeing the storm? I climbed the tree and worked at getting the arrow out of the trunk. It was too wedged in and too visible from the channel.

From where I crouched, I saw the Antiquities emblem on the approaching boat. I dropped into the water, swam toward my log-boat, and curled into a ball behind a nearby tree to reduce whatever infrared signal they might get from me.

Winds were unsettled, coming from the east and south, as if they couldn't make up their minds. A wave bounced the patrol boat closer to shore. I didn't move. When the wave retreated, bright lights shone on the trees around me. Voices sifted in on the wind.

"Since that clever rat removed her tracking chip," Coarse-face said, "we'll have to search every island until we find her."

"We've already caught twelve," another voice said. "We should go before we get dashed against the rocks."

"Shall I relieve you of command?"

"No, Chief Inspector. But it won't matter if we crash."

"Let me worry about that. If you hadn't been so skittish, we could have had her by now. Letting her make a fool of you won't look good on your record. She's running. She'll soon learn there's nowhere to hide."

Shivering in the heat, I clung to the tree and strained to see the faces on board. Sure enough, Coarse-face looked over the side with binoculars. *What's your interest in me?*

The woman in the gray uniform next to her was the one who had helped insert my implant. I recognized three of the girls from my school, chained to the port railing. It wasn't too late to let them rescue me, too. Except the girls looked waterlogged and frightened, not relieved.

Then I froze. Behind Coarse-face was the last woman I expected to see on a patrol boat. *Mom!* Her hair matted against her face. She wore the same blue outfit she did on those Sundays when she left Colleen and me. Her eyes looked tight and angry. Mom, unbound by chains, approached Coarse-face. She leaned in as if to whisper. She didn't look like a prisoner.

I couldn't breathe, couldn't move. Even if I'd wanted to surrender for a chance to see her and escape the storm, I couldn't make my aching limbs budge. My voice failed me.

Mom? What's going on? You said I should never let patrols find me. Now you're with them. What happened?

Coarse-face turned to speak to Mom. I strained to hear, but the wind shifted. Before I saw or heard anything else, the patrol boat motored up the channel out of sight. If there was a cove or ledge, they could land and search the island. If I left, the current would drag me away.

I returned to the tree that held my arrow and worked the arrowhead free with my knife. Then I swam back to my boat. I couldn't believe Mom was with Antiquities agents. It made no sense. Marginals rarely wore anything but green, yet Mom wore blue outfits on Sundays when she disappeared. Now she wore that same blue and whispered to the inspector. Instead of staying with her family during the storm, she'd sneaked off in the middle of the night to be with Coarse-face.

Now that the storm surge had retreated, my log-boat hung eight feet above the water, looking like a twin to the tree's trunk. Sitting on a rocky ledge nearby, I reeled in my precious fishing line.

My hands shook. I'd felt betrayed when Mom left us during the storm, and now this. I didn't want to believe what my senses suggested. Six days a week, Colleen and I went to school while Mom did whatever she did. On Sundays, she often disappeared, leaving me to watch Colleen. I'd always felt closer to Mo-Mere than to Mom, a rift that had grown intolerably wide after Mom and I argued over my donor mother. Could Mom really be a spy, the biggest Antiquities spy ever?

I threw up and sat against a tree, trying to steady my breathing. I took in rainwater to clear the taste. Was there no one I could trust? Mom and Mo-Mere had known each other since coming to the swamps. Were they both involved?

Wake up! Stay alert.

The patrol boat could land. Agents could scour the island. With those thoughts, I pulled in the last of my fishing line. My world was tumbling upside down, with the storm showing me things I wouldn't otherwise have believed.

I secured reel, line, and arrow in the back compartment of my log-boat. A moment later another vessel approached, with the dirty growl of high-powered engines used by pirate scavengers. Despite heavy rains and choppy waters, the boat headed straight toward the island. Leaving my log-boat in the tree, I climbed onto dry land. Well, as dry as it could be during a storm.

By the time I'd crawled up the muddy bank, the boat had stopped on the north side of the island. Girls stood chained to the port and starboard railings. I made my way along a low ridge and found two cabins in the center of this island and several boats on the north shore. The nearest boat let off six women in black wetsuits: bounty hunters, or froggies, as we called them. They often raided the Richmond Swamps for girls to sell into servitude. In a moment of exhaustion and desperation, that sounded better than dying.

Yet I knew better. Mom said the Federation denied my donor mother basic medical care, leaving her to die. Now they hired bounty hunters to take girls like Colleen and me.

The second boat looked as if a giant had battered its hull. The third carried familiar markings on the side, exactly like the one Aunt Vera and Colleen had been on. My heart sank. The bow had splintered into kindling from smashing against rocks; it lay open like a gaping gator mouth. There were several gashes down the port side. I was surprised the boat hadn't sunk or washed away. The surge must have pushed the remains up on shore.

Colleen, are you here?

I got to my feet and ran to the tree line nearest one of the cabins. Two froggies in their thin black wetsuits ran up the path carrying weapons and waterproof chemical torches. Four more froggies approached from the other side. They surrounded the two homes. I slid behind a tree and held my breath. I needed my crossbow.

I slid down the slippery path to my boat, climbed the tree, and found my bow and quiver of arrows. With those in hand, I scrambled up the path to the tree line.

By the time I reached the clearing, the froggies were spraying chemical fire on the cabins and lighting them with their torches, which sizzled in the rain. At first the rain protected the cabins. Then the chemicals seeped into the wood and the cabins burst into flames.

Three women emerged from the nearest cabin. One was Aunt Vera; I didn't recognize the others. Then Colleen stepped outside and curled up into a tight ball on the ground. It was all I could do to keep from running to her. If they caught me, we were both doomed.

Aunt Vera talked to one of the froggies. I couldn't hear above the whistle of the wind. Wiping rain from my eyes, I tried to keep from shaking.

One bounty hunter with a fierce, ruddy complexion picked up Colleen. Another escorted four more girls, including Aunt Vera's daughters, toward their boat. They stopped at the tree line to my right. The ruddy-faced bounty hunter dropped Colleen and returned to where Aunt Vera was arguing. Ruddy-face pressed a handgun to Vera's chest and fired, throwing her backward like a sack of flour. Shot her like shaking hands, as if it were nothing. I couldn't believe … I had to rescue Colleen.

I moved closer to where the five girls sat. The froggie with them was gazing toward Aunt Vera. I notched an arrow and aimed. My heart raced. The crossbow shook in my hands. I'd killed animals for dinner, but never a person. Before I could decide, my finger twitched.

The arrow struck the black-suited woman in the neck. A wave

of shock and horror swept over me. Too late. I couldn't take it back.

She tried to yell. When she couldn't, she pulled the arrow from her neck and fell to her knees, then onto her side. I sprinted faster than I thought possible. I grabbed Colleen's arm, motioned for the other girls to follow, and ran through the bushes toward my boat. Then it hit me: The log-boat wasn't big enough for six, and we couldn't outrun a bounty boat.

"I knew you'd come for me," Colleen said, clinging to my hand.

"Shush." I pushed through thick bushes in the gray darkness with rain filling my eyes.

A metal trap bit my left leg with such force I was certain it had cut off my foot. Stifling a scream, I fell onto my side and dropped my crossbow and quiver. Colleen fell on top of me, screamed, and tumbled away.

The foot pain was worse than when I'd pulled my own tooth, worse than anything I could have imagined. Shaking, I pushed my face out of the mud and reached for the trap. Pain radiated in every direction until I couldn't be sure what part of me hurt.

A black boot kicked my side, sending new waves of pain. "Serves you right, you little muskrat. These five will bring us 800 credits each. Lame one like you isn't worth the trouble."

I squinted upward. The ruddy-faced bounty hunter who shot Aunt Vera shined a light on my trapped leg.

"Don't leave me." Colleen said. She crawled next to me and took my hand.

"Please, ma'am," I said. "She needs me."

"Cut your whining. They'll place her in a home where she'll eat a darn sight better than out here. If you're a good girl, we'll come back after the storm passes."

The murderous bounty hunter picked up Colleen and carried her away. I heard my sister's screams all the way to the boat. Poor Colleen. Three times I'd failed to protect her. I was no better than Mom.

Rain splattered my face. I shivered despite the heat and fingered the turquoise necklace, the only thing I had left of my sister and mom. I should have given it to Colleen, but then the froggies would have taken it.

The bounty hunters left me as damaged goods, unwanted by

real people across the Barrier Wall. Rain splashed into my wounds. The pain grew so intense my mind went blank.

* * *

I woke with a start. It was still raining and growing darker. If I didn't do something soon, I risked becoming some critter's dinner. I considered cutting my foot out of the trap, as I'd dug the implant from my arm, but I liked having two legs. Lame Marginals didn't fare well. At least the trap wasn't a Federation genetically-enhanced alligator. Then it would have half eaten me already.

Sitting up, I wiped my eyes and studied the trap. I wanted to kick it and make it let go, but it wasn't an animal you could motivate. It was a simple, spring-loaded model like those Mom and I set around home to catch rats, coyotes, and scavengers. Digging in the mud, I found a couple of rocks and forced one between the teeth at the edge of the trap. Then I found a branch with enough stiffness and pried it between the teeth on the other end. When I sat on the stick to anchor it, pain radiated. I had to steady my breathing before continuing.

With both hands, I pulled up on the top of the trap until the upper teeth let go of my foot. Raising the teeth hurt as much as when they'd clamped down. I was tempted to pull my leg straight out. If I slipped, it would chew up more of my foot. Instead, I kicked a large stone between the widened teeth and made sure it wedged in. Wincing, I lifted my foot up off the bottom teeth. My throbbing foot shook so much it almost kicked the rock out. I slowly lifted my foot out of the trap without scraping the teeth.

Hungry for its meal, the trap snapped shut on the rock. I fell back and took a deep breath. My foot felt as though it was on fire. Trembling, I removed the bandage from my left arm, wrapped it around my ankle, and passed out.

I didn't know how long I was out. When I woke, it was growing even darker. Aunt Vera leaned over me. Blood soaked her green canvas clothes from her chest down.

"Child, I bandaged arm." Her voice sounded weak and gurgled, as if her lungs had filled with fluid. "Cleaned leg. Re-bandaged."

I noticed material missing from her sleeve. "Aunt Vera, I thought—"

"Sorry we couldn't get you. Bounties chased. Wave dashed us on rocks." She wept. "Find my babies. Promise."

69

"I promise, Aunt Vera. I saw Mom."

She collapsed in my arms and let out a ghastly sour breath. I held her. It was all I could think to do. I held tight for Mom and Colleen, for Jasmine and Aimee, and for myself.

I checked Aunt Vera's pulse and breathing. Found neither. Her chest stopped oozing blood. I didn't know what to do with such a large wound. Then it sank in. She was dead. I was alone, completely on my own.

ELEVEN

Inspector Joanne Demarco's Mesh-reader vibrated. It had to be Governor Wilmette.

Shielding her eyes from the rain, the inspector motioned toward the twelve girls chained to the railings of the patrol boat. "Don't let these swamp rats out of your sight," Demarco told one of her agents. "They have ways of slipping their chains."

Demarco turned to the Chinese Marginal woman she'd picked up on her return from Charleston. She had proven useful during the storm, but now she was a distraction.

"We've done well tonight," Lola Deng said. "We should take these to safety before we attempt to collect more."

Demarco held up her hand. "Urgent call." She climbed down into the captain's cabin, locked the door, and sat before answering her Mesh-reader. The round face of the 300-some-year-old governor filled the screen. The lips moved without sound. Demarco tried not to grimace while she maintained the required amount of eye contact so she didn't offend her benefactor.

The distorted image looked as if photo-manipulated between images of a striking youthful woman and a corpse. All the fancy meds and genetic therapies preserved the illusion of vibrant health, or perhaps only a hint of such. In fact, all those medical miracles enabled a decrepit old woman to linger well past her expiration date, beyond when she should have been recycled. Demarco didn't get to make that decision. If she had, well …

Perpetual life isn't for everyone, Demarco reminded herself, trying to avoid showing any emotion. Those who possessed the rights—GODs—rarely carried the effect well. Unfortunately, the therapies hadn't begun until the Grand Old Dames were well into middle age. Perhaps applying treatments to younger women would have yielded better results.

Demarco waited for the governor to finish whatever business distracted her and turn on her microphone. It was all she could do to keep her small fish dinner down. She tried to read the governor's lips, but all the medical treatments left them so stiff they barely moved.

The more Demarco saw of the governor, the less she fancied signing up for longevity. Oh, the governor plied herself with every sort of makeup to hide the effects, but beneath all those creams and layers was decay. Yet decay could yield new life. The promise of better circumstances motivated Demarco to hitch her fortunes to the relic for now.

"I expect you to answer when I call, not keep me waiting," Governor Wilmette said. The frown did little to improve her appearance.

"I was in the bathroom, Your Majesty. You might try riding the waves during a storm."

"That's what I have you for. Speaking of which, why haven't you called with news on the Shen girls? My lab techs tell me we've consumed their samples in tests and need more."

Demarco bowed her head, even though she wasn't in the physical presence of her benefactor. "We've been busy dealing with tens of thousands trying to breach the Wall."

"That's why you have staff," the governor said.

"They're spread thin protecting the Wall and hunting girls. Good news: we have final test results on the Shen girls' DNA."

"Then why didn't you say so? What do they show?"

"They have healthy reproductive markers," Demarco said, "and none of the defects found in previous samples."

"Great. When can I see them?"

"I'm making a sweep of bounty hunters. I believe they've captured the twelve-year-old, Colleen."

"I thought you tagged them with trackers," the governor said. "How hard can this be?"

"The storm makes it difficult to pick them up."

"Bring me Colleen."

"As soon as I have her in custody, Your Majesty. Remember, she's only twelve."

"I know, I know. What about the older one?" the governor asked. She furrowed her brow, which bunched up the cakes of makeup. "Don't tell me you've lost her."

"She removed her tracking chip. I've received word she's alive. She has nowhere to hide. We'll find her."

"You'd better."

"I have every resource on it," Demarco said. "Now, if we'd launched replacement satellites, we could have restored aerial surveillance."

"Don't start on that again."

"I'm just saying, Your Majesty, that we would have had her in custody already with satellite tracking."

"Do I have to repeat myself?"

"No, Your Majesty." Demarco hung her head. There were uphill battles and lost causes. The premier in Antarctica controlled all satellites, and no other governor wanted that much control so close to the Antarctic governor. Stalemate.

"What I started to say earlier," Demarco said, "is Regina's DNA markers are much stronger than her sister's. The girls only share one mother."

The governor's face turned pink under layers of makeup. Her eyes made up for that with a fiery gleam. "Don't clutter my mind with details, just bring the girls."

"Yes, Your Majesty."

"They could alter the course of history. Remember, if I rise, you rise. Don't make me repeat what happens if you fail me."

The inspector didn't need reminding. There would be no throwing her back over the Wall. For those born as Marginals, punishment meant confinement, deprivation, and torture. All that happened before agents fed you to gators.

* * *

I pushed myself up into a standing position. My left foot howled at me to stop. I groped for anything to soften the blow as I fell onto my side. Clouds above me turned dark plum. Rain filled my mouth. I swallowed, choked. Rivers of rain churned mud all around and splashed my face.

My hand grasped a thick branch with a cleft that would do as a crutch. I used it to push myself up. Rain washed away some of the mud. After scooping up my crossbow and quiver, I poked another stick ahead of me to test for more animal traps while I limped toward the clearing.

To steady my breathing and rest my leg, I stopped often. The canvas bandage Aunt Vera had provided was soaked pink. My ankle throbbed as if still in the grip of that trap. *I'm still alive*, I told myself over and over. I'd survived the surges, so far. I'd escaped Coarse-face. Yet the thought of her brought images of Mom on that boat, talking not like a prisoner but like friends.

I pushed forward. *Deal with what's in front of you: find water, food, and a safe place for the night.*

When I reached the clearing, both cabin fires still smoldered beneath sheets of rain. The chemical-induced flames shed some light. The bounty hunter I'd hit was gone, as was their boat, and Colleen. My arrow lay in the grass nearby. I wiped off the blood, placed the precious arrow in my quiver, and hobbled toward the nearest cabin. Two women lay in front of it, in a pool of blood. I would bury them later. First, I needed to check out the island. I didn't see anyone else, and thankfully, no more bodies.

The smoke was too thick for me to search the cabins for salvage or refuge. If it hadn't been for my useless leg, I would have tried, but it was all I could do to take one step at a time. My stomach cramped from sobbing. *Mom, why did you leave? What have you done?*

I dropped onto a tree stump across from one of the cabins. All I had left in the world was a gimp leg. "Stop feeling sorry for yourself," Mo-Mere would say. "Swamp critters prey on the lame."

She was right, as usual. If the storm hadn't taken it, I also had my log-boat, but I needed food and water before making the journey down to find it. I also had to wait out the storm or the sea could still claim me.

Taking a deep breath, I hobbled around outside of the cabins, looking for anything to eat, drink, or barter for survival. The water purification tanks stood intact. I limped over, pain pulsing with the bounce of each step. The tank was full, so I took a long drink from a tap on the side and reveled in precious clean water. Then I filled the water jug on my belt. With fresh water came hope. Food next.

A washed-out garden stood behind the cabins. It felt good to dig my hands in soil. Like fresh water, soil was life-giving. I found tiny carrot buds, a few turnips, and a small spud. Sitting on a rock, I gorged on the vegetables, such as they were, and considered saving the spud. Hunger won out.

Rains stopped. Winds shifted from the south, bringing sticky heat that mosquitoes loved. The fiery cabins left me no shelter for the night. Trees were my next best refuge from ground critters, but not with this bum leg. The water tanks had a ladder leading up to a solar paneled roof. If the tanks had been enclosed, I would have taken shelter inside, but there were no walls, only four posts holding up the roof. At least it was off the ground.

With my walking stick strapped to my back, I pulled myself up the ladder using my hands and one good leg. Rolling over the rim, I plopped down on the tarred wooden frame around the edges of the solar panels. I unfastened the ladder's latches and pulled it up to be sure no one could follow.

From the solar platform, I watched what remained of my world. Off in the distance, boat lights moved across the horizon. They could have been patrol, scavengers, bounty hunters, or Marginals looking for dry land. A boat passed close to the south shore and panned a floodlight around the island. The light came to rest on the charred cabins. The boat moved on, leaving me in darkness.

A dry place to sleep would have been paradise, but no such beast survived in our swamps. Wet was our constant, what defined us, what gave us character. *But why, oh Blessed Mary, couldn't you make us Marginals amphibians, so we could better endure it?*

* * *

I woke with a start to loud banging. While the sky remained charcoal gray, the rains had stopped. The eastern clouds grew paler. It had to be morning.

My heart stopped. Torches lit the cabins and surrounding area. A scavenger boat had docked next to the boat wrecks. Those vultures would pick clean whatever they found. All six of them carried rifles, and scavengers could be just as vicious as bounty hunters. Something clanged beneath me. Seven. When they got around to reclaiming the roof, I would be trapped.

Mo-Mere had told how, early on, some Marginals chopped every tree on their island for firewood until they had no fuel or protection from even mild storms eroding their land. Those people died or became bounty hunters and thieving scavengers.

My leg throbbed beneath the mushy bandage. I needed it dry or infection would take hold. Rotating on the tarred section of the water tank roof, I watched scavengers poke through the cabins. They pulled out kitchen pots, and utensils I could have used for barter. The charred furniture was only useful for firewood. Any food was beyond edible. Clothing and bedding useless. The sum total of these families' lives littered the mud.

Banging continued beneath me. It rattled the posts that held up the roof, and rattled my nerves as well. Someone grunted below; hammer blows followed. The fresh water tank rolled away from its mountings and into the clearing. Two scavenger women dove out of the way. On second glance, they were girls the age of my giggly classmates. They weren't scary, but the dark-skinned woman who ordered them back to work looked seasoned by too many storms.

Throat parched, I took a quick drink from my jug. It didn't help, and there would be no more fresh water on this island.

The girls dug in the garden, finding a few immature vegetables I'd missed. I was tempted to beg them to take me with them, but scavengers had no use for a gimpy girl who couldn't bring them much in barter. A Marginal's survival depended on how useful she could make herself. Right now, for me, that didn't amount to much.

Mosquitoes buzzed. I couldn't swat without shaking the platform and giving up my hiding place. There was more pounding below. The second tank rolled away, shaking the wooden frame until I thought it would spill over. I clung tight to the rim while four scavengers, including the girls, rolled the tanks down to their boat. Two women collected the pitiful remains of these homes. In minutes they'd picked the island clean, except for solar panels and the tarred roof that would make poor firewood. They even stripped Aunt Vera and the other dead women of their clothes, leaving their bodies to rot. I couldn't let that happen.

A smaller boat pulled up to the island, a motorboat only uppity Marginals could afford. I scooted to the side of the roof for a better view and squinted through slits in the rim that framed the roof like a picture.

Two bounty hunters in black froggie wetsuits stood at the bow of the motorboat holding rifles. Three more faced the scavengers in a standoff. Leaders from both sides argued. The words sounded like bees buzzing until …

"Just let us check your damned boat." It was the ruddy-faced Bounty-killer, the one who had shot Aunt Vera. "You can keep your scavenged goods."

Evidently the scavengers agreed. They moved away from their boat to let the bounty hunters board. Both sides stared each other down with guns pointed at the ground. I strained to see if Colleen might be on the bounty boat, but the railing held no chained girls, and it was too small to hold much below.

My stomach lurched. What had Bounty-killer done with my sister and Vera's girls? I didn't know what to do. There were too many guns, too many desperate angry people. *Mom, it was your job to look after Colleen.*

With the tanks removed, there was nowhere to hide if I were to climb off the platform. To make matters worse, the latches for the ladder faced the clearing and the boats.

As soon as the bounty hunters finished checking the boat, the scavengers scurried on board and motored off. They were the bottom feeders of our Marginal scum. Five bounty hunters in black scuba gear hiked up from their boat toward the burned cabins.

"They reported no one left on the island," said a woman with creased leathery skin.

"I don't give a damn what they said." Bounty-killer held her rifle ready to shoot. "Check the island for hiding places and boats."

"We should've taken the injured girl when we had the chance."

"Shut up and find her. She can't have gone far."

I was tempted to take a shot at that dreadful, ruddy face. Four other armed froggies convinced me otherwise. Trembling, I notched an arrow just in case. My heart raced. I couldn't breathe. I'd never really known hate before, but that's what I felt toward this demon. I wanted her dead.

Younger froggies entered each of the two cabins. Another headed to where my log-boat hung from a tree, while Leather-face went down the south side of the island. Bounty-killer poked around the supports to the water tank cover. She rattled a support beam until I was certain she'd knock the roof, and me, onto the clearing. I held onto the rim, although this made my fingers visible. She fired two shots up into the middle of the roof. Solar panels shattered, sending glass spewing over my back.

Twitchy, I pressed my face into the sticky tar to stifle an involuntary yelp.

"Damned bitch!" Bounty-killer said.

I couldn't be sure who she was referring to: me, one of the scavengers, Leather-face. She fired again. Wood splintered next to me. *Will you kill me like Aunt Vera? Is this because I shot your friend? Where did you take Colleen?*

Fear kills. Think.

The wooded area by the shore was too far away. A clearing surrounded the platform to provide sunlight. Too visible. The other bounty hunters returned from scouting the island and cabins, cursing the mosquitoes and the lack of anything to salvage.

"We should have taken from those scavengers," said a young froggie, her hair covered by the wetsuit.

"Too many guns," Leather-face said. "Too messy."

"Nothing inside the cabins." A twentyish blonde adjusted her wetsuit cap. "Anyone caught inside would have been cooked."

"We'd have smelled that," Leather-face said.

"Did you find the girl?" Bounty-killer asked.

"No sign of her or a boat. If I were her, I'd have found a way off this island."

"You're not her."

"We have nothing," Leather-face said.

"Then we take this." Bounty-killer pushed on the roof supports, making the platform sway.

Clinging to the rim, I looked around. The platform was halfway between the cabins and the tree line. Three fruit trees stood nearby. The closest was an orange tree, picked clean of fruit.

The other bounty hunters joined in pushing the platform supports. I spotted two of them through blast holes and moved away.

"Count of three, everyone push," Bounty-killer said.

The contraption swayed wildly, almost tumbling me over the side. The ladder slid along the edge to the opposite end.

"Push," Bounty-killer said. "Did anyone find the trap?"

"Yeah," an older froggie said, out of breath. "With bits of skin and blood. The woman you shot was next to it. She must have helped the girl escape."

"Okay, listen up. The girl had to arrive in a boat and we found none. We take this firewood and hunt her down, island by island."

"You couldn't even kill that stupid woman," Leather-face said. "You're slipping."

The platform stopped rocking. I began to feel seasick. The ladder was propped on the opposite edge from me, near the orange tree. On two good legs, I could have gotten to it and used it to what? Jump into the tree? It beat tumbling into the clearing.

"This is getting us nowhere," Bounty-killer said. "You're right. I didn't shoot to kill. If I had, she wouldn't have moved. I also didn't know this was the Shen girl Antiquities was after. Otherwise, we would have taken her, bum leg and all. Before you get any ideas, what were you doing while all that was going on?"

They must have hit the supports in unison. The platform swayed toward the orange tree, bouncing the ladder up off solar panels toward the tarred roof. I held tight to the rim until the roof swayed back, and then I scooted to the ladder. When the platform moved the other way, wood cracked below and the platform moved as if it had become fluid like the stormy seas.

Instead of swaying back, the platform continued forward, collapsing toward the orange tree and the ground. After pushing the ladder against the rim, I clung to the top, pushed off with my good leg, and swung out into the orange tree. While the solar platform cracked and collapsed beneath me, I caught hold of a branch. The ladder fell away, leaving me dangling from the tree. Like a squirrel scurrying for its life, I climbed higher.

Several bounty hunters vanished beneath the collapsed platform. Bounty-killer dusted herself off and looked at the shattered remains. "Get up, gather what you can, and get it to the boat. Then check the wrecks one more time."

My bandage had slipped during my climb. The wound bled again, dripping onto the ground below. I curled up against the trunk and fought the stinging pain to move the ragged green canvas over the sore.

Below me stood Bounty-killer, examining the blood in the dirt, my blood. She looked up. I held my breath and didn't move. Through the leaves, I saw one of the froggies bandage her own arm. Bounty-killer kicked dirt over the blood and helped the others move the support beams and tarred roof to their boat. They left the shattered solar panels.

Leaves blocked most of my view. Were they leaving? No. Bounty-killer returned. She walked the perimeter of the tree, looking up and down the trunk and into the leaves. I pressed myself against the tree trunk, legs crossed, until I thought my wound would burn a hole through both legs.

I couldn't see her ruddy face through the leaves and branches, but it continued to haunt me. I figured she would bring an ax to chop the tree for firewood. There wasn't even fruit for me to suck on while I waited.

TWELVE

My legs cramped, and my foot fired off waves of burning pain. Bounty-killer examined the tree bark and kept looking upward. I couldn't recall when the bandage had slipped. Had it snagged on a tree limb while I scrambled for a handhold? She lingered, as if she smelled something.

I waited for the ripping sound of a saw. Then I heard nothing but the wind. No longer able to hear or see any hint of her below me, I strained to pick up flashes of her between the leaves. I could just make out the wrecks by the shore, but no motorboat next to them.

I removed the strip of material Aunt Vera had torn from her canvas top as a bandage. The wound wept, but it didn't look infected. Yet. Aunt Vera must have cleaned it, even while dying.

"Find my girls," she'd said.

And Colleen, I added.

Without dry material, I refolded the blood-soaked cloth and re-bandaged my leg. Then I looked through leaves at the ruined boats. Was the bounty-hunter's boat really gone? Had all five bounty hunters gotten back on board? I couldn't find out while sitting in a tree.

I had to find my boat, assuming the bounty hunters, scavengers, and storm hadn't taken it. I scooted out on the limb for a better look at the wrecks. The bounty boat was definitely gone. I didn't see anyone, but the scavengers might return now that their foes had left.

I returned to the trunk, climbed to the lowest branch, and dropped to the ground. Then I leaned against the trunk until the pulsing pain lessened. I removed the walking stick strapped to my back and hobbled over to the woods where Vera lay, dead and naked. Her last act had been to help me. Nearby was the wretched trap that snared me and kept me from taking Colleen to safety.

No time to dwell.

The trap had saved me from Bounty-killer and whatever Coarse-face had in mind. It had also increased my determination. The harder they hunted, the more I had to fight to remain free.

Using stones and a branch, I dug a shallow grave to bury Aunt Vera. I barely knew her, but it felt like we had a bond. I said a prayer, limped over to the other two women, and dug two more graves. When I finished, I looked over the cabins and surrounding area. Scavengers and bounty hunters had already picked the place clean. The water tanks were gone. The place no longer offered any food. It was time to leave.

As if to reinforce that thought, two large alligators nosed around the boat wrecks that rested on their sides in receding water on the beach. I prayed there were no bodies.

There were no other boats in the channels around the island, so I limped down the path. I reached the tree where I'd tied my log-boat, but didn't see it. My heart sank. It wasn't in the channel drifting away or in the mud between the trees.

In despair, I looked up at the clearing sky. Of course. When the waters were higher, the boat had seemed only eight feet up; now it was even higher. I would have to climb after all.

With my walking stick strapped to my back, I pulled myself up limb by limb to the branch where I'd tied the mooring rope. Arms ached, heart raced, foot throbbed. Leaning against the trunk of the tree, I looked toward open waters to where my home had been. Most of our island was under water.

It didn't matter. The storm had scrubbed our home clean of any evidence that we'd lived there. Scavengers would pluck anything worth taking, including the foundation and trees. Between rising seas and eroded lands, the waters looked to have risen five to ten feet. That was the way it went: no change for a year or three then a storm took another chunk. It was hard to tell if the seas were rising or the land sinking. It made no difference. These weren't the best of times and if they weren't the worst, what else could I expect?

I gazed farther southeast toward my school, which was too far to spot. Ten feet would have swamped it and Mo-Mere's plastic-wrapped books. Maybe they survived. *Take hope where you can.*

I untied the mooring rope and lowered the log-boat. My calluses burned as I tried to keep the log from falling. Even so, it dropped the last few feet. I hoped that hadn't damaged anything. I'd spent too much time carving the boat by hand and sealing it to see it destroyed.

The ground nearby moved. A gator crawled toward the log to inspect it. The animal wasn't big, but up close they all looked huge. Carefully I lowered myself branch by branch. I didn't fancy becoming the critter's dinner. I admired gators. They were so versatile that they could live on land or in water. Fearless, they ate just about anything, thanks to the Federation's genetic manipulations.

The gator waited while I descended to the lowest branch. My bad foot throbbed, reminding me to stop putting weight on it. The red bandage attracted every bloodsucker around. Flies swarmed, wanting in.

The predator watched me with big, attentive eyes. Staring back, I notched an arrow into my crossbow and leaned over the branch. The gator reared up to snap at me. I loosed an arrow and hit the animal's right eye. The creature wiggled like a snake coiling and uncoiling. I fired a second arrow and hit the skull between the eyes. The steel tip must have hit brain matter. The gator twitched, retreated, and stopped moving.

I waited, but not long. I couldn't afford some other critter grabbing my catch and two of my arrowheads. I poked the gator with my walking stick. When it didn't respond, I dropped on top and jabbed my knife into the other eye. I dug out the first arrow and wiped it on the gator's hide. The second arrow had lodged into bone.

I plunged my knife into the skin around the arrow to work it free. After it came loose, I carved off some of the gator's tail. Cooking it would have made it softer and tastier, but damn it all, the wood was wet. Hunger won out. I cut up and gulped the meat raw.

Now some said gator tasted like chicken, but this was greasy, dense, and tough. Still, it was food. With my fill of protein, I limped with my log-boat down to the water. I scanned the area for boats and gators, then climbed in and paddled away from this island of death and misery.

For a moment I reveled in moving fast without my injured leg slowing me down. Then my thoughts returned to Colleen. I didn't want to think about what those bounty hunters would put her through or where she might end up. If lucky, Colleen could be a maid or cook in a nice home with a roof and good meals. If not, they could put her to work at age twelve in the mines or reclamation facilities.

I circled half of the island, crossed the channel, and headed northwest. Paddling was hard against the current, but I put my back into it. It felt good to make something go right for a change. *I'm still alive.*

Yet I didn't feel special, at least not in the way Mo-Mere kept telling me. Maybe there was nothing unusual about me except I was the statistical one in a thousand who lived to tell my tale. So far. If I'd stayed on Vera's island after the storm took the houses, I could have floated out to sea without a raft. Coarse-face could have grabbed me. If I hadn't flown that kite long ago, I would never have found home and my log-boat. If I hadn't gotten my foot in the trap, Bounty-killer would have taken me. Maybe in another universe, things went differently and my tale vanished with me.

Surviving meant I could contemplate my story while many brave girls disappeared, taking their stories with them. Classmates and sister salvagers came to mind. I wept for them and hoped they'd survived. As for me, I wanted my family back, and to understand why Mom was with Coarse-face.

* * *

Spooked by a patrol boat lingering near the island I'd left, I paddled hard until late morning to reach Aunt Vera's. I checked around for gators, scavengers, bounty hunters, and patrols, before setting foot on the island, which was noticeably smaller than when I'd first seen it two days earlier. The water purifier tanks hadn't survived either the storm or scavengers, which meant no clean water. It had been worth a look. There was also no sign Mom had come back. No, she was with Coarse-face.

Sipping from my water jug, almost empty, I took one last look around. Except for firewood, there was nothing worth salvaging. Two rats scurried away before I could make a meal of them. My bandage oozed, telling me I needed meds. I didn't want to lose my foot. Gimp Marginals died. Without four good limbs, it was too hard to get food and water or to barter for survival.

Back on my boat, I paddled west, toward higher ground where survivors might have gone and faced uppity Marginals. Those snooty devils, including barter groups and scavenger clans, didn't welcome their less fortunate neighbors.

Canoeing in my log-boat, I resembled flotsam drifting down after the storm. By late afternoon, I neared a large tree-covered island. It was one of the tallest I'd seen and situated off the main channel, meaning it hadn't seen the worst of the storm surge. I circled upstream to where the harbor had flooded. Four boats floated near a makeshift dock. Ten women in ragged green canvas clothing worked to tie up the boats.

They didn't look like scavengers or bounty hunters, so I paddled into the little harbor, hoping they wouldn't be tempted to barter me for scraps. Coming here was a big risk, but without meds and water, I didn't have much choice.

Several of the women were bailing out a waterlogged boat. Others pulled ropes, bringing another boat closer to the shoreline amid rocks, tree branches, and debris.

"Hola," I called out.

A tall, burly woman moved to the edge of the new dock and studied me. "Where you from?" An alligator-hide skirt hung from a belt around her waist. Her fresh green top looked new. She also wore a gun holster.

I pointed downriver. "Storm took our water tanks."

"Sorry to hear," the woman said. "You have anything to barter?"

"Nada. I'm searching for family. Have you seen Zola or Colleen Shen?" I pulled in close to shore so the woman could check for weapons, yet far enough so she couldn't grab me.

"Zola visited two days ago. I haven't seen her since." The alligator-skirt woman leaned toward me. "That foot looks nasty. Let me examine it. You got a name?"

"Regina Shen. Zola's my mom. Did she say where she was heading?"

"I assumed back home to prepare for the storm," the woman said.

I started to say something about Mom being on a patrol boat, but without knowing why, I hesitated to share that with a stranger.

Besides, two days earlier would have been before she left Colleen and me. "Have you seen Vera Morton or her daughters, Jasmine and Aimee?" Speaking Vera's name made my throat tighten.

Shaking her head, the alligator-skirt woman held out her hand. "Great family. I haven't seen them since the storm."

I tied my boat to a tree at the end of their new dock, secured the paddle to latches in the bottom, and crawled out with my walking stick.

The alligator woman pointed toward a wheelbarrow sitting on the dock and helped me climb in. "Call me Therese." She pushed me across the wooden dock.

"Do you know my mom?"

"She comes to barter now and then. I was hoping you might have something to help with repairs."

With muscles bulging, she pushed me up a paved path that was missing a few stones. We reached a clearing with a cluster of eighteen large log homes and a washed-out gravel street between them. At the end of the road were log and stone buildings, bigger than I'd seen on other islands, more like stores and offices I'd seen in Mo-Mere's books from before the Great Collapse. Not only were these buildings larger, they looked sturdier than our home, Vera's place, or Mo-Mere's school. I'd stumbled into one of the wealthier Marginal communities.

Windows and wood-plank roof sections were missing from several houses. Green-clad women and girls as young as Colleen were repairing them. The damage to this community was trifling compared to islands on the main channel. These people hadn't experienced the same storm I'd lived through and were high enough that they could repair and carry on. "You have such beautiful homes," I said.

She smiled. "We've been fortunate, so far."

Either that or they worked with bounty hunters and scavengers.

THIRTEEN

Therese pulled me inside what looked like Mo-Mere's schoolroom. It had shelves along three walls filled with milky-white plastic trays stacked like books. Most of the containers were too small to hold anything bigger than flimsy pocket paperbacks. I could only dream.

Therese parked the wheelbarrow next to a cushioned table covered with a thin sheet, and helped me move over. While she removed Vera's canvas bandage, I gritted my teeth. Unwrapped and indoors, my leg gave off a rotten fish odor I hadn't noticed before.

"You should have taken better care of that foot," she said. "You could lose it."

I shrugged. "I had nothing else to wrap it with, and no way to keep it dry."

She threw the bandage into a bucket, pulled a thin beige sponge from one of the plastic trays, and dabbed the wound. It stung like jabs from a thousand knives. My foot throbbed. My eyes watered. I wanted to scream but didn't make a sound. Mo-Mere would have been proud.

Therese stuck a needle into my rump, put ointment on the wound, and wrapped it with a fresh linen bandage from another bin. "Clean this daily and keep it dry. Now, what can you do to pay for this?"

Pay? I took a deep breath and reminded myself I was a Marginal who had to pay her own way. "I'm a hard worker."

"With a bad leg."

"I can cook, wash pots. How much do I owe?"

"A day's work should do." Therese smiled. "Kitchen's across the street. Grab a bite to eat first, but not too much."

I nodded.

She helped me to my good foot and handed me my walking stick. I didn't expect charity, but now I was indebted, and I had to pay that debt before I could hunt for Mom, Colleen, and Vera's girls. "Thanks for fixing my leg."

"Don't thank me yet. You could still lose the foot."

I stared at the crushed-pebble floor. She was right, but what else could I have done?

She raised my chin like Mo-Mere did, forcing me to look at her. "I'm not scolding you. It's not fixed, but our herb ointment and antibiotics can help. You lost your home, didn't you?"

"Yes, ma'am."

"As long as you work hard, you can stay."

"Thank you, ma'am."

Therese helped me limp across the gravel street to a long log building with stone pillars and a big sign: Therese's Kitchen. She sat me down to a small bowl of possum and turnip stew before putting me to work next to her daughter, Carla. Older than me, the chubby girl grimaced.

"I don't need a gimp," she told her mother. "There's nothing worse than a Marginal gimp."

"You asked for help," Therese said. "Dinner's in an hour. Put Regina to work."

"Do we have to share our food?"

"Yes. Now get to work," Therese answered and left.

I propped my walking stick in the corner and leaned against a sink basin full of dirty dishes. "You want me to wash pots?"

"Yeah, whatever."

Facing a window that opened to the log wall of another building, I washed iron pots covered in baked-on food that would have cleaned better with soaking. As dinnertime approached, Carla acted frazzled, moving back and forth. With no economy of movement, she dashed between preparing buckets of stew and setting out plates and spoons, jumping from one task to another without completing either.

I put aside another clean pot. "How can I help?"

"Why don't you take that useless leg to gimpland?"

When I followed her, my foot pulsed with pain, screaming for me to put it up and let it heal. I couldn't. I had to earn my keep or starve, which would happen for sure if I lost the foot. That had happened to a classmate after the last storm. Dana broke her leg. It didn't heal and within months, she'd lost a quarter of her weight. I tried to bring food, but her mother and aunt sent me away. Then she died. I suspected her family starved her since she couldn't work. Her entire family perished in the next storm.

Carla carried pots of stew into a large dining hall and over to a table where green-clad women and girls had begun to line up, the same women I'd seen working at the docks, on the roofs, and at the broken windows. I limped over with loaves of bread.

"Come on. Hurry up," said a gray-haired woman, wearing an alligator skirt like Therese's. "We have more work to finish today."

There was grumbling behind her over our slow meal service. Many of the faces looked similar. This might have been an extended family or clan, though a few of the younger girls could have been refugees like me. Still younger girls trooped in for dinner with their families.

Hobbling over to Carla, I whispered, "Let me stand and serve, at least."

"Whatever." She handed me the ladle and returned to the kitchen.

While I scooped what looked like chicken stew to more than a hundred women and girls, my mouth watered. We rarely had much food at home unless I caught it. I ignored the burning pain in my foot as I smiled at each customer and said, "Bless you, have you seen Zola Shen?" No one had. "Have you seen the Morton family?" Same answer.

I wasn't sure I wanted to see Mom. She'd grown so distant over the past six months, ever since I'd started pressing her about my donor mother. I couldn't understand my own obsession. Yet my ambivalence over her leaving created a deeper pain inside.

* * *

After serving the last customers, a grey-haired woman and a girl whom I took to be her granddaughter, I dished a bowl of stew for Carla and hobbled with it into the kitchen. She glared at me, lowered her eyes and took the bowl. Behind her stood her mom.

"I'm sorry," I whispered, for whatever I'd done.

I sat across a scratched wooden table from Carla and ate tasty turnips seasoned with real salt, fresh carrots, and noodles. I wanted to hate her. She didn't have the lean, hungry midsection most of us had, which meant she had plenty to eat. She'd been mean to me when I couldn't imagine having done anything except upset her world by being here.

After her mom left, I put my spoon down and looked up. "I'll only stay until my leg's well. I don't want any trouble."

"You are trouble." Carla glared at me. "Just wait until bounty hunters come. Even with that gimp leg, they'll barter us something."

"Why do you hate me?"

Carla's face twisted into rage. "Why don't you behave like Regina?" she said, mocking her mother's voice. "She's been through hell and back, yet she smiles at people."

I gobbled the rest of the vegetables, ate a slice of rosy apple, and noticed two chunks of chicken hiding beneath spuds. I wanted to let them linger in my mouth and savor them, but as a Marginal, you ate when you could, and quickly. You never knew when you might have to run for your life.

Biting into the chunks, I realized it wasn't bird after all but gator, which might have explained why I hadn't seen any by the dock. Boiled, the meat tasted so much better than raw, and did have a similar texture to chicken. I finished by drinking the broth.

Carla glared at me. "Mom thinks I should be friendly."

I shrugged. You needed friends to survive in the swamps, but friendships rarely lasted. Yet Mom had known Mo-Mere for over fifteen years. Their bond puzzled me.

"Did you hear me?" Carla yelled.

"I don't want to make problems for you. I can't help this foot. I landed in a trap during the storm."

"Do you have any idea how depressing it is to get up, make breakfast, clean up, make lunch, clean up, make dinner, clean up, every single day? And now I have to share our measly food with you."

I hadn't considered getting angry or depressed. Life was what it was. As a Marginal, it was, well, marginal. Get over it. The only person I'd known get depressed was Gail, the girl who skipped class and lost her legs and her life to a gator. Maybe she couldn't help her condition, but it cost her life.

I didn't know what to say to Carla. I didn't mind serving and cleaning if it meant food, a place to stay, and clean bandages. I wouldn't have minded cooking, either. It sounded a darned sight better than starving or washing out to sea. Better than a gator eating you, and having the critter begin to digest you while you're still alive. It beat getting stuck in a trap and bleeding to death in a storm. Getting depressed or angry wouldn't fix my foot or feed my belly. I didn't say anything. I didn't want to give her more reasons to hate me.

Carla ate in silence and left. I washed the pots in the kitchen. In the dining hall, everyone had gone. My foot begged me to lie down. Instead I limped with a tray to gather dishes, and washed them so they'd be ready for breakfast.

As I put the last spoon in a drawer, Therese joined me. "Where's Carla?"

I looked around. "She must have taken a break."

"She bugged out, didn't she?"

"Pardon me?"

Therese's eyes narrowed. "Carla never cleans the kitchen at night. She's gone, isn't she?"

"I wouldn't know, ma'am. I'm just doing my work."

The woman took my hands and raised my chin until our eyes met. "There's something different about you. You have fight, yet you don't flaunt it."

"No, ma'am."

"Let me change your bandages." She handed me my walking stick.

"I don't know. If I have to pay you a day's work each time, I'll never pay you off."

She laughed. "You're a good worker. We could use you around here. I won't charge you tonight."

"I don't want charity. I'll earn my way like the others."

"I'm sure you will, but you'll do better with a healthy leg."

She helped me limp toward the door and across the street. Night had fallen. Fists full of stars surrounded a half-moon. Lamps illuminated the gravel street connecting all the homes to the dining hall, infirmary, a storehouse, and two other large buildings with no signs. This village was larger than Mo-Mere's school community, and much better off.

"Are you the chief?" I asked.

She helped me onto the infirmary table. "I'm the mayor, which means I'm responsible for the livelihood of the entire community. Let's see how you're healing."

When she unwrapped the bandage, my foot was angry to the touch. Bleeding had stopped, no oozing pus, and it no longer had the rich aroma of decaying fish.

"I think we can save this," she said.

She put on ointment, re-bandaged the wound, and gave me another injection in my rump. Hating needles, particularly after what Coarse-face did to Colleen and me, I tensed up until she was done.

"I need to hunt for my family," I said.

"You're not going anywhere until we save this foot."

Her voice sounded protective, in ways Mom or Mo-Mere might talk. Yet I didn't know this woman. That got me worrying about Carla and her talk about selling me to bounty hunters.

Therese showed me an indoor toilet with a seat and a pull-chain for water. After I finished using it, she helped me onto a cot in the back of the infirmary. "It's not much, but you need rest."

I sat up. "How much will I owe for the bed?"

"How about you work in the kitchen until your foot heals in exchange for food, the cot, and my treating your foot?"

My breath caught. She'd offered a fabulous deal, as good as any I could have bartered, and yet … "Why are you being so kind?"

"You seem like a good girl, down on her luck. I've been there. We need extra workers. Do we have a deal?" She held out her hand.

I studied her eyes with suspicion and didn't see anything that raised alarm. With no other options, I shook her hand, and then held it tighter. "Please don't barter me to bounty hunters. I'll work extra hard for you."

Therese laughed. "You couldn't work hard enough for what bounty hunters pay these days. Get some rest."

Is that your game: to fatten me up for sale?

She turned out an electric lamp run off solar panels and left me alone with the ghosts of others who had visited the infirmary. *Oh, Colleen, I pray you're safe somewhere.*

I woke to every creak of the infirmary building, the swish of the wind, and the sense of constant swaying to the waves and gales during the storm. Finally, I cried myself to sleep and dreamed of Coarse-face chasing me across the swamps.

FOURTEEN

Therese rocked me at first light and examined my foot while I lay on the cot. Her touch didn't sting as much. The wound had begun to heal despite ugly bruises, which tended to look worse before they got better. The cut looked deep, though it no longer bled.

"Well, Regina, our herbal ointments and antibiotics seem to be working," she said. "A few more days and you'll feel better."

I wasn't so sure. The foot throbbed the moment I placed it on the floor, protesting having to carry my weight.

Therese helped me stand and offered to wheel me across the street.

"I need to do this myself," I said, not wanting to be more indebted to her.

While I hobbled onto the gravel street, Therese walked beside me. A few other women stirred. Otherwise, the town was as desolate as the swamps after a storm. The sun peeked over the horizon between trees, hinting it would be another steamy day, even warmer in the kitchen. At least I could move on my own and my foot wasn't rotting off. That was something.

"Carla will be along soon," Therese said. "Let's get the cookers started and the dishes out for breakfast."

"Therese, please. Your daughter already hates me. Let me do the work."

"Hate is a strong word." She sighed. "As you wish."

She fired up the wood burners while I carried clean plates and spoons to the serving table. It took a dozen trips to get everything

93

set up. When I finished, I turned to Therese, who had laid out pans on top of the stove. Carla still hadn't arrived.

"What do we make for breakfast?" I whispered.

"Let me find out what's keeping Carla. Set out biscuits from the cupboard. Don't start the eggs for another ten minutes, otherwise they'll get cold."

"Eggs?" I'd never cooked those before.

Therese shook her head. "Break the shells over a bowl, toss the shells in that pan, and mix the eggs until smooth. Then stir them in those pans."

"Sounds easy," I said. It might have been if I didn't have to hobble around.

Therese left.

By the time Carla showed up, I had everything on the serving tables and a second batch of eggs on the stove. She looked like the storm itself, as if she'd spent the night wrestling gators.

Without a word, she shoved me away from the stove. I landed on my bad foot. Pain radiated out. I stifled a scream, fell to the floor, and scooted away.

"See where a gimp leg gets you?"

I reached for my walking stick. She kicked it away. I grabbed hold of the wooden countertop, pulled myself up on my good foot, and hopped around the kitchen island to get my stick. She grabbed it, opened the wood burner, and pushed my makeshift crutch into the fire.

"Don't, please," I said. "I need that."

"You want it, get it."

I limped toward the burner. Carla blocked my way. Then she turned her attention to the stick, which was too long for the stove. She pushed it around, stirring the fire, but couldn't seem to figure out why it wouldn't fit. By the time she pulled it out, the stick was burning. She held it up, uncertain what to do next.

The gray-haired alligator-skirt woman who had grumbled the day before poked her head into the kitchen. "Where's our food?"

Carla threw the stick at me. "The gimp ruined breakfast."

On the stove, the eggs had turned into black scum that sent up smoke.

"Get that off the stove," the woman yelled to Carla.

"Your feet are on fire," I said, moving away.

Carla had knocked logs out of the wood burner. Their fire

lapped at her boots. She jumped, kicked the firewood, and ran out of the kitchen.

The alligator-skirt woman moved the pan of eggs and used fire tongs to put the logs back into the burner. Then she turned to me. "If you serve, I'll cook. By the way, I'm Jen."

Nodding, I limped out to the dining hall, where the line stretched out the door. Women and girls had helped themselves to muffins and rolls.

"Where's the food?" a middle-aged woman asked, pointing to the empty egg tray.

"Carla's ill. I'll bring more when they're done."

I hobbled into the kitchen and carried out more muffins. By the time I finished, Jen brought the eggs. Then she ate and left me to serve and clean up.

Limping around without my stick, I had to make extra trips to clean the dining hall. I'd just finished the last of the pans and dishes from breakfast when Carla showed up to start preparations for lunch. I picked up my charred walking stick and leaned on it. The wood snapped under my weight, so I discarded it on the woodpile.

Carla glowered at me.

"Everything's ready to start lunch," I said.

Her pudgy face twisted into a well-practiced scowl. "I don't know what you're so happy about. This is three times a day, every day of the year. Just because I fed them yesterday doesn't mean I get a day off today. No, they expect me to feed them again, and they complain because the food is cold or too watery or too dry. All they do is complain."

"I don't mind. I'll serve and listen to their grumbling."

Carla moved closer, towering over me. "I've asked around. Bounty hunters will pay a hundred credits, even for a gimp."

"Why do that when I'll do your work for you?"

She pointed her stubby finger at me. "You're darn right you'll do my work. I'm management. You're a Working Stiff."

I could live with the promotion.

So, for three meals a day, I baked muffins and rolls, cut vegetables and meat for the stews, served the line, cleared the dishes, and washed up. Carla sat in the kitchen stewing over what else she could get me to do. I tried to act friendly so Therese didn't send me away, but Carla made it clear she didn't want anything to do with the lower-class Marginal Working Stiff.

Nights and mornings, Therese checked my leg. The wound scabbed over. Bruises took on purplish colors she said meant healing. I found a new walking stick, though by the third evening, I got by without it in the kitchen and dining hall.

On the third night, while cleaning pots, I considered staying with Therese. I wouldn't have books, but I could handle this in exchange for food and shelter. Except, now that my foot was healing, Therese could barter me for 800 credits. I couldn't top that. Heck, I was tempted to collect that bounty myself.

No, staying wasn't an option. Aside from my need to find Colleen, Mo-Mere believed I should hope for more, much more. It was a curse more than a blessing to think you should have more than your lot in life. Yet I couldn't deny how her dreams motivated me to persevere when I thought I couldn't.

The same faces every day brought no word on Mom, Colleen, or the other girls. Now that my foot was getting better, it was time to move on before I grew too comfortable and let my guard down. As the sun set and I soaked the last of the pots from dinner, Therese came in, agitated.

"Leave those." She wrapped my hands in a dry towel.

"I agreed to work."

"We have company." She gave me the look Mo-Mere did when I wasn't to ask questions.

"What's going on?" I whispered.

"Bounty hunters."

"I promise to work even harder. Please don't barter me."

"Hush," she said.

She opened the pantry door, pulled out sacks of flour, and lifted a metal panel that revealed blackness below. She nudged me into the pantry and helped me down. "It's a four-foot drop. Not a sound."

When she placed the panel over my head, the cellar became dark as tar. Something dragged over the panel and a door closed. I struggled for breath. I felt closed in, a prisoner in her dungeon, caged like chained girls on bounty boats. Could I really trust her?

FIFTEEN

The floor beneath me was rock hard and clammy, the ceiling so low I had to crouch down. I found a drier place to sit, and stretched my legs. Darkness shrouded my eyes. Someone banged at the basin above and hummed.

I had to get out. Bounty hunters were coming. Carla had threatened to barter me twice, which made no sense. She couldn't think past hating me to take advantage of how I did her work. Carla didn't strike me as stupid, but she couldn't think through her hate to her own best interests. She had to know about this cellar.

Unwilling to stay and wait to see what happened next, I felt around for a stick, anything to use as a tool or markers to feel my way around. I listened for the sounds of rats. I heard only humming.

Footsteps sounded on the floorboards. Dust fell over my face. I stifled a sneeze. *Not a sound.*

"We've come to barter for girls," said a familiar voice: Bounty-killer.

"We have none to spare," Therese said. "These girls are our daughters."

"In the past we've left you alone because you've cooperated, Therese. Don't force my hand. Your daughter mentioned a stray that interests me."

"We took in an injured girl after the storm. She healed and left this evening. In fact, she left these dirty dishes, which my daughter should have cleaned instead of telling stories. Perhaps I should ... no, she's my blood."

"You think this is a joke?" Bounty-killer asked. "Do you have any idea how hard it is to scrape by on what the Federation pays?"

"We suffered damage during the storm. We need every hand to rebuild."

"You say this girl is gone. Then you won't mind if we look around."

"As long as you don't mind an escort," Therese said. "We don't need what little we have disappearing."

Footsteps moved across the boards above me, followed by silence. I couldn't see anything. Critters that thrived in the dark moved around. I hadn't seen how big this underground room was, but it felt large. With Carla wanting to barter me, I was tempted to break out, but not with bounty hunters nearby.

Heavy boot-steps pounded on the kitchen floor and echoed in the room around me. "Regina, it's safe to come out now." Carla. She banged cupboards and the pantry door. "Come out before the rats get you. We grow big ones, and they're attracted to blood and raw meat."

She pounded, moved, and pounded again. "Mommy says it's okay. Those bad bounty people are gone. Come on out."

Sticky dampness swept over me, adding to my sweat. That would attract rats. I tucked my feet up next to me and fingered the knife on my belt.

"Come out, Regina. No one will harm you."

"What are you doing?" Therese asked. "Do you realize if they found strays, they'd punish me by taking you?"

I imagined Carla's frozen, confused look, like when her boots were on fire. She might have been a Marginal, but she'd insulated herself from the hardships of the swamps. She'd grown soft and vulnerable.

Carla's heavy boot-steps retreated from the kitchen.

I expected Therese to let me out. Instead, she walked out the back. Different footsteps approached, lighter than Carla's. The pace and tone sounded like two individuals. They pounded on walls, kicked floorboards, and banged doors.

"Let's burn the place down," Leather-face said. "Then we'll see what scurries out."

"Save that thought," Bounty-killer said. "If we find the girl Demarco wants or any strays, we'll send all these girls into bondage and turn this place over to scavengers."

"For a price."

"Naturally. The mayor's daughter was convinced the Shen girl is still on the island. Did you find her boat?"

"No," Leather-face said. "All boats are registered with the Department of Antiquities."

"Spend the night. Search the island. Offer our cartel partners a piece of the action. This girl's worth a fortune. They've doubled the price three times since the storm. That's almost a tenfold increase."

It's nice to know someone wants me. My attempt at humor didn't stop my shaking. Sweat streamed down my back. That set me to shivering in the heat, which caused me to sweat more. I hadn't asked for this attention.

The two sets of footsteps moved toward the door and faded away. The whole conversation made no sense. They knew who I was, or thought they did, and I was worth a fortune. That couldn't be. They had to have me confused with someone else. Then again, if they offered a steep price, could I count on Therese or anyone not to turn me in?

Time to go before she changes her mind. The front of the cabin faced the street and too many eyes. The sides faced alleys between buildings. The bounty hunters could check from the street. I faced the back of the dining cabin and crawled, keeping my left leg up off the stony floor.

Nearby, rats scurried. Enough of them could kill you. It smelled of dust, damp animal fur, and decayed food that made its way down here. The floor squished beneath my hands and knees. Rats or something nipped at me.

When I reached a wall, I pushed at moist dirt over stone and felt between the wall and the ceiling. Boards cross-supported to hold up the cabin. This must have been how they kept the cabin dry during heavy rains. To do so, they needed a drain, and not toward the street.

At one end of the back wall I came to a corner that ended in two stone walls, the support beams above me, and no way out. I worked my way to the other corner, similar but with one difference: a drainage channel out the back at floor level. These were clever people, like Mo-Mere building her schoolhouses on stilts.

I dug at the channel until rocks in the wall came loose. One by one they fell away until I could scoot sideways into the groove. The channel opened up to stars. Across a clearing, lights moved down toward the shore. This might have been a big island, but it wasn't too big to search. These bounty hunters were being thorough.

Voices from the cabin startled me. "I said open it." Bounty-killer sounded angry.

In the woods lights stopped and scanned. More lights reflected over the diner's roof. There was nowhere to run. Behind me, the panel to the pantry opened. Light flooded the cellar, which was one large room under the entire cabin with posts to hold up the floor. There was no place to hide.

I crawled into the drainage channel and dragged myself along on my side. When I cleared the wall, I pulled my legs out of the cellar and rolled behind a stack of firewood.

"Looks like digging over there," Bounty-killer said from inside the cellar.

"Damn," Therese said. "Rats removed the grill again. They're attracted to scraps."

"And why do you have this hiding place?" Bounty-killer asked.

"It's not a hiding place. It keeps our cabins dry and cool. I'll have someone check all the grills. We don't need vermin in the dining cabin."

"Show me where this leads to out back," Bounty-killer said.

Lights continued to move in the woods across the clearing. Climbing the solar paneled roof would be too noisy and visible. Taking the only other path, I rolled into the ditch and pulled myself into the cellar. I was heading the wrong way, into a cage like a trapped animal.

The cellar was dark again. Recalling the layout, I crawled along the back wall to the far corner. Taking the rope from around my waist, I weaved the cord between nails in the floor joists. I pulled myself up onto the makeshift hammock and hung over the floor. The ropes tore at my flesh through my canvas clothing.

A light shone down through the drainage channel. The wall lit up. Rats, roaches and spiders scurried. I raised my boots and prayed the ropes didn't pull loose while the beam panned the dirt-covered floor all around. It hovered beneath me. Then darkness enveloped me again. Voices murmured outside the drainage opening. Light flooded the room again.

I held my breath as curious rats lurked beneath me.

SIXTEEN

It was not a night for sleep. I dozed between stray noises, scratching feet, faint murmurs of rats, and footsteps. But as uncomfortable as the ropes were, they kept me off the damp floor.

Morning brought enough light to make out the stones on the wall next to the drainage channel. Stiff from hanging on ropes, I crawled off my harness, unfastened the rope, and looped it around my waist. It was time to get off this island and see if I had any family left.

I needed my bandage changed, but bounty hunters could have been anywhere. I crawled to the drainage channel and dragged myself through to the outside. When my feet cleared the wall, I turned to climb out and bumped into Therese.

She held out her hand. "We haven't much time. They'll wake soon."

Therese helped me out of the ditch and leaned me against the cabin wall, behind the wood pile. Kneeling next to me, she propped my leg on a log, pulled off the bandage, and examined my ankle. "It's healing. You should be very happy. You must have strong genes."

"Why are you helping me?" I studied my leg. The swelling was down, though the bruises looked ugly. Most important, it didn't hurt to her touch.

She put ointment on the wound. "You mean when it puts our whole village at risk?"

I nodded. "I can't thank you enough. My foot thanks you as well."

Therese laughed and wrapped my leg in a fresh bandage, thinner than before. "The bounty hunters and their overlords believe you're someone special."

"I'm nobody," I said. "I'm a Marginal nobody."

"I doubt that." She finished the bandage and made sure it wouldn't come loose. "In any case, they wouldn't say why you're so important. I guess you deserve a chance to find out for yourself."

Again I recalled Mo-Mere talking about my destiny. "Am I some forgotten princess everyone neglected to tell me about?"

"Heavens, no. But I do think you're an extraordinary girl." She helped me to my feet.

I put weight on my left foot to make sure it wouldn't buckle. While the leg was unsteady, it didn't scream at me.

"You're a good girl," Therese whispered, helping me across the clearing to the woods. "I wish you every success in your journey."

We reached the trees and she helped me down to the shore. My log-boat lay beneath some bushes.

"Here, take these." She handed me a package and a jug of water. "It's chicken jerky and apple chips. After the dust settles, you're welcome to return."

"I should find my family. I've put yours in enough danger already." I limped to the boat and pulled it into the water.

"I'm sorry about Carla. She's a good girl, but she feels privileged. That leaves her weak and insecure, which makes her angry all the time. With me as mayor, she doesn't think she should have to work in the kitchen, but everyone works or we all suffer."

"I didn't mind," I said.

Therese smiled. "Don't forget to keep that leg clean and dry. No swimming until the skin heals."

I hugged her and held on. "Thanks for everything."

"If you can't find family, you're welcome to settle here."

But my future lay elsewhere. I smiled, hugged Therese again, and climbed into my boat before I broke down. She was my only connection now, and I was leaving. It took all my resolve to paddle away from shore. When I turned to wave, Therese was gone.

I pulled hard across the channel to a small island, a dead island. Scavengers had stripped whatever the storm hadn't taken, including water tanks. Only the mountings remained. Its promised sanctuary offered false hope.

Hidden by partly submerged bushes, I spotted a patrol boat with the gray Antiquities emblem motoring toward Therese's dock. Coarse-face.

Careful not to entangle my log-boat, I took the long way around the island. Paddling felt wonderful after being stuck on land. Thankfully, the kitchen work and digging my way out of the cellar had kept my arms strong.

I couldn't be sure Therese hadn't gotten me off the island to protect her village before bartering me, if only to get bounty hunters and patrols to leave her alone. After all, bartering in salvage goods was illegal, and Therese was heavily into barter.

Each island I passed had signs of storm damage. Matted and uprooted vegetation lined their shores. Drowning trees and bushes washed back and forth. They swayed in the flow of the channels, which were wider than before the storm.

Taking a sip from Therese's jug, I looked for signs of life and potential salvage. Nothing. I kept moving, steering clear of gators and snakes. Now that the storm was over, they were hungry. So was I, but I held tight to Therese's bundle for more desperate times.

When I reached the next channel, I froze. A big boat rested by the shore, a bounty hunters' powerboat by the looks of it. Its painted hull gleamed in the morning sunlight.

* * *

Therese had just escorted the bounty hunters to their boat when an Antiquities patrol boat pulled up to the dock. She wasn't happy to see Inspector Demarco, yet she couldn't offend such a powerful official.

While Therese escorted the inspector up the hill, Antiquities agents fanned out across the island, rechecking what the bounty hunters had already done. Therese couldn't help wondering why the injured girl so interested Antiquities, the Federation, and her. Regina was a tough girl, a survivor, not unpleasant in the way other desperate souls became during and after storms. It had been the lack of guile that convinced Therese to help her, that and not wanting the girl caught on the island.

Inspector Demarco entered the infirmary, shook her head, and examined the wall shelves, the examining table, and the cot.

"Therese, I expected better from you of all people. We go back a long time. I've made it clear to agents and bounty hunters that you're off limits. On this matter, even I can't save you. You know the penalty for harboring fugitives."

Therese scanned the infirmary for any evidence of Regina's stay. She'd burned the blood-soaked bandages the moment she'd spotted the bounty hunters. When they'd questioned her, she told them the rags were contaminated. "We can't afford to spread disease."

Regina hadn't slept in the bed since Therese made it the morning before with clean sheets. The little urchin didn't have any clothes or possessions except for what she wore, and that rope she kept around her waist.

Therese turned to the inspector. "I cooperate with posted alerts. I haven't seen any since the storm."

"We've been busy."

"The girl looked like dozens of others who lost everything. I didn't see anything to report. Despite her injury, she worked hard for her food and meds. She must have seen the bounty hunters and fled."

Demarco examined the bed sheets. She moved from shelf to cabinet, studying contents. "How long was she here?"

"She arrived three days ago with an injured leg. She was a hard worker."

"I'm not interested in her work habits. I want the girl."

"Of course," Therese said. "It would be a relief to get her into a good home across the Wall. I'll tell everyone to watch for her."

"Therese, I've looked the other way while you salvaged and bartered."

"For which I'm grateful, and pay a share to you."

"I need that girl." Demarco looked worried, even scared.

"What's so special about her? She was barely alive when I found her."

"What condition was her leg in when she left?"

"Healing," Therese said. "If she keeps it dry, she could save the leg." She wondered how well the girl could do that on the river all by herself.

"Why didn't you report her for removing her tracking chip?"

"I'm sorry. With everything going on, I didn't examine her arm, only her ankle."

Demarco shoved another container back onto the shelf and turned. "Where did she go?"

"She talked about finding her mother, though she had no idea where to look. The storm shuffled everything around."

"What type of boat did she travel in?"

"She didn't take any of ours," Therese said. "She arrived in a leaky canoe. I can't imagine it would take her far."

"We will find the girl. If you have any delusions of helping her, don't."

Demarco received a call and returned to her boat.

SEVENTEEN

At the sight of the bounty hunter boat, I paddled into the cover of nearby cattails. The boat swayed, tilting awkwardly. I spotted a gaping hole in its side: a shipwreck.

Not seeing anyone on deck, I paddled across the channel and up the shoreline, hidden by vegetation. The island to my right was big, like Therese's, though with less damage from storm surges. That was one benefit of being off the main channel and farther west. Trees obscured the top, and this side of the island had no docks or boat moorings. Closer to the bounty boat, a body floated face down in the water. She wore a black froggie wetsuit. Another bounty hunter lay in the water between the boat and a rocky ledge. It must have crashed there.

One of the curses of my photographic memory was remembering numbers as well. Those on the side of this boat matched the one that took Colleen.

I hid my boat among bushes, grabbed my crossbow and arrows from beneath my seat, and crawled onto a fallen tree trunk. From there, I climbed up one of the mooring lines that dangled over the side of the bounty boat. A jagged tear ran down the middle of the deck. I gagged from the stench of feces and death.

Six girls dangled from the railing by their chains. I limped across the shattered deck to examine each. All dead. Thankfully, Colleen wasn't among them. Their flesh moved with flies and maggots. I couldn't tell if they'd died from injuries during the crash or afterwards. A terrible thought struck me. What if they *had* survived the crash but couldn't break their chains to find food or water? The pungent odor and maggots told me they'd been dead for days. Surprisingly, no predators had crawled up to take advantage.

Eyes watering, I covered my mouth and nose and looked over the railing into the tree-lined coast for any sign of bounty hunters or survivors. A third froggie dangled upside down in a tree.

Colleen! Where are you?

Across the cracked deck, stairs led down into darkness. I crept below. The stench was overwhelming, but I couldn't turn back. Behind a locked cage door, five girls floated in inches of water. The small sleeping cabins on both sides of a narrow passage were empty. In the last cabin, larger than the others, the body of a woman in black lay twisted on the floor.

Fishing in the dead froggie's pockets, I found keys that opened the cage. Holding my breath, I checked each of the girls. None was Colleen or Vera's girls. All had been dead for days. I rushed up onto the deck and threw up, thankful I hadn't eaten; I couldn't afford to waste precious food. The taste of vomit and smell of decay lingered. I wanted to bury these girls, but I had to find Colleen.

I climbed over the side onto the rocky ledge where the boat had come to rest. Two more women in wetsuits lay sprawled among the rocks, for a total of six dead froggies. So far, all I knew was that Bounty-killer and Leather-face had survived. If they'd survived, Colleen and Vera's girls might have been on that motorboat when they'd returned to the island looking for me.

My mind swirled, unable to focus. Colleen's fate was my fault. I should have done more. Yet if I'd remained with her on Vera's boat, this could have been my fate. She wasn't among the dead here, though she could have floated to sea, where she wouldn't get a proper burial. *Oh, Colleen. I'm so sorry. May the Blessed Mary take your soul and guide you to a better place.*

I refused to give up hope, though. *I can't.* I grabbed hold of branches and rocks to pull myself along the muddy shore, while keeping my bandage dry.

"Colleen," I whispered, not sure if bounty hunters lingered nearby.

A narrow path led away from the boat and ended where the storm surge had. Beyond were trampled bushes where someone had pushed inland.

"Colleen." I held my breath and listened. Water lapped against the wreck behind me. A gentle breeze fluttered tree leaves above. Crows sang a sad tune.

With a stick, I probed the underbrush for traps and pushed forward. I stopped to notch an arrow.

"Halt," a voice said, "unless you want to lose a foot." A thin, dark girl wearing green canvas lay on the ground. "Traps everywhere." Her voice sounded strained and weak.

I scanned her slender rag-covered body down bare legs to a trap like the one that had snared me. "Who's with you?"

"Froggies grabbed me. Ship wrecked. Two froggies took survivors."

I propped a stone between the trap's teeth and wedged in a tree branch. It looked as if, after the trap caught her foot, she'd fallen awkwardly. "You got a name?"

"Fran. Get this damn thing off me. I can't reach it."

Standing on the branch, I pulled up on the top jaw with both hands. When she lifted her foot out over the bottom teeth, the trap snapped shut onto the rock and branch, almost taking my fingers with it.

She cut a strip of cloth from what was left of her green canvas top and wrapped her ankle. "Who's Colleen?"

"My sister. You want me to look at that?"

"No!" She grabbed a stick and pushed herself up to her full height. She was taller than me.

"Do you know if Colleen survived?" I reached out to help her.

She put up her hand to keep me away. "I don't know names, and it was too dark to see faces."

"Only two froggies survived?" I asked.

"Don't know. Two came with us." She used her stick to check for traps and limped farther up the hill.

"I know a good healer."

"Leave me alone. I don't do friends, so stop pretending. You want info on your sister. I have none. So there. Buzz off."

I followed. "What if the bounty hunters are on this island?"

"Then I'll kill them, one by one." Fran sounded gutsy, yet she had to be in a lot of pain.

My foot stung, too. "Maybe we can help each other."

"I don't need anyone holding me back." She poked her stick in my chest.

"You don't have to be ungrateful." I pushed the stick aside, which threw her off balance.

Fran recovered. "Oh, you saved my life, so I owe you. Fine, thanks for saving me. I'll owe you in the next life." She turned, limped forward, and checked the path with her stick.

"I need to find my sister. She's only twelve."

"I doubt she made it."

"How did you survive four days without food and water, and not figure how to get out of that trap?"

"Are you always a smartass?" she called over her shoulder. "I couldn't reach my foot to open the damned trap. I found mushrooms, bugs, and a pool of muddy water. Now, if you insist on following, shut up."

I limped after her, checking both sides of our narrow path for signs of Colleen. The bushes ended at a plateau with a cluster of four nice homes. I half-limped, half-ran to the nearest house. Two women in flowered canvas trousers and tops worked in a nearby garden.

"Hola," I called. I didn't want to startle them and get shot.

The flowered women rose and hurried toward me. A dark-haired woman in a blue uniform approached from the front of the house. I froze.

The blue-uniformed woman held a revolver. "What brings you to our island?"

"I'm looking for family," I said. "Colleen's twelve. Bounty hunters grabbed her and crashed here."

"I'm sorry." Blue-uniform lowered her gun. "I don't know anything about bounty hunters, but after the storm, two women came through with their kids."

"Could one—"

"They didn't give names, and I didn't get a good look in the dark. Would you like to come in for breakfast?"

Fran limped up next to me, her face tight with pain. "Where did they go?"

"They traded for a boat and headed upriver," Blue-uniform said, looking Fran over. "I see you've injured your foot."

"One of your traps got me."

"Now, now. I'm sure you can appreciate how hard we work, and how scavengers threaten to take from us. Why don't you let me look at that?"

Fran pulled away.

"Have you seen Zola Shen?" I asked.

The woman looked surprised, and then smiled. "You must be Regina."

I nodded. "Have you seen her?"

She hesitated. "She trades up this way. I last saw her before the storm, looking for supplies. She mentioned you and your sister, Colleen. She asked me to look after you if you got lost." She grabbed hold of my wrist.

"Really? Do you know where she went?"

"Not so fast," Fran said. "Exactly when did you last see her?"

"I ... uh ... don't recall." Blue-uniform grinned and pulled me toward the house. "She insisted I help you. I'm sorry about the trap. We have meds to help." She looked at me as if I were the one her trap had snared.

I pulled back and looked for bounty hunters. Were they here? Were they holding these families hostage?

"Don't give me any trouble," Blue-uniform said. "Your mom would be very upset if I let you run away."

Fran got behind the uniformed woman, grabbed her gun, and pushed her away. "We don't do charity, and you're lying about my friend's mom and the bounty hunters. You barter a lot by the looks of it. You're probably in bed with froggies and scavengers."

"I swear," Blue-uniform said. "I didn't know those two were bounty hunters."

"And it wouldn't have changed anything if you had," Fran said.

"Come on," I said. "Let's go."

"Listen to your friend," the woman said. "You know what we do with criminals."

"We're all criminals," Fran said. "That's what being a Marginal is. Look around. This is a penal colony."

Blue-uniform moved toward the house. "Take what you want and leave."

"I'm sorry," I said. "All the bounty hunters have us on edge. We only came for information." I limped backward toward the woods, holding my crossbow with arrow notched.

"What's it going to be?" the woman asked. "Are you going to shoot us in cold blood?"

Fran pointed the gun. "I'm thinking about it. You planned to capture us and barter with the bounty hunters, didn't you? That's how you pay for all this."

Reaching the woods, I dropped to my left knee to ease the pain. Fran turned as if to say something and glared. Shaking her head, she hobbled my way with her walking stick.

Blue-uniform ran into the house, while the two flowered women returned to gardening. I waved for Fran to hurry. When she reached the woods, I stood and checked the trail behind me.

The blue-uniformed woman returned.

"She's got a shotgun," I yelled and ducked behind a tree.

Fran turned to shoot and must have thought better of it. She scrambled behind a tree as buckshot ricocheted all around. The woman fired a second blast.

While she reloaded, I moved down toward the boat, using my stick to test for traps. When I glanced back, Fran was limping at a good gait.

"We could have taken her," Fran said.

"I don't steal."

"Then we starve."

I kept moving, holding onto bushes and tree branches when the trail grew steeper. A second pair of shots ricocheted all around. Ducking down, I came face-to-face with a trap.

EIGHTEEN

Chief Inspector Demarco couldn't believe Regina Shen had eluded capture for almost a week, and that intrigued her. If it hadn't been for all the sightings, she might have thought the girl dead. Instead, Regina had been quite resilient. Quite a surprise, considering she'd looked like a frightened urchin back when she was tagged. Regina had ditched her tracking chip at an opportune moment and escaped without a boat. She'd turned the misfortune of injuring her foot into a way of evading scavengers and bounty hunters.

In short, there had to be more to the special nature of this girl than DNA. Maybe the myths surrounding a Marginal girl who would rise up held an element of truth. Until that moment, Demarco had imagined those myths referred to herself. After all, she'd risen from Marginal orphan to Chief Inspector of the Department of Antiquities with the governor's ear.

That wouldn't last if she failed to find the girl. Demarco knew, in her core, that nothing she'd done with her life would matter if she didn't deliver Regina.

Yes, the girl had been resourceful, but it couldn't last. Riots would add another lethal dimension to famine, disease, predators, and trigger-happy guards on the Barrier Wall. "Don't waste ammo," the inspector had told them, though when faced with a desperate mob, panic gripped even the steadiest of hands. The worst was not over yet.

While she waited for the bounty hunter, Isabella, Demarco reflected on how close she'd come to closing this matter with the governor. The fearsome bounty chief had Regina, foot in a trap, unable to escape, but she'd only pursued the quick cash of healthy girls. She hadn't wanted a cripple slowing her down during the storm. She'd figured the girl wasn't going anywhere. That turned out to be a blessing, since she'd wrecked her bounty boat and lost most of the captured girls. Now she begged to meet in person, no doubt to ask a favor.

Demarco stared at the sleek motorboat while she accepted Isabella aboard her patrol boat. The chief inspector avoided looking at the red, blotchy face, some allergic reaction to the swamps. "Nice boat, but you can't carry much."

"That's what I wanted to talk to you about," Isabella whispered.

The inspector saw none of Isabella's fearsome reputation in the woman who cowered to curry favor, though she had no doubt the bounty hunter was a killer. Demarco settled in for disappointing news while she took the bounty hunter down to the captain's quarters. Closing the door, she stared out at the channel. Two weathered bounty boats floated by. "Do you have the girl?"

"I have two girls to barter."

"Do you have *the* girl?"

Isabella slumped onto a bench. "We covered every inch of the island where we found her. There were no boats other than the wrecks. No hiding places. Scavengers took everything worth taking."

"Could the girl have gone with them?"

"We searched every hiding place in their boat twice. I don't think so. Yet no one could survive on that island without water, food or a boat." Isabella sighed and stared at the floor.

"Then why are we meeting?"

"I'd like to barter two swamp girls for your permission to take the scavenger boat apart." She gave Demarco the boat's call number. "It's one you've sanctioned as hands off."

Demarco stared at the bounty hunter's blotchy face and considered the numbers. "You called me away from important business for trifles? Bring me the girl and you can keep the scavenger boat and their possessions. Sell off their families for all I care. Stop wasting my time. Bring me Regina Shen!"

While Isabella motored away, Demarco cuffed two girls to the bow railing of the patrol boat. They couldn't have been twelve, no family resemblance, and too young to bring top dollar from the mines or reclamation. She examined teeth and decided neither girl was clean or healthy enough to place as a caregiver in a Professional or Elite home. She just might have to throw these two back if she couldn't find someone to pay.

* * *

I rolled away from the trap, got to my feet, and hurried down the path. Recalling what Mo-Mere and Therese said about keeping feet dry, I moved my boat to a ledge to make it easier for Fran to climb in.

She stared down. "Does that driftwood float?"

"It does fine. Are you getting in, or do you want to wait for the Blue-uniform and her shotgun?"

Fran climbed into the front of the boat. When I pushed off, she pulled the second paddle off the floor latches and got to her knees to help. She was strong for someone who'd been trapped for four days with little food or water.

"What were you thinking, grabbing her gun?" I asked. Other than the wreck, the only boat on the channel was a local skiff with three women in green canvas.

"Put your energy into paddling. She can still shoot us."

A shot rang out, followed by a sharp scream and a child's wail. A second shot followed with more howling, a wounded cry.

"I think she found the trap," Fran said. "Serves her right. Let's leave this dump before their friendliness rubs off."

"She could have bandaged your leg."

"Blue uniforms work with froggies. That's why they have the nice house and why froggies went there. I bet they've got a cage in their cellar."

I let that sink in. The cage on the boat had killed five girls. I didn't know why Colleen wasn't with them, but I was glad. Then it hit me. "Could that Blue-uniform be holding Colleen?"

"Those bullies wouldn't hold anything that could cause them trouble."

"I saw the bounty hunters who survived. They had a regular motorboat, which they probably got here."

Fran shifted position and kept paddling. "I told you they're working together."

"They didn't have any girls on deck and little room below."

"Okay, maybe they held your sister for a day. Trust me. They've moved her for cash."

"How can you be so sure?"

"It's a cash business. Forget what you're thinking. It's suicide to go back. I'm sure they contacted their bounty friends already. Besides, with Blue-uniform in a trap, you can bet they're arming themselves."

After we crossed the channel, I looked back at the island. Through the trees, I saw Blue-uniform with several others. As much as I wanted to go back, two lame girls didn't stand a chance. Fran was right. They would have bartered Colleen by now.

Stifling tears, I pulled the log-boat deeper within the cover of sunken vegetation and headed upstream. I hoped beyond reason to find Vera's girls, and maybe Mom, or even Colleen.

Facing me, Fran draped her foot on the side of the boat and winced. I checked for boats on the channel and studied my companion. Her dark complexion didn't exactly match images in Mo-Mere's books. At first, I imagined Fran to be Hispanic, and then decided South Asian.

"We need a bigger boat," Fran said. "We can't salvage much with this."

"I haven't found anything to salvage since the storm, and this is easier to hide."

"I'm just saying. Without salvage, we don't stand a chance."

"Where's your family?"

"Dead. Thanks for reminding me," Fran said. "Where are you taking me?"

"I need to find Colleen. If she's not on that island, maybe she escaped. Maybe she made it to one of the refugee camps." I crossed a channel marking the end of Blue-uniform's island with the wrecked bounty boat.

Fran tucked the pistol into her belt beneath her torn canvas top. "It's just that people get worse the farther west we go, more suspicious of outsiders."

"There's nothing downriver except open seas. We lost another five or ten feet."

"I figured. But salvage is better back there if you know where to look."

"Not with an infected foot," I said. "You'd attract gators and sharks."

Wincing, she looked away.

We passed a gator with three spears in its back. Five women in green canvas dragged it up onto shore. Gators were about the only plentiful food left in the swamps, other than fish.

Fran's bronze skin glistened in the sunlight. She stretched and dozed while we moved up the channel toward the Great Barrier Wall. I hadn't visited the Wall before. It was a mythical place, like the Great Wall of China in Mo-Mere's books. After we passed another cross-channel, the Wall loomed ahead like a massive tidal wave.

From the distance, the Wall didn't look so mythical. A gray line of concrete studded with towers stretched across the horizon. I ducked into cattails when I saw a boat. Most were local skiffs that traded up and down the channels. Storm losses increased the need to barter for those who could afford to replace lost food and shelter.

Fran woke, groaned, and twisted her body to look forward. "You've got to be kidding. The Wall! What are you thinking?"

"I have to check refugee camps."

"What the heck?" Fran pointed toward the Wall. "Water cannons?"

I squinted. Sure enough, huge hoses hung over the Wall, pouring water into the channel. "They must have flooding on the other side."

"You think? Let's go. I don't need trouble."

"Are they looking for you?"

"Bounty hunters look for all of us." She pointed to her left shoulder. "They injected an implant before the storm. I refuse to work on their farms or in their damned mines."

"Then dig it out." When the thrum of a motor crept up behind us, I scooted into the cattails. Through the grass, I identified it as a local salvage boat looking to barter.

"You're on." Fran drew out a thin blade and pulled off her shoulder bandage. She dug at the knob on her arm. Blood streaked down. She looked at it as if studying someone else's cut and dug out the tracking chip. Fran dipped it in the water, cleaned it, and looked closer. "Amazing what they can do with tracking technology, and we can't feed people." She held the chip over the water.

"If you drop it, the chip will sink and they'll know you took it out." I found a thick twig and handed it to her. "Lodge the chip into this and let it float downstream. They'll track you out to sea."

She frowned. "You're not as dumb as you look." She took the twig and did as I'd suggested. Then she tossed it into the water and watched it float away.

We drew closer to the Wall. One of the towers directed its hose toward a group of women gathered below. The wind carried mist our way; it clung to us in the humidity.

From where we floated, the Wall was an abnormal rip in the natural world, as big of a tear as the storm surges that took our land. The top remained level to the horizon in both directions despite the natural hilliness of the landscape, as if engineers had gauged the top to be so many hundreds of feet above sea level back when they built it. The Wall was the color of pale gray of clouds on a rainy day, yet it had an unnatural uniformity, a cancer that spread, severing us from fertile land. Even so, its sheer monstrosity inspired awe. The Wall represented a power we couldn't challenge, and no one had in over a century.

"There's a camp up ahead." I moved the boat toward shore. "I'm going to ask about family. You can stay if you promise not to steal my log."

"This junk? I'd better come along to make sure you don't get into trouble."

* * *

Demarco had just delivered the two immature fishes, frightened girls whose lives were about to get a whole lot worse. It seemed reclamation had need for little hands for dangerous cleanup in and around sewage treatment facilities that had flooded. She doubted they would survive, but the credits were good.

She was just enjoying the positive turn of luck when she got an agent's call. After she disconnected, Demarco ordered the captain to head toward the Wall.

Sometimes bad news came with unforeseen benefits. The agent on the other end had reported an argument on an island farther west. Two girls assaulted the island's mayor, pushing her into an animal trap. The injury required eighteen stitches, antibiotics, and a leg splint, more detail than the inspector needed.

On a positive note, the mayor identified Regina Shen as one of the girls. She was alive, limping without a crutch, and in the company of an older girl who took the mayor's gun. Now the girls were armed and dangerous, likely to be shot on sight. Demarco needed to reach them before they got themselves killed, and with them, any future for the chief inspector.

The last thing the mayor reported: Regina in a canoe paddling west, toward the Wall.

Demarco put in a call to all agents to contact their bounty hunter connections. "Get everyone on this. I want that girl by sundown."

NINETEEN

I helped Fran out of the boat and onto the grassy shore, hoping we could find a healer for her leg. She refused to let me help her walk, so I limped next to her along an overgrown path, a couple of gimp Marginals who weren't ready to give up.

Fran poked the ground ahead of us for traps until we found a well-worn, pebbly trail. She winced with each step yet kept up with me. I offered her water from my jug. She drank until I thought she'd finish it. So much for her tale of finding water while in that trap.

We reached a gravel path and encountered two women in green canvas rags shuffling along like the walking dead. One carried a baby. Two thin girls, five to six years old, followed her. The other woman looked to be her mother.

"Where you from?" I asked.

"All gone," the younger woman said without looking up.

"Where are you going?"

"Food, water."

"Have you seen Zola Shen or her daughter, Colleen?" I asked.

"Nothing left." She seemed in shock.

Fran tugged my arm to move on. We limped ahead until we caught up with other small groups. Soon we reached an opening, a large field beneath the massive Wall. Water cannons sprayed women who approached the Wall with their hands out. A blue-uniformed woman stood where the gravel road met the field. She motioned for newcomers to move toward the left.

She looked as weary as the women we'd passed, as the women who trudged before us. "Keep moving," she said. "Off to the left. Find a patch of ground and settle in."

"Will they give us food?" a woman before us asked.

"We're doing what we can," the uniform said, meaning no.

"I'm looking for Zola Shen and Colleen Shen," I said.

"Good luck," the blue uniform said. "Move to the left and find a spot."

"Then what?" Fran asked. "What are we waiting for?"

"Assistance," the uniform said. "Be patient."

I asked the woman about Jasmine, Aimee, and Mo-Mere. Without looking at anything, the woman shook her head.

"You don't have anything to offer these people, do you?" Fran asked.

"I'm sorry for my friend," I said. I tugged Fran away. "Don't antagonize her."

"Why not? This is a load of alligator dung."

We moved to a spot of grass and looked back. The blue uniform sent more people our way. The Wall was less than a mile away. Wall guards hosed women who got too close. Everything from the river on our right all the way to the horizon on the left was open field covered with small groups of women and girls, a sea of faded green canvas. When I looked closer, I saw lots of women and few children. Maybe the bounty hunters had taken the rest.

"It looks so easy," I whispered to Fran. "Instead of gathering in this field, just swim under the Wall."

"Well, my little salmon, the river is walled off. What you see is water they pump through steel grates to prevent us from trying. They use blades to push the water. Bodies show up now and then along the river. It's tempting, but it's suicide."

"You can stay and wait," I said. "I came to find family." I headed toward the Wall.

Fran limped after me. "Don't be an idiot. Let's go downriver, steal a boat, and do salvage. Maybe we'll find something that gets us out of this rat hole."

We stopped a quarter mile from where the uniform wanted us. I yelled at the top of my lungs, "Zola Shen! Colleen Shen!" I faced in each direction, yelling as loud as I could.

No one took any notice. Women sat on the ground, keeping their girls close. I moved another quarter mile and yelled again, repeating this until we were near the Wall.

I'd never seen anything so monstrous. The concrete rose 300 feet toward the sky and stretched to the horizon in both directions. Its enormity separated us from food and clean water. Surrendering to bounty hunters sounded tempting, but I couldn't help thinking life on the other side wouldn't be any better.

I headed south and away from the Wall in a checkerboard pattern, shouting until I was hoarse. Over a hill, the field ended at a tree line that went up to within a few hundred feet of the Wall and spread south. Gray-uniformed guards looked down from one of the towers. A hose rotated in our direction. Fran pulled me away before the guard hosed us into the mud.

The field behind us sprawled with despair, women with nowhere else to go, no food, no shelter, no water, and no hope. My heart ached for them. Maybe Colleen somehow escaped the bounty hunters and reached one of these camps, but I doubted it. Truth be told, she wasn't the escaping type.

I'd read in Mo-Mere's books about Marie Antoinette being this callous toward starving women and children. I imagined Marie on the Wall, hosing our women. The Federation had no intention of feeding us. I'd heard that they refused to provide food after the last storm. They took the children they wanted and left the rest.

"I'm sorry," Fran said. Her eyes saddened. "Don't give up hope. At least you have family."

I wasn't so sure.

A silver-haired woman approached wearing a tattered canvas skirt and top. At first, I imagined her as Mo-Mere, bent by the flood, but she didn't have Mo-Mere's smile or round face.

"I couldn't help overhearing," she said. "You're looking for family. I hope you find them."

"Do you know Zola Shen?"

The woman's face took on a grayish cast as she shook her head and whispered, "You might try camps farther south, where channels meet the Wall. A friend left me here a few days ago to look for family."

"I'm sorry," I said.

"She said conditions across the Wall aren't much better. I have nowhere else to go. We could fight neighbors for scraps, but what's the point?" Her face looked like weathered alligator hide.

"Have you been to the other side?" I asked.

"Born there. I've been here fifteen years. They said this would be a death sentence. I guess they were right."

"Why?" I started to ask.

"They built walls to hold back the sea, but their crops were devastated, too. They've had floods and droughts. Find a different place to survive, before bounty hunters catch you."

"Come with us."

"An old woman like me would slow you down. Survival is a young girl's game. I've had my life."

"What about up north?" I asked.

The woman sighed and shook her head. "Fighting and riots. Patrols intervened. I don't think there were many survivors."

"Please come with us."

"You're sweet to ask." She kissed my forehead, stuffed a small packet into my hand, and pushed me along. "Watch for bounty hunters and patrols." She returned to the middle of the large field.

"Don't mind her," Fran said. "Let's go find your family."

I did mind. I wanted to help the woman, but Fran tugged me into the woods and headed south.

Stopping, I turned to Fran. "We need the boat."

"We travel faster without it."

"Until we come to water. Besides, I can paddle better than I can walk right now."

I was surprised Fran didn't head off by herself. Maybe she didn't have anywhere to go.

The sight of all these people giving up ripped at my guts. Yet I couldn't even take care of myself unless we found food and fresh water.

We walked along the edge of the field, which was lined by trees stretching for some distance away from the Wall, more trees than I'd seen in one place before. We reached the woods across from where the blue uniform had sent us. An Antiquities agent approached that corner of the field. I pulled Fran deeper into the woods. We hobbled behind the cover of bushes and trees until we approached the gravel path that led to the field.

An Antiquities patrol boat moored on the channel. Two gray uniforms joined their companion in the field. I couldn't see faces; the one talking to the blue uniform could have been Coarse-face. The blue uniform pointed to where she'd sent us and looked mystified that we weren't there. I looked at the patrol boat for any sign of Mom. I didn't see her, but she could have been below deck.

I returned my gaze to the field. The lead agent walked among the small groups sitting on the ground. It was Coarse-face. She scanned the area with binoculars. An old woman used her hand to trace my path up and down the field. A sky-skimmer drone buzzed along the channel. It banked left and flew low over the field.

"Something you're not telling me?" Fran asked over my shoulder.

"Or you?" I said. "Let's go."

* * *

While Coarse-face interrogated women eager to barter our whereabouts for scraps of food, Fran and I moved through the woods away from the field. Fran didn't complain, though she winced with each step. It was the Marginal mantra: *Never show weakness or you'll get left behind.*

As we neared where I'd left my log-boat, I crouched down. Two women Mom's age dragged themselves along the path. I looked at faces and didn't recognize them, just more Marginals who had lost everything.

The women passed and disappeared around the bend. I motioned for Fran to go. When she was halfway across the path, I half limped, half ran to the other side and stumbled.

Fran grabbed my arm before I fell into the water. "You got a death wish?"

When she let go, I poked around the tall grass until I found my boat. I climbed in. It felt good to get off my foot.

Pushing off, we floated downstream through rush and cattail. I felt twitchy. At every noise, I pulled deeper into tall grass and looked for gators.

"We'll never get anywhere at this rate," Fran said.

"You could help."

She picked up the other paddle.

"Wait!" I whispered. "Patrol boat."

Seeing the gray Antiquities emblem flap on the boat's forward flag, I crouched down and watched for hungry gators. After the hum of the inboard faded downstream, I sat up and looked around. No more boats.

We both paddled until we reached a cross channel. We hugged the shoreline along the west side until we reached another channel that led toward the Wall. I couldn't be sure if what we were paddling around was a very large island cut in half by the Wall, or a peninsula.

My small, shallow boat allowed us to follow closer to shore and hide when skiffs and motorboats went by. Most headed upriver toward the camps. I studied each for signs of Mom, Colleen, or Aunt Vera's daughters. No luck.

Halfway to the Wall, we turned the log around, and Fran paddled while I rested. She was strong, and within an hour we reached a path with groups of women approaching the Wall. Fran pulled into cattails on the northern bank.

We joined a group of women walking the pebbly path. I asked the same questions and received the same answers. They hadn't seen my family or Aunt Vera's girls. Before us, guards on top of the Wall sprayed with big hoses. Fields on both sides of the river had turned to mud beneath clusters of storm survivors, more people than I'd ever imagined. Several called out for food and water.

A blue-uniformed woman greeted new arrivals. The other women on the path trudged toward her. Fran and I slipped into the woods, crossed the wooded hillside, and reached a clearing that stretched to the Wall and from the river up a hill to the right. The clearing was jammed with mud-covered women and a few girls.

I stood at the edge of the field and yelled for Mom and Colleen. I barely heard my own voice above others. A disharmony of names mingled with steamy heat as women moved from group to group asking about loved ones.

"This is impossible," Fran said. "We should go before we get trampled. We need time to hunt."

"Someone has to be collecting names." I hoped.

We walked the northern side without finding any help. Finally, we took the boat across to the southern bank. There we bypassed the blue-uniformed woman directing newcomers and found a makeshift set of tables. A dozen women stood, helping long lines of refugees. I got into the line for the end of the alphabet while Fran looked around.

"This is crazy," said a thin woman with a wrinkled face. "Last time the Feds at least gave us fresh water and bread. This time they spray us with foul water."

"Yeah," another old woman said. "With all the rain, you'd think they could at least give us fresh water."

"We should storm the Wall," a third woman said.

I looked up at hundreds of feet of concrete and shook my head.

"That's enough," the blue uniform said from behind us. "One more word and we'll send you away."

The first woman waited until the uniform left and whispered, "Like that would be worse."

The woman in front of me left, shaking her head. I approached the table. A woman Mom's age had dark circles under her eyes. Mud covered her arms and cheeks. "Who you looking for, missy?" she asked in a soft, mechanical voice.

"Jasmine or Aimee Morton."

The tired woman shook her head and looked down. These women didn't even have Mesh-readers, which required batteries. "No one by that name has come through."

"What about Mo-Mere? I mean, Marisa Seville?"

"I haven't heard that name, either. What's your name, in case they come asking?"

"I'm Regina Shen," I said. "Have you heard from Zola Shen or Colleen Shen?"

"Why don't you wait here while I ask around?" The woman left.

TWENTY

Other women pushed close behind me. "Where did she go this time?" one grumbled.

I felt feverish in the afternoon heat with all these people closing in around us. There was no fresh air, just the muggy spray from the Wall.

"What's taking so long?" someone asked.

I felt guilty and hopeful.

Fran grabbed my arm. "I found something."

"I can't leave."

Fran pulled me around to the other side of the tables, alongside a group of women heading across the field.

"What's going on?" I demanded.

"I have a surprise for you."

We moved away from the information desk. Then Fran turned left and hobbled into the woods.

I pulled on her arm. "What's the surprise?"

She pointed toward the information desk. Two blue uniforms joined the woman behind the table. A gray-uniformed Antiquities agent stood nearby.

"That woman skunked you out," Fran said. "Care to tell me what kind of trouble you're in?"

So much for finding family. The search was futile anyhow. Bounty hunters had taken Colleen. Mom was with Coarse-face. Not far away, three women who looked healthier than the other desperate souls were moving across the field.

"I don't know," I said. "We've got to go." I stepped toward the wooded path that led to my boat.

Fran stopped me. "Have you killed anyone?"

"No."

"Stolen from someone?"

"No."

"Then what?"

"I think they're after my mom," I said. "I don't know why."

Fran sighed, put weight on her foot, and winced. "Forget the log. We can make better time if we keep going."

"You can. I'm not leaving my boat."

The sun began to set behind the Great Wall, casting long shadows.

"Could we at least try to catch some dinner?" Fran asked.

We trudged through the woods, limping and hobbling until we reached the gravel path that separated the woods from the channel. We waited for several groups of women to shuffle past before we crossed. Then we hid in the bushes and tall grass looking for the log. Twilight gave us shadows to hide among, but it also made hunting difficult.

"Maybe someone took your boat," Fran whispered.

"People are heading this way, not east."

"Maybe it got loose."

"I tied it well," I said. "You know what we haven't seen for a while?"

"Friendly people? I warned you."

"Gators. There should be dozens. We've only seen one."

"Being killed, as I recall. People are eating anything. I'm surprised they haven't turned cannibal."

Voices approached. We crouched down and watched a sky-skimming drone fly low over the channel, heading west. Women along the path groaned. When their voices faded into the steamy breeze, I pushed aside cattails to check for gators. There was my log-boat, moored to exposed roots of a tree.

"There, see?" I said.

We slipped into the boat and floated down the channel, keeping within the cover of rush and cattails until we reached a jut of rock with no grass to hide within. A patrol boat motored past, followed by bounty boats, scavengers, and skiffs. I tied the log's mooring line to a bush on shore and squirmed to get comfortable as twilight turned to night.

Stars brightened above us. We cast two lines while boats of various sizes moved up and down the channel. After a while, I caught a single bass. We split it and ate it raw, sushi the ancients would have called it. Another Antiquities patrol boat sped by and stopped near the entrance to the camp. More bounty boats motored up and down, shining floodlights all around.

"I told you we'd do better over land." Fran lifted her leg onto the side of the log.

"Not with drones checking every clearing."

"Then we should go downriver where fishing's better."

"That patrol boat has nowhere to go when they're done except back down. We'd do better to wait."

"I'm just saying."

In the distance, a sky-skimmer buzzed along the Wall, casting shadows from floodlights shining down on the field. Fran and I curled up in the boat while the drone scooted over the channel. We weren't going anywhere, though if temperatures dropped enough, they could catch us using infrared.

After the drone was gone, we tried to stretch out, but the boat was too small. I tucked my legs under me until they cramped. Fran draped hers over the sides.

"You'll attract gators," I said.

* * *

Unable to sleep, I stared up at the star-studded sky and at boats passing up and down the channel. I missed Colleen, mostly looking after her, but somehow I couldn't miss Mom as much as I'd expected. Fact was, I rarely saw her, particularly over the past six months. School took up six days a week with no holidays, and on Sundays she left us alone. The most I'd seen her was getting ready for school and quiet dinners at night. Inside, she'd vanished long ago.

"Is your home under water?" I asked.

"Which one?" Fran said.

I didn't answer. Instead, I stared at the sky, wondering if Federation citizens ever looked at the stars. Our superstitious ancestors thought they were pinholes of lights stuck in the heavens. Before the Great Collapse, they'd shown enhanced images of those points as suns like ours. Maybe the Federation had unified the

Earth under a single government with peace, but there had to be other ways. If nothing else, history and science taught me that, though I'd seen little evidence here in the swamps. Still, when I looked up, I saw images from Mo-Mere's precious books and longed to see more.

"This is the same sky we had in New Mumbai," Fran said.

"India?"

"Surprised? My mom and a friend got a boat to find a better place. After months at sea, we landed here. Some improvement."

"Isn't Mumbai on the coast, under water?" I asked.

In the dim light I couldn't see her expression. "Mumbai sank beneath the sea. Inland, they created New Mumbai. We lived on the sea-side of their Great Wall, just like here. It was much worse, if you can believe it. More people on less land."

"I'm sorry."

"For what? You didn't build the damned Wall. At least this swamp was less crowded before this storm."

Fran told stories about New Mumbai with longing. She entertained me with adventures of her journey around the world to our very own Richmond Swamps, and spoke with despair over the number who died from dehydration during the trip. It seemed a tall tale to me, stories I could have told of my home here, with a few embellishments from Mo-Mere's books. I didn't say so. It was nice to have someone to talk to.

"We should sleep," I said, "so we can leave at first light."

If there had been alligators nearby, they could have feasted on me and I would have been too comatose to have stopped them. I didn't even wake to boats on the channel.

Something jabbed my foot and sent splinters of pain up my leg. I looked up into Fran's face, barely visible in the early dawn. She pointed to a patrol boat moored across the channel from us. I turned to shore nearby, expecting Coarse-face to jump out.

My legs cramped. "We can't use the channel." I pointed inland.

Fran nodded, grabbed her stick, and crawled onto a rocky ledge. She moved toward the gravel path. I secured the paddles in the bottom of the boat and climbed out, keeping an eye on the patrol boat across the way. A single gray-coat stood at the stern, gazing downstream.

Keeping low, I pulled my boat out of the water and into the bushes along the shore.

Fran returned. "Looks quiet if you hurry." She went ahead.

I dragged the boat across the gravel road and into the woods. Fran blocked my way. "You can't be serious. That'll slow us down."

"I'm not leaving the boat. We'll need it." I limped forward, pulling the log-boat behind me.

Fran leaned on her walking stick and followed. Beyond the pebble path, we climbed a hill to stay clear of the expansive campsite. I didn't want to relive the suffering we'd seen yesterday, and wonder who had died. Also, too many people there would barter us for favors with all the froggies who'd converged on this section of the Richmond Swamps.

We headed south, parallel to the Wall, which we couldn't see until we reached the tops of hills. I imagined peeking over the Wall, but it was too far away. Although the fields below hadn't begun to stir, water cannons flowed freely. So they weren't just hosing women approaching the Wall. They had to be dealing with their own floods.

Well beyond the refugee camp, we came upon crop fields. Desperate people had trampled and scavenged them down to their roots. The land looked barren, with not even a squirrel in sight. If trees had been edible, they would have been gone as well.

Small groups of women wandered the field, picking at what they thought might be edible. Mo-Mere had warned us about poisonous fish and mushrooms, as well as plants that caused severe dehydration. Fresh water was scarce. We'd had no rain since the storm, and water coming through the Wall was muddy.

"We won't find any food," Fran said. "We should return to the river and catch some fish before we starve."

"You want to rest?" I asked, straining under the weight of dragging my boat. I was dehydrated, barely sweating in the heat.

"Drop the log so we can make better time."

I was tempted, but in our waterlogged world, a boat was a necessity.

Fran's limp was getting worse. She hobbled to a muddy rock to rest her foot. The scavenged land filled me with the horror of what the storm and the Federation had done to us. Mo-Mere would say everyone should start their lives in our swamps for a better appreciation of our world. Live off the bugs and moss. Except for mosquitoes, I didn't see either. Picked clean.

131

I handed Fran half of Therese's food and savored the rest: chicken jerky, apple slices, and bread. It was best to eat before the heat made it inedible or someone mugged us for it.

Fran wolfed hers down. Though she looked hungry, she didn't ask for more. She was a stubborn one, a tough gator. And she hadn't ratted me out, or left like Mom did.

I looked for snakes, birds, anything worth catching. Scavengers would have killed and eaten any coyotes or other big predators. The only animals around were human. I prayed it didn't come to that.

Then I spotted a scrawny squirrel in the tree overhead. I notched an arrow into my crossbow.

"I claim that," said a woman's voice behind me.

Turning, I saw a leather-faced woman next to a dark-tanned blonde girl about my age. The girl looked familiar: thin, hungry face covered with splotches of mud. She wore a torn and faded green canvas skirt and top. Her eyes had long since given up hope. She was, after all, a typical Marginal after a storm.

The woman pointed a shotgun at me and then up into the tree. Neither the woman nor the girl looked as if they'd eaten since the storm. She fired up into the tree. Leaves and branches scattered. The thin gray squirrel fell. The woman reloaded the gun and picked up her catch. "Why don't you two come join us for a meal?" She pointed the shotgun our way.

This morsel wouldn't feed one of us, let alone all four.

"Come on," the woman said. "Time's a-wasting." She motioned with her gun for us to head toward the big camp.

Fran must have been weak with hunger, because she followed the woman. I grabbed her arm.

She pushed me. "Don't touch." Wincing, she limped a few steps.

The blonde girl backed away from the woman and broke into a weary jog toward nearby woods. The woman turned, aimed, and then swiveled toward us.

I aimed my crossbow at her head. "Take your ill-gotten squirrel. Go before you lose everything."

The leathery woman pointed her shotgun at me and then at Fran, who now held her gun. "Damn it all," the woman said, "no one pays for cripples." She hurried after the blonde.

I dragged my boat, heading south. Fran limped next to me,

looking now and then toward the woman. "I told you overland was a bad idea."

"When was that? Yesterday you were all for it. Today, there's too much traffic on the water."

"There's nothing to eat."

"You want to go back?" I asked. "Then go."

Fran winced with each step. "It's just that we could make it to the river. At least then we could fish."

"You want to sell me to bounty hunters?"

* * *

I dragged my boat south through woods, out of sight of the Wall. It was hopeless. Colleen was probably slaving in some safe place where she had food and water. Being sweet and innocent, she wouldn't mind as much as I would. Mom had gone up north where there'd been fighting and then joined Coarse-face. I headed south.

Mo-Mere would call what kept me going destiny, but I wasn't so sure. I felt like flotsam drifting downriver. We crossed barren fields, walked through woods without sighting a single crow. When we veered too close to the Barrier Wall, we saw water cannons spraying a muddy ditch along its base. From a distance, it looked like a moat.

We moved east under cover of trees to avoid sky-skimmer drones. We hobbled forward for hours, slowing bit by bit, until I could barely put one foot in front of the other.

The ground leveled off, then sloped downward. In the distance I spotted a ridge. In between, I hoped, there might be a stream or channel where we could fish. Fran was right. We needed water and food before evening. My throat parched, I drank from my water jug and gave the last to Fran. I spotted the tanned blonde. She moved behind a tree that barely hid her slight form.

Fran waved her walking stick. "Off with you." She favored her bad leg too much to give chase.

The blonde hung her head and ambled toward us. "Please don't send me away. That woman made me steal. Then she wouldn't even feed me."

"That's not our problem," Fran said.

"Please, I just want to get away from her. She's a bounty hunter."

"We don't have anything," I said. "You can follow if you'd like."

"Are you serious?" Fran asked. "She's a scavenger."

"I won't send her back, and we have nothing for her to steal," *if you don't count the heavy boat.*

I lifted the log and crossed another field, picked clean by scavengers. When we reached the next tree line, I stumbled and collapsed beneath the log.

Darkness embraced me as the log-boat swallowed me into its hollowed-out interior. My arms were too weak to lift myself, let alone the boat. I felt as if I were in a coffin over an open fire. After hours of dragging the boat, I still had the sensation of motion, and getting nowhere.

The next thing I knew, Fran carried the boat, limping forward with her stick, and pulling me by the rope tied to my waist. The blonde trudged along beside me. The sun set over the Wall to our right, turning wisps of clouds purple. We were trudging downhill and south.

Nothing focused the mind like death, the prospect of oblivion. You were only ever a trap, a hungry predator, an angry bounty hunter, or an unfortunate fall away. I'd seen death: the moment when the breath of life left Aunt Vera, the girls on the crashed bounty boat. Even though I mostly obeyed the Twelve Commandments, I didn't find any comfort that would allow me to lie down and wait for the end to come, or whatever hereafter awaited me. I wasn't ready. Something inside was like a wormy parasite that refused to let go. That devil kept me alive, moving my good foot, then my gimp one, when all I wanted to do was drop and rest.

Feverish, I felt both heavy and light, as if I could blow away at the slightest breeze. The air was like steam off a tea kettle. I fell, yet remained in motion. Then I was in my boat drifting downriver. Waves were choppy, bumpy, as if shooting rapids up north. Thump, thump, thump. Above, the scarlet sky drifted to gray with puffy clouds all regal and dry, and then to black.

The starry heavens spread out above me. Floating, I yelled how free I was. My voice croaked, barely making a sound. Sticky sweat glued me down. I hadn't the strength to shoo mosquitoes or pesky black flies that swarmed my face. The heat felt like we were sliding into the depths of an active volcano.

It's not my time, I told myself and continued to drift.

TWENTY-ONE

I woke, wondering whether I'd reached heaven or hell. The space around me was unbearably hot and sticky, so I guessed the latter. A moist breeze blew over my face. The flies were gone, though I itched all over from mosquito bites. I lay in a bed, an honest-to-goodness cushiony mattress with a heavenly pillow.

As I opened my parched mouth, my lips threatened to split apart. A hand placed ice chips to my lips, real ice. It sent chills. I had to be dreaming. I smiled. Shards of pain shot through my face. I sucked on the ice and tasted blood.

When my feverish eyes tried to focus, the Blessed Mary hovered over me. No, it was Mo-Mere's face, wrinkled with worry.

"Don't try to speak," she said. "You're a very lucky girl, though you probably don't feel that way." She dabbed my forehead with a cool, damp cloth.

I reached up and touched her arm: tough and firm, not a mirage.

She squeezed my hand and placed it on my stomach, which grumbled with hunger.

"I thought I'd lose you to fever," Mo-Mere said. "You've pushed yourself too hard."

"Colleen?" I croaked.

"I haven't heard from her or your mother since the storm. Fran was very brave. She saved your life." Mo-Mere smiled, which did little to soften her worry lines. "She told me how you saved her from that trap, and she owed you. She almost lost her leg to infection while dragging you and your boat to the camp. The moment I heard, I got you out of there. What a den of vipers preying on young girls."

"Where?"

Mo-Mere placed more ice on my lips. "Fran left after I treated her leg. Said she'd repaid her debt. She borrowed your boat and half the fishing line but left your bow and arrows with me."

"Why?" I managed.

"Fran's too much of a loner to stick around. Her mother was willing to pay for school, but Fran kept running off."

I finished the ice chip and sat up. "What are Colleen's chances?" My voice scratched at my ears.

Mo-Mere gently pushed me back down. "We must have faith that your sister survived."

"Did you know my donor mother?"

She looked surprised. "What brought that up?"

"She wouldn't have abandoned us."

Mo-Mere shook her head. "Don't worry about that. Get some rest."

I held her arm. "Are you my—"

"No, dear. I'm not your donor mother. But there is someone who wants to see you."

The tanned blonde who had followed us stood on the other side of my bed. She took my hand and bit her chapped lip.

"You?" I pulled away and tried to focus on her face.

"You may not recognize Wendy," Mo-Mere said. "She's a year behind you at school. She helped Fran carry you here."

I squinted. "Thanks. What about your family?" I tried to remember her.

Wendy shrugged. "Mom died in the storm along with my sisters. Her last words were to go to the Wall. For days I foraged and escaped bounty hunters. Then that horrid woman grabbed me. She said she'd barter me for food if I didn't help. The squirrel was yours. She didn't see it until you got ready to shoot." Her gaze turned from me to the floor. "I'm sorry."

Shivering from the ice, I took her hand. "Thanks for saving me."

"Thanks for not sending me back to that bounty hunter. I recognized you from school. Everyone talks about how smart you are, skipping two grades. That woman wasn't going to give me any squirrel. I was so hungry I had to get away." Wendy broke down, her body trembling in my grip. She leaned in and hugged me.

There must have been some instinct in my fuzzy brain telling me to let her join us, some remembrance. My mind burned too feverish to bring it into focus. I patted her back. Then my arm fell limply at my side. My insides boiled.

When Wendy pulled away, she handed me a turquoise necklace. "You were holding this. It's very beautiful. You should wear it."

My hand tightened around the stupid beads, a cheap string Mom had made out of colored stream pebbles for Colleen's birthday. "It belongs to my sister." My eyes ached to tear up, but they were too dry and scratchy. "It's all I have of her and Mom."

She closed my hand over it. "Then best we don't lose it."

I looked at Mo-Mere. "Did the school survive?"

"I rescued what I could. You'll be schooling here now."

"We're not at the Wall?" I looked out the window, too high to see more than treetops, blue sky, and no clouds.

"For heaven's sake, no," Mo-Mere said. "I brought you to a cabin your mother and I built in case of another flood. The flood came sooner than expected."

"My mom?"

"She's committed to your education. She provided me enough to ensure I could guide you through the rest of your schooling. And here you are, like iron filings to a magnet."

Until that moment I hadn't realized it had been Mo-Mere I'd been searching for. "Are you sure you're not my donor?"

"Sorry to disappoint you, dear."

"What about the other teachers and students?"

"You're the only two I've found. I've put out word at the refugee camps, but I'm not hopeful. It's a tricky business. Bounty hunters worked through the storm collecting girls. People are desperate. They're selling their own children for relief. There must be a great need for cleanup crews across the Wall."

"Colleen?"

"Let's hope not. If they place her in a home, she'd have food and shelter as long as they need her. It depends on whether they want permanent housekeepers or temporary childrearing."

"You mean they could dump her back over the Wall when they don't need her?"

Sadness filling Mo-Mere's eyes. "Unless they find her another home in need of her help."

"Only those who are useful survive," I said. "The weak die."

"I'm committed to making you and Wendy strong. Rest up, but stay alert. Bounty hunters have been quite persistent."

* * *

I faded in and out of fever and chills. Mo-Mere hovered over me with ice and a damp rag. Wendy sat and talked to me. Her words glided over me like a cool blanket. I couldn't recall anyone feeding me before, but Wendy propped me up while Mo-Mere fed me sweet porridge that slid down my scratchy throat like honey.

As if part of some strange ritual, they grabbed my arms and legs and carried me out of the bedroom. I floated through a place of unfamiliar shapes before they laid me on a floor made of chipped and polished stone. Mo-Mere dragged me by the arms through a narrow passage where walls looked like floor. She set me down on my side in a space tighter than the channel under Therese's dining hall, and boiling hot, as if fires burned all around me.

My arms and legs felt paralyzed. Walls pressed against my back and stomach. I couldn't move or breathe. Whatever fever I'd had before shot through the roof.

"Stay put," Mo-Mere said in a soft whisper. "Don't make a sound and do *not* move."

I couldn't if I'd wanted to.

Something scraped nearby. The opening through which they'd dragged me closed. Polished rock surrounded me with gray plaster the color of the Barrier Wall. Sweat beaded on my forehead, neck, and back. I was roasting like alligator steaks. A single voice shocked me into total alertness.

"Marisa, this isn't a social call," Coarse-face said. "I trust you wouldn't harbor fugitives, but we must take precautions. You understand."

Escape. I had to leave, but I couldn't move.

"Of course, Inspector," Mo-Mere said. "Feel free to have your agents look around."

"They already are. The Federation needs girls. I could offer this one a good home."

"Wendy's young. She'll have much more to offer if you allow me three years to groom her."

"Marisa, don't try my patience. You may have survived this storm."

"We've been lucky," Mo-Mere said.

"That luck won't hold. Let me help her."

"I have much yet to teach her, and she can help me fix this place for when she leaves."

"Why bother? The next storm will demolish it," Coarse-face said.

"Why are you taking Wendy's blood?"

"The Federation keeps track of its people, including those on this side of the Wall. I'm pleased to see you've done well. Marginal life suits you."

"I make myself useful," Mo-Mere said. "I doubt the Federation would take me back."

"Good solid stonework, but why build a fire when it's already so hot?"

"To cook a stew."

Voices faded, or maybe I did. I woke in bed. Mo-Mere stood over me with more ice. Wendy stood on the other side mopping my forehead.

"That was close," Mo-Mere said.

"Why was she here?" I croaked.

"You know Inspector Demarco?"

"She's the one who tagged me."

"Ah," Mo-Mere said. "The inspector has a personal interest in you. She offered some nonsense about you attacking a peaceful family up north. According to Demarco, you took a gun, threatened them, and stole items to barter."

I shook my head. "When they tried to turn us over to bounty hunters, Fran took their gun. We didn't threaten anyone, and we left with what we brought."

"And the gun."

I shrugged.

"People do desperate things in desperate times. I'm sorry about the fireplace, but the heat masked their infrared scans. Otherwise Demarco would be taking you for a ride."

"We have to go before she returns." I sat up.

"No, my dear. You need to rest. You're burning up."

* * *

School began the next day when Mo-Mere roused Wendy and me with the announcement that it was time to take a walk around her island, our new home. Though my fever had broken, my arms and legs felt stretched to the breaking point.

Sunshine poked through my window. The air dripped with humidity at the start of another muggy day. At least an electric fan blew over me. Mo-Mere must have had solar panels or a wind generator.

The room where I awoke had the soft bed with mosquito netting and a chest on which sat bandages and a wash basin. The air carried freshness, smoke-free, which meant no cooking fires upwind.

Dressed in a fresh green canvas top, Wendy helped me to my feet. "Mo-Mere wants us to start training," she whispered.

Despite my weariness, my left leg held weight better than it had since I stepped into that trap. Wendy helped me out of the bedroom. I'd never had a bedroom before, let alone one all to myself.

"My room's next door," Wendy said. "Mo-Mere's room is down the hall."

Our teacher stood in a large room with a kitchen corner on one side and a small classroom on the other. The room was larger than Mom's house. Two desks faced a chalkboard with the message: *Life begins now.*

Mo-Mere helped me out onto a new wood-plank porch that had withstood the storm. The sun rose over the seascape beyond the trees, on an island bigger than Aunt Vera's. "We have two cabins and space to build more in case other teachers and students arrive." She pointed to a second log house. "For now, you're my family. You'll treat me with respect as your teacher and as your surrogate mother. Is that understood?"

Wendy nodded.

"Yes, Mo-Mere," I said. "How will we get by with no one paying?"

She stepped off the porch onto the grassy clearing between the cabins. "Lesson one. We *will* become self-sufficient. It's a rule of our swamps that you should never forget. You'll spend part of your days honing survival skills of hunting, fishing, and salvage under my direction. You'll work the garden, and harvest apples and oranges from trees out back. You'll devote the rest of your time to studies leading to university."

Now I remembered Wendy from school. She looked thinner than before the storm, though her face had regained some color. A quiet one who kept to herself, she looked too frail to have survived the storm and sixteen years in the swamps. Yet here she was. Like me, she was that statistical improbability, one in a thousand. I smiled.

From where we stood, I gazed through the trees at channels on three sides. Water surrounded us, besieged us. It penetrated every fabric of our lives. This school had to be the last in the entire Richmond Swamps.

"We have no university on this side of the Wall," I said, "and the Federation doesn't accept Marginals."

Mo-Mere smiled. "Lesson two. You'll learn to speak, act, think, and dress as a Federation citizen, so when the time comes, you'll have a choice."

"You can do that?"

Mo-Mere led us to the edge of the clearing, where the ground sloped down into the water. "It's what both your mothers wanted for you, why they sent you to my school. Life in the swamps teaches you survival skills in this world but little else. There's more to life than avoiding death. That's what I hope to teach you."

"Is that lesson three?" I asked.

"Yes, my precocious one. But first things first. This is a modest island. It's rocky, high enough, and off the main channel to avoid the worst of the next storm surge. We may only have a few years before this, too, is lost."

"And the Antiquities agent returns for Wendy," I reminded her.

"She'll return well before that. Count on it. In the meantime, let's make the best of what we have." She fanned her hand toward the trees. "You won't find game here, so you'll need to fish and plant a garden. We'll barter for more seed."

"Do we have a boat?" I asked.

She pointed north, alongside one of the cabins. "We have a tidy cove with a skiff and a motorboat. They're hidden from view, though anyone with half a brain could circle the island and find them."

"How did you get to be so smart?"

Mo-Mere patted my shoulder. "It's good to have you back, my dear. I was a college professor, at a branch of New Harmony University in the Federation. That's where I met your mother."

"You knew her over there?"

"We both hoped my knowledge of the Federation could help

you make a better life over there. You need to learn caution, as you have here in the swamps, only different. Learn to separate what's real from what the Federation says is true. Know when to use which knowledge."

"Truth is truth," I blurted out, then hung my head. "I know; using truth to hurt others is a bad truth."

"You *were* listening. Good. Let's get to work."

"I feel weak," I protested.

"No time to waste. Predators are at our doorsteps."

And so mornings began with Wendy and me walking the island. We looked for evidence of trespassers, alligators, and other critters. We checked traps, boats on the channels, and useful debris that washed up on our shores or floated close enough to snag.

To preserve our trees, we gathered branches that floated downstream and dead limbs for firewood. Then we checked our trees for ripe fruit before the birds got them.

Wendy followed my lead as Colleen used to, not saying much, yet observing everything I did. It seemed strange that she was a year behind me in school, since she was a year older. The sadness in her eyes mirrored my own. While she didn't want to talk about her family, I knew she missed them as much as I missed mine. Well, Colleen, at least.

After our morning island survey, we fished with what Fran left me of my line and fishing wire Mo-Mere provided Wendy. The bass, carp, and catfish were plentiful, though small. We should have thrown them back, but we only took what we needed. Then Mo-Mere had us work in the garden, planting seeds she'd saved from her schoolhouse.

Only then did we begin lessons on life in the Federation. Working Stiffs were like Marginals, at the bottom of the official caste system. They worked in small groups on farms, in mines, in factories, or as servants in better homes. If they didn't obey, the Federation threatened to dump them over the Wall. Other than having meals and a roof over their heads, they didn't have much that we didn't.

Mo-Mere wanted us to become Professionals. Then we could vote, have our own homes, and drive motorized vehicles. I'd seen sky-jumpers, motorboats, and sea-skimmers, but never anything motorized on land.

"Every Professional has a Mesh-reader with access to much more than we do," Mo-Mere said.

"Are they really trusted with information?" I asked.

"In the Federation, no one trusts anyone, though Professionals get more respect than Working Stiffs."

"Elites get more," I said. "GODs have access to everything."

"Ah, my dear. Even that isn't so. Behind the scenes, GODs fight among themselves. Think of them as individual bounty hunter groups, each vying to be on top."

"They're pythons and gators then."

Mo-Mere laughed. "Never get between two quarrelling GODs. They'll do anything to stay on top, including betraying their closest family and friends."

While I was thankful for Mo-Mere's wisdom and absorbed as much as I could, I couldn't see the relevance to my life. Even so, every day, she pushed us harder than the day before.

Even after a few days of regaining my strength, by the end of chores my body begged to sit and rest. Then Mo-Mere filled my head with knowledge of a world I'd only read and heard about as we scanned the horizon for patrols, bounty hunters, and scavengers.

TWENTY-TWO

By the end of the week, I was growing restless. Before Mo-Mere could sit me next to Wendy for another mid-morning schooling session, I pulled our teacher aside. "Shouldn't we salvage the old school?" I whispered.

"I've saved my books, my dear. I'm sure the rest of that rickety place washed out to sea."

"Then elsewhere. We need things to barter."

"Don't be in such a hurry. You're in no condition to salvage." Mo-Mere pointed at my seat by her chalkboard. "Your job is to focus on your studies. That's what your mother wanted."

"She abandoned us."

"Regina! Respect. We can't know what's in another person's heart or mind unless we face them. Until we know otherwise, don't think ill of her."

"She was with that inspector."

"Regina, you're very special. Don't waste that." She glared at me.

"Why did she even have me?"

"Enough."

I suspected Mo-Mere knew something she didn't want to share. I couldn't be sure how close she'd been with Mom, nor whether that extended to Coarse-face, who had used Mo-Mere's first name when she'd visited. Were they friends? If so, why hadn't Mo-Mere turned me in?

"Why do you keep telling me I'm special?" I said. "I don't feel that way, and don't want to. Special stands out. Those who stand out get caught."

Mo-Mere smiled. "I see I'll have my hands full with you. Maybe you didn't ask to be special, but you are, both in terms of survival skills and intellect. Being special brings responsibility to use your talents as best you can, not only for yourself but for those around you. Sit." She nudged me toward a wooden seat facing the board.

I sat next to Wendy, who forced a smile. I felt sorry for her. She seemed lost without family. Me? I was used to taking care of my sister and myself. I was angry at Mom for leaving and being with Coarse-face, but I didn't miss her, and that made me sad. I wanted to miss her. It was the right thing to do.

Mo-Mere stood over Wendy but stared down at me. "Your mothers want you to pay close attention. They counted on me to look out for you if anything happened."

"Yes, ma'am," I said.

Nodding, Wendy looked ready to cry.

"I make no guarantees," Mo-Mere said, "but I'll use every bit of my knowledge and strength to prepare you for a better life in the Federation."

"What about you?" I asked.

She sighed. "One issue with getting older is you acquire a reputation. You become recognized. The Federation has my DNA, fingerprints, facial recognition, and a dozen other ways to identify me. I have no expectation of returning. They cast me out for life. You two, with tracking implants removed and no Federation records, have a chance to become most anything you're willing to work for."

I looked at Wendy's arm and saw a new bandage over where her chip had been. "You removed hers? That's illegal." Then I rubbed my arm—no lump and a big scar.

"When the Federation is free to capture girls, being a free Marginal is illegal."

"Why do people put up with the Federation caste system and hierarchy?"

"Perception creates its own reality," Mo-Mere said.

"What does that mean?"

"When people believe obeying gives them a better life than

rebelling, they obey, no matter how bad their circumstances. Starving peasants in France grumbled about their conditions and added their numbers to the revolution, but they didn't lead. The powerless rarely do unless they've had a taste of a better life. They believe they have more to lose—their lives and families—than to gain."

"But they have the most to gain," I said.

"Maybe so, but they have little experience with a better life to inspire them, and they've experienced punishments that come with protest: prison, dispossession, and starvation."

"Then who does lead rebellions?"

"Regina?" Wendy said. "What are you thinking?"

"The way the Federation treats us isn't right."

"No, it isn't," Mo-Mere said. "They've developed choice rationalizations for what they do, centered on saving civilization. What you should ask, only among yourselves, is whether they did save our culture, and what culture they saved. Every regime seeks to perpetuate itself. Some do this by helping people, some by oppressing in order to hold on to power."

"It's our primate evolution," I said. "We compete to dominate groups in order to dominate our environment."

"While that *is* a function of our primate heritage, you're getting off topic. Rebel leaders believe they have more to gain from change than by clinging to the devil they know. They're bold, and often better fed than the downtrodden they claim to speak for. Unlike those on the bottom, they've tasted a better life and often had it taken from them."

"Like you did," I added.

"As I did. You see around you starvation. People give up and sell their families and souls for scraps. Why? They've bought into the illusion that they can't save themselves, and if they try, they could lose what little they have. Give a woman fishing line and she'll fish. Give her a dozen and she'll barter for a better life. Why don't Marginals revolt against their conditions? The Federation beat them until they believe there's no hope. They don't know any better. You do."

I shrugged. "I don't know anything about a better life."

"You will. When the time's right, and if you demonstrate excellence in your studies, I'll help you create Federation identities and get you into the university. Then you can make your own destinies."

"Doing what?" I asked.

"You could become a doctor, an engineer, a professor, a genetic researcher."

"If I don't ask too many questions."

Mo-Mere nodded. "People in power don't like embarrassing questions."

"What if I don't want to be a Professional?"

"With your mind, your mother and I hope you will."

"And you?" I asked. "Since our moms can't pay, why are you doing this?"

"So full of questions. Okay, when you live long enough, you think about what survives you."

"So Wendy and I are your legacy."

"I want to pass on what I've learned," Mo-Mere said. "I hope you'll do well, and in some way, I'll take pleasure in helping you. Is that asking too much?"

I shrugged and looked out the window for any boats coming up the channel. "With bounties and Antiquities looking for me, it helps to know why."

"I guess vicariously I'll take joy in you getting into the Federation when I can't. In time, the seas will gobble up all our land. I may have lived out my life by then, but you're still young. You girls have opportunities. I've seen the other side. Professional is a much better life."

"It's just."

"If you're not prepared to give this your all, don't waste my time," Mo-Mere said. "If you promise to follow my directions, I promise to prepare you as best I can."

Wendy looked up and gave her full attention. After all, she had nowhere else to go. Tears filled her eyes. I felt sorry for her. Having lost her mom, she needed someone else to look up to, someone to look after her. I swore I'd never let myself be that weak again.

Thank you, Mom.

"The most important key to surviving on the other side will be to profess belief in the Community Movement. Memorize their Twelve Commandments. Don't mumble as you do in class. Read their bible until you can recite the passages that sanctify the Community Movement as the one true path, and convince anyone that you believe all that rubbish."

So went our lessons, while I was itching to get out on the channels and salvage.

"What's the point of planning for a Federation university when we could die or Antiquities agents could grab us?" I asked.

"If you don't plan for a better future," Mo-Mere said, "opportunities will pass you by. I make no guarantees except to do my best if you'll do the same."

TWENTY-THREE

While Wendy used the outhouse behind our cabin, I pulled Mo-Mere aside. "Why won't you let me talk about my mother?"

"There's nothing to be gained by dwelling on questions you can't answer."

"During the storm, she was with the Antiquities agent who tagged me."

"Are you sure?" Mo-Mere asked. "It was chaotic, and you were feverish."

"I didn't hallucinate that, Mo-Mere. She stood on the port rail of the Antiquities patrol boat talking with that agent like they were friends."

"Inspector Joanne Demarco."

"How well do you know her?" I asked. "She used your first name the day she came here." I couldn't read Mo-Mere's pensive expression.

"Demarco was born up north and knows the swamps well. While working as a bounty hunter, she impressed a senior Antiquities agent who hired her. She moved up to inspector covering the Richmond Swamps. I'd heard the governor promoted her to Chief Inspector over all North American Antiquities activities."

"Mom was with her."

"Before you jump to conclusions, let me do some digging. Not a word to Wendy." She held up her hand before I could say more.

Wendy joined us. Mo-Mere took us out to the clearing in front

149

of the cabins. The sun beat down, not a cloud in the azure sky, and no wind. The ground had dried to where floods became a distant memory. We had to pump muddy water over the garden and fruit trees if we wanted anything to grow.

"There'll be times when you'll need to know how to fight to protect yourselves," Mo-Mere said, "and when and how to act the calm Professional. First, you must learn to endure uncomfortable conditions. For this exercise, you'll stand in the heat. The one who falls first will get extra chores. The one who remains standing will get a treat." She moved up onto the shaded porch and sat in a lounge chair.

"You can't be serious," I said.

"I can and I am. You're gutsy, but you need to control that before you get to the other side. Otherwise, you'll betray yourself. If weakness can doom you on this side, wait until you reach the Federation."

"Then why go?"

"Learn not to ask so many questions," Mo-Mere said. "Federation citizens are suspicious of anyone who threatens to take what little they have."

"And questions threaten them?"

"They do," she said. "By keeping citizens in fear, the Federation keeps them in line."

"You're not—"

"Pretend I'm the Department of Antiquities, and I've captured you. I'll question each of you to find out who helped you."

"I'll never tell," I said.

"Are you sure? You can't stand two minutes in the sun without spilling your guts. Now, how do you address a sister Professional?"

"As ma'am," I said.

"You address your mother, teacher and superiors that way, including Elites and Goddesses. How do you address an equal?"

"By first name if I know them."

"If you don't?" Mo-Mere asked.

"By their last?"

"Is that a question?"

"I'd address you as Ms. Seville."

"If I wasn't your teacher that would be correct."

While we stood in the sun, she grilled Wendy and me on Federation social mores. Sweat trickled down my neck. My legs

150

were rubbery. At least my bum leg felt stronger. Wendy began to sway. I'd imagined myself as the weak one. After all, I'd collapsed while hunting for family, yet she'd been near death as well.

Wiping my forehead, I shifted from one leg to the other. I felt feverish again. Wendy's eyes pleaded for help. Shaking, she snapped to attention, and then fell toward me. I grabbed hold of her and we both tumbled onto the ground. I cushioned her fall and banged my shoulder.

Mo-Mere ran to my side with a wet cloth. She dabbed my forehead and draped a cloth over Wendy's face. "That friendship could save your lives. Hold on to it. Nourish it. Learn how to depend on each other and how to watch each other's backs. Alone you can only become so strong. Together, you could achieve so much more."

Understanding and yet not, I stared up at Mo-Mere. No words formed in my parched throat. I hated her for putting us through this, even while, deep in my heart, I felt a strong bond to Wendy, stronger than toward anyone outside my family and Mo-Mere. Concern for Wendy had been there when I let her follow us on the trail. I leaned over and held her hand. "Will she be okay?"

Mo-Mere nodded. "I won't apologize for making you strong to survive. You two need to work together. Help each other become stronger than either of you believes possible."

She handed each of us half of an orange. The juice tasted sweeter than usual, as if it were a special medicinal fruit. Yet it had to be one I'd picked that morning. I savored the last of the juice and licked my fingers until the taste vanished.

No sooner had I finished the orange than Mo-Mere had us watch while she demonstrated martial arts. "Something I picked up in my youth," she said.

I'd had to fight scrappy scavengers who grabbed my salvage goods, on the rare occasions when I didn't simply dump my treasure and skedaddle before they brought friends. When Mo-Mere made me face Wendy, my friend stood like a cornered rat in a trap.

"This is important," Mo-Mere said. "On the other side of the Wall, you won't have water on your side. If you have to fight, you need to be prepared."

"Professionals fight?" I asked.

"No, but don't let yourself feel intimidated. You can't walk in fear among Working Stiffs or they'll recognize you don't belong. Then they'll drag you down. Learning to defend yourself builds confidence."

Mo-Mere taught us to punch instead of slap and to find pressure points. "If you have to fight, finish it quickly to conserve your strength. Never fight if you can avoid it. But don't back down from a fight you can't avoid."

She was teaching us to be stronger in the swamps as much as for the Federation. Every day, we watched the channels around the island for boats. Patrols came through mornings and evenings.

"Don't let their regularity lull you into complacency," Mo-Mere would say.

Every day we drilled on the best ways to hide from patrols, bounty hunters, scavengers, and others who might wish us harm. We went to the narrow passage behind the cooking fireplace, or hit the water and swam away from the island, if alligators weren't waiting.

I grew weary of living in fear. This wasn't worth surviving for. There had to be more.

* * *

Over the next week, we lived on a diet of fish, garden vegetables, and Mo-Mere's teaching. She taught us to fight and to think. She provided us with a wealth of information on life in the Federation from her years on the other side of the Wall. Yet she wouldn't share what got her cast out as a Marginal.

Whenever we complained that she expected too much, her reply was the same. "I want to give you girls what I can no longer hope for, a better life." Her legacy.

At times I wondered if she kept us to fish and garden to make her life easier. What disturbed me most was that Mom knew of this island and didn't come for me. That reinforced the image of her working for Coarse-face.

On our second Sunday, Mo-Mere took Wendy and me down to the dock. "I need to barter for seeds, clothes, and chickens." She put a brown package into her motorboat.

"Can we come with you?" I asked, thinking of how Mom used to leave Colleen and me on Sundays.

"Too dangerous. Patrols and bounty hunters are still collecting girls. You have safe places here. Out there you'll be exposed."

Alarmed, I grabbed Mo-Mere's hand. "But we could help." I

stared past her at waters breaking over nearby rocks. The channel called to me, begging me to resume salvage work.

"Not today. You have your routine. Make sure to do your daily reading and hide the books when not using them."

"Yes, Mo-Mere."

She threw the mooring ropes into her boat and climbed in. "I should be back by mid-afternoon. If not, don't come looking for me. At the first sign of trouble, you know how to hide. Do not, under any circumstances, leave this island. Is that understood?"

Mo-Mere motored away as gray clouds blew in. It could be a false alarm or the beginnings of a bigger storm. I prayed that it wasn't the latter. Mo-Mere's leaving felt like Mom's. Wendy slipped her hand around my arm as if to say she'd watch out for me. We stood in the cove until Mo-Mere's boat disappeared behind a neighboring island.

"It'll be fine," Wendy said. "As long as we're together."

I nodded, but it didn't quell my squirming gut.

At least with Mo-Mere gone, we wouldn't have to work in the blazing sun or practice martial arts. Wendy put up a good show for Mo-Mere but her thin arms didn't build muscle. I even had to do part of her garden work. I didn't complain. She didn't whine over working all the time and she didn't quit on me. I knew she worked as hard as she could so I'd like her better and want to be her friend. It reminded me of my bond with Colleen, a memory that left a gaping hole inside.

Not seeing any boats in the channel, I led Wendy to the cabin. We ate dried carp, checked the garden, and caught catfish for dinner. While she watched both fishing lines, I chiseled the insides of another log, turning it into a boat.

"You want to read?" Wendy asked. She looked forward to reading with me so she could ask all sorts of questions about what she didn't understand. I got the impression she pushed to read fast to keep up and wasn't absorbing the words or their meaning. I was too restless to read.

Wendy hooked a worm. "I wish we could live this way all the time and not worry about the Federation." She cast her line.

"You mean never grow up." I thought of Peter Pan. No. I felt like Tom Sawyer, and could relate to *Life on the Mississippi* and other works of Mark Twain.

She shrugged. "I don't know. I like it with you and Mo-Mere, especially you." She turned away, though not before I caught her blush.

"I like it, too," I said. "But what about when the next big storm …" I couldn't finish the thought.

"Thanks again for not leaving me with that horrid bounty woman."

I caught a catfish, and with it, an idea. "You want to help me salvage? We might find something to trade for a new pair of boots." I pointed to where her toes poked through.

"Mo-Mere said not to leave the island."

"We're almost adults," I said. "Old enough to make our own decisions. Besides, this could be fun." I pulled in my line and gathered the fish we'd caught.

"Regina, please. Don't."

"Come on." I pulled in her line.

"Mo-Mere said no salvage."

"I'm going. You can stay if you want." I ran into the cabin, thankful my limp was fading.

In my room I found my dive goggles and breathing bladder.

Wendy joined me. "Mo-Mere said to stick together."

"Then come with me." I headed toward the dock.

Wendy pulled on my arm. "I don't like diving."

"That's where the best salvage is."

"I can't swim well."

"You've got to be kidding. I'm sorry. That sounded mean. You don't have to dive." I pulled her toward Mo-Mere's skiff.

"I almost drowned during the storm. I …"

I squeezed her hand. "It's okay. You can help by remembering our way back. The storm changed the area, making these channels tricky."

She smiled. "I can do that."

From the ledge above the skiff, I checked up and down the channel. Not seeing any other boats, I climbed in.

"Can't I convince you to stay?" Wendy asked.

I held out my hand. "Come on. You need new boots. We can't expect Mo-Mere to do all the work."

With her on board, I pushed away from shore. The skiff's boxy shape and bigger size made it harder to row than my log-boat, though we'd have room if we found anything. We floated out onto the main channel, where there was less land than before the storm, and headed southeast toward a tree-marker that reminded me of school.

Instead of going directly, I zigzagged from island to island, sticking as close to shore as possible without floating within reach of anyone hiding in the cattails. A few salvage boats were out reclaiming anything that survived the storm. I didn't see a single gator. How could our entire ecology have changed overnight?

Dark clouds blew in. We approached a marker I recognized as a pendant for our school. I rowed close to the shore of a nearby island. A sky-skimmer drone flew low over the area. I pulled a green canvas wrap over us and hunkered down until the drone's hum faded away.

"We should go," Wendy said.

I wasn't about to lose a salvage opportunity.

* * *

Across the channel, a ridge some six feet above the old shore had become the school's new shoreline. Gone were the roofs and walls of the schoolhouses. A bigger house atop the rocky hill had turned into kindling.

The island stood high enough above water that someone could have made it habitable, but scavengers had other plans. One of the water purification tanks was gone. The other lay on its side, dangling from pipes. A woman stood next to the tank, working on it. With no water purifiers, no one could stay on the island for long. It surprised me that no one claimed this island. I wanted to tell Mo-Mere, but our new island was better protected.

Other scavengers buzzed the shoreline like mosquitoes. I didn't recognize any of them from school or my salvage trips. Most were Mom's age. A skiff pulled up to the shore, and a woman lugged logs and branches into her boat. They would do as fresh firewood.

"There's nothing left of our school," Wendy said.

"I want a closer look."

I rowed around the island. The eastern shoreline was the worst, having caught the brunt of the storm surge. The entire island suffered from uprooted and drowned trees, as well as tangles of boards and logs from the cabins.

I rowed into an empty cove to hide the skiff. "I'll take a quick look. Stay in the boat, stay hidden, and don't talk to anyone."

"What if patrols come?"

I closed my eyes. *Always patrols.* "Tell them you're alone and wanted to see if your school might reopen. Since it won't, you need to go home."

"Please don't go." She clutched my hand.

I pulled away, put on my diving goggles, and filled my breathing bladder.

"Regina, please."

"I won't be long. You'll be fine. Remember what Mo-Mere taught us."

I handed her the oars and waited until she sat in my seat. Seeing no gators, I dived. Underwater was clear. Riverbed silt from the storm had settled. I swam through submerged bushes and trees to the remnant of the wharf where school cabins had been. The ring of schoolhouses was gone except for submerged foundations that stubbornly remained. I moved into the trees, surfaced, and took a deep breath.

While I filled the breathing bladder, I looked around. The darkly tanned woman who had filled her skiff with firewood rowed away. Another moved in to take her place. They would strip the island of trees and vegetation for firewood. That would doom this island.

I swam to the foundation of Mo-Mere's schoolroom and apartment. The sea had scraped everything from above the foundation, including her wood-burning stove. The floor platform itself drooped between stubby stilts yet remained mostly intact. The trap door was still beneath where her stove had been. I opened it and held my breath as I pulled up a plastic-wrapped package and laid it on the platform.

The first time I'd salvaged books from sunken homes in Richmond, I'd been amazed that their owners took such care to protect their books in plastic yet hadn't carried them to drier ground. Of course, if they had, the Department of Antiquities would have destroyed what the water hadn't. I was thankful for these owners' foresight. It meant I could read *Tom Sawyer*, *Kidnapped*, and other books that provided helpful tips on living in the swamps as well as views of other lives.

Beneath the battered floor, I pulled up a second bundle, and a third. I took a breath and reached far under the platform. Nothing else. That was good. Books were heavy, and it took all my strength to drag them with me behind the cover of submerged trees and scramble to the surface for air. After I pushed the packages up on the rocky shore, I refilled the breathing bladders. I attached my full bladder to my belt and took the rope from my waist to tie the bundles together.

By the time I'd gathered the packages and moved to the tree line, the second firewood collector finished and headed out. A sea-skimming patrol boat approached with two gray-uniformed Antiquities agents. I breathed easy. Neither was Coarse-face. The scavenger dropped her oars and threw up her hands.

Pulling the books with me, I swam underwater toward Wendy and surfaced behind bushes. She had her hands in the air. A second sea-skimmer pulled up next to her. Standing by the rail was Coarse-face. I strained to see who was with her. They all wore gray uniforms. None had Mom's Chinese features.

I tied Mo-Mere's packages to my waist and swam underwater to the boats so I could hear.

"You shouldn't be in these waters," Coarse-face said.

"I was hoping our school might reopen," Wendy said.

"It won't."

"I thought these people had come to rebuild."

"This is off limits," Coarse-face said. "Aren't you the girl with Marisa Seville?"

Damn. I inhaled from the breathing bladder, but instead of breathing out bubbles that might give up my location, I breathed into the bladder, diluting my oxygen. I looked for anything on the bottom of the skiff to hang on to. Toward the bow was a metal loop intended for an anchor, except this skiff didn't have one.

"I'm not doing salvage or anything illegal," Wendy said. "I was checking my school."

"Wouldn't your teacher know the school isn't reopening?"

I untied the rope from my waist and struggled to keep from sinking. I swam up and held onto the loop while I pulled the rope through the hole and tied a knot, anchoring the books to the boat.

"Who is with you?" Coarse-face asked.

"Just me. I was waiting for those scavengers to leave so I could go home."

I took a breath from my bladder. Already the oxygen content was dropping. If I didn't surface soon, I might pass out.

"Have you seen this girl? I believe she was a classmate of yours."

There was a long pause. My lungs ached.

"She looks like any ol' Marginal girl in green canvas," Wendy said. "She wasn't in my class."

"You'd best get rowing. Tell your teacher I'll stop by."

"Yes, ma'am," Wendy said.

The skiff moved. While Wendy was not a strong rower, I struggled to hold on to one of the loops. Water swirled beneath the sea-skimmer as it lifted and moved away. When I could no longer hold my breath, I knocked on the bottom of the metal boat. The skiff stopped. I swam to the bow and gasped for air. The patrol boat had approached another skiff near the island's sunken harbor.

"Regina?" I heard sobbing in Wendy's voice.

"Stay in your seat and row." I filled the bladder and kept an eye on the patrol boat. "You did great. Let's go home."

Wendy put her back into rowing. She rowed stronger than I'd imagined she could. When the boats were out of sight, I climbed into the skiff and took over the oars.

"Don't ever do that again," she said, hugging me awkwardly. "That awful patrol agent showed me your picture. She's the one who came to our cabin. She said she'll come back."

I released her grip and rowed. "Keep your eyes out for boats and landmarks."

At times like this, Wendy reminded me of Colleen. I realized how much caring for my sister had transferred to Wendy. I smiled. "I'm proud of you."

But why was Coarse-face so focused on me?

TWENTY-FOUR

When we reached the last channel crossing before home, we spotted a big boat docked behind a nearby island. I eased closer to shore for a better look. The boat didn't have the gray Antiquities emblem or the shape of most bounty boats, yet chained to the rails were several terrified girls. I recognized one from Colleen's class.

Gunshots rang out, a rarity in the swamps. I cringed. Wendy cowered lower in the skiff. The boat had to belong to froggies, though it was bigger and boxier like a barge, and open in the middle where the helm should have been. A large crane rose up from the stern. Its arm dropped over the side. Then it lifted something: an alligator, a big one.

The animal twisted, trying to break free. Four bounty women hauled the gator into the middle of the boat. Another shot rang out and the gator stopped moving. The crane dropped the reptile into the center of the boat and came to rest. The boat motored away before I could figure out how to help those girls. And who was I kidding, going up against bounty hunters?

When the boat was gone, we crossed the channel to the south side of Mo-Mere's island and took the long way around to the cove. This shooting and crane boat could explain the absence of alligators, but why? Gators were as much a part of our lives as the water itself, and a threat genetically engineered by the Federation.

Then it hit me. Without gators, we would lose our source of skins, and food for those who had a taste for their meat. Things had to be pretty desperate for the Federation to sanction killing them off. I'd never seen bounty hunters go after gators before.

When we reached the cove, Mo-Mere was waiting. She helped me tie the skiff to the trunk of a tree, took a large, brown-wrapped package from her motorboat, and handed it to Wendy. Then she studied the bandage on Wendy's arm.

"I removed the protective foil from the chip as you showed me," Wendy said.

"Good girl. Only shield the tracking chip when you're on this island. Take this package into the house, set it on the table, and prepare dinner."

While Wendy headed up the path, I dove under the skiff and untied the rope holding the books. I pulled them to shore and handed them up to Mo-Mere with the greatest sense of pride. I'd salvaged her babies.

She dropped the packages into the skiff and helped me out of the water. "I told you not to leave this island."

"You said you'd saved all your books."

"I said that so you wouldn't salvage them yourself. Do you realize what you've done?"

"Those books are priceless," I said.

"Not as priceless as your life. Did you run into patrols?"

I nodded.

"Now they can identify you and connect you to Wendy."

"I was in the water." I hung my head.

"They saw Wendy and the skiff."

"I'm sorry, Mo-Mere. I thought—"

"I know what you thought. I told you not to leave so the patrols wouldn't catch *you*."

"Wendy needs new boots. We need something to barter. The storm destroyed the school. There were scavengers, so I checked your priceless books."

"I know, child, but everything I do is for a reason."

I looked up. "I hate being stuck on this island. I feel useless. There's nothing more useless than a Marginal with nothing to offer."

"You have much more to offer than your salvage skills."

"What are you protecting me from?" I asked. "Why me?"

"You have the potential to go farther than anyone who has come from these swamps."

"Farther than Inspector Demarco?"

"Much farther," Mo-Mere said.

"But—"

"Enough."

"You bartered today." I pointed to packages in the motorboat. "I could help find salvage."

"If you can't follow directions, I can't help you. You're free to leave. Take the skiff. If you do, don't return."

"Mo-Mere!"

She lifted her packages and headed up the path. "If you bring those books, you'd best find a good hiding place. I'm not ready to share them with Wendy. That's one reason I left them. I had them protected for the time being."

"Until someone salvaged the foundation for lumber."

"The books were a darn sight safer where they were. Never put all your treasure in one place if that place is vulnerable."

I shrugged. "Yes, Mo-Mere. Any word on my mom or Colleen?"

She stopped to face me. "No, dear. If they've taken Colleen across the Wall, we'll never hear. As for your mother, she'll contact us when she can."

That made her absence more damning.

* * *

During the next week, Mo-Mere drilled Wendy and me on hiding places. She liked the slot behind the fireplace, though only if there was a fire to heat it to body temperature; otherwise, we risked Antiquities infrared sensors spotting us. Clefts in the rocky ridge near the shore on two sides of the island were good hiding places if the patrols didn't use infrared. Finally, we had diving equipment to allow us to slip into the water and swim away. That didn't help if several patrol boats surrounded the island.

"You're running us ragged," I said to Mo-Mere the next Saturday in the middle of martial arts training. "I'm not doing this anymore. After all, what's the point if I can't salvage and patrols can grab us any day?" I moved out of the sunlight and collapsed into a wooden chair on the narrow porch.

She sent Wendy to her room, took my hand, and pulled me toward the tree line that formed a perimeter around the clearing. She lowered her voice. "I've asked around. No one knows why Antiquities is so interested, but their focus is clearly on you."

"I'm a Marginal nobody."

"The prophesy said a Marginal nobody would rise and change our world. I doubt that means our Antiquities Inspector."

"I figured you made all that up to get me to believe in myself," I said.

"The prophesy is real. Well, it didn't start with me. It dates back hundreds of years. Maybe it *is* only wishful thinking. That doesn't matter. What does is that I believe in you and your potential, with or without prophesy. The Department of Antiquities must think you're important, too."

"Is that why you keep me cooped up here?" I asked.

"I'm worried for you. You're too young for all this pressure, and yet I'm reminded of Alexander the Great."

"Are you my Aristotle?"

"No, dear," she said. "I would never presume to be in his league, but I am your teacher as Aristotle was to Alexander until he was sixteen."

"I know. Alexander became regent and heir apparent at age sixteen, helped defeat the Greeks at eighteen, and became king at twenty."

"Like him, you need to prepare for whatever gets thrown your way. That's why I push and train you. I don't know about prophesies, but it's disturbing how hard they're looking for you. You're smart and clever. You survived the storm when many didn't. Yet the Department has no way of knowing what I see. I've told no one, and your classmates haven't seen your potential."

"Then why are they after me?"

"If I had to guess, I'd say their fertility clinics are failing. With declining birth rates, they're raiding the swamps for our girls."

"They've taken so many already. Why me?"

"Excellent question. When the inspector implanted the tracking chip, she took blood, didn't she?"

I nodded.

"Then they've discovered something in your blood they believe can help them. It could make you popular, or confine you to a lab for the rest of your life."

"You mean indoors?"

"If I'm right, they plan to confine you and run all sorts of experiments. I don't want that life for you."

I stared out at water flowing past our island, eroding the land bit by bit. "I'm in a cage here. I want to find Colleen. I want to know why Mom abandoned us and why she was with that Antiquities inspector. I want to thank Fran for saving my life, and to find Jasmine and Aimee for Aunt Vera." I looked at Mo-Mere. "Is that asking too much?"

"It's understandable and commendable, but the moment you let your guard down, a gator gets you."

I laughed and then recoiled at the memory of a schoolmate who lost her legs. I hung my head in remembrance. "Bounty hunters are killing gators."

Mo-Mere looked stunned. "So that's why they've become scarce. Curious. Antiquities used them to reduce our population. Evidently, they've changed their minds."

"We have to do something."

"I know you want to break loose, but you need more training. I beg you not to put yourself in danger again."

My eyes burned. I couldn't be sure whether they wanted to burst a torrent of tears or fire sparks at Mo-Mere. I tensed up and clenched my fists.

She held my shoulders tight against her. "Patience, my dear. I'm doing my best. I can't watch over you all the time. If I had a daughter, I couldn't imagine a better one."

I pulled away to face her. "Why did Mom do this? Why? Why? WHY?"

"She's trying to barter for Colleen. I don't think she'd abandon you on purpose. She cares too much. She's told me often."

"Not good enough. What mom abandons her daughters during a storm?"

"Your mother has two daughters," Mo-Mere said. "We both know Colleen can't take care of herself."

"Neither can I. What good am I if I can't salvage and pay my own way?"

"You're only fifteen, dear."

"I've carried my weight since I can remember," I said. "Let me go with you tomorrow. I promise to stay hidden. I need to do more than train."

"Not tomorrow, dear. Give yourself another few weeks and we'll find a way for you to salvage. I promise."

I needed more than promises.

* * *

By the time Mo-Mere left in her motorboat that next Sunday, I'd finished my new log-boat with Wendy's help. It had a larger compartment in back for my crossbow, arrows, diving gear, and fishing line. I made it longer so two people could stretch their legs.

Wendy stood and admired it. "I can't believe you turned that log into this fine canoe. It's like the one you used to take to school."

"Grab your gear. Let's take it for a ride."

"We can't," she said. "Remember how angry Mo-Mere was last week."

"Then we'll have to make it back early so she doesn't find out."

Wendy held my arm. "I can't."

"Then stay. It's not right that we're stuck here while she goes out."

"What about patrols and bounty hunters?"

"Camouflage," I said. "I found a couple gray-brown wraps we could put around us. We'll look like debris floating along the channel."

She helped me carry the log-boat to the west shore and followed as I gathered my crossbow, arrows, diving gear, and food. All the while, she tried to talk me out of this insanity. "Where would we go? Not back to the school."

"Off limits, remember? Never let patrols tell you twice." I loaded my things in the slotted compartment and climbed into the back. "Come or stay."

Wendy sighed and climbed in. "I couldn't bear it if you didn't return. We have to stick together."

I had mixed feelings. I liked her company but didn't want to get her into trouble.

A patrol boat with gray markings puttered east along the north shore. Wendy and I headed southwest, across the channel to an island that seemed to grow farther away with each passing day. I imagined that as an optical illusion, though I'd lived in the swamps long enough to know the seas always won.

When we reached the other island, I pulled into the cover of sunken bushes and watched Mo-Mere's island. A bounty boat passed, heading east. A scavenger boat appeared, with a large open deck for loot. I hoped they didn't scavenge our island. Mo-Mere said if that happened we should let them take what they wanted. "Things aren't worth dying for," she'd said, but to me, home was worth fighting for.

The antenna of the patrol boat stuck out between the trees along the north shore of Mo-Mere's island. It sported the gray Antiquities emblem and the chief inspector insignia. "Lucky thing we're not there," I said.

Wendy shrugged. "What if they declare our island abandoned and we lose our home?"

"What if you'd been there and they took you? I'd have to fight them off. Then they'd have both of us."

"I couldn't bear that."

To avoid traffic on the northern channel, I headed south. I wasn't sure what we'd find, but it was great to be paddling again. Keeping to quieter channels, we made our way close enough to see the Wall looming gray in the noon sun. Gone were the water cannons and the throngs of women. This channel was narrower and farther south than I'd gotten before. Now that the Federation wasn't pushing excess water over the Wall, the land had dried out.

We pulled within sight of the grounds beneath the Wall. The fields looked empty. The stench of rotting flesh hung like a low fog.

"We should go," Wendy said.

But I needed to see. I pulled the boat amid cattails and tied it to a bush that clung to shore. I crept through thick bushes toward a pebbled path and crouched down facing a field that stretched to the Wall. Gone were the throngs of women waiting for help that wouldn't come. In their place lay a field of oblong mounds. Halfway to the Wall, bodies lay in the field. Small bands of bounty hunters dug shallow graves. They didn't look happy with their new work.

Well, when you work with the devil, you get the devil's work.

Wendy tugged my arm to leave. I couldn't. This could have been us. This could have been Aunt Vera if a bounty hunter hadn't killed her. I hoped Fran hadn't returned here to die.

Groups of bounty hunters worked their way, row by row, across the field. One group of three approached the woods. Two women dug and yelled at a girl Colleen's age to work harder. The thin, fair-haired girl didn't bear any resemblance to either woman, so she was likely one of their catches. Were they working her before they turned her over to Antiquities patrols? That gave me an idea.

We returned to the log-boat, where I grabbed my crossbow and arrows. "Stay and watch the boat," I told Wendy.

"Please, don't do this."

"Stay out of sight."

I gave her a hug, then crossed the path and moved through the woods near to where the three were digging. With an arrow notched, I aimed my crossbow in the direction of the bounty hunters. Wendy bumped into me, holding a stick and a rock. I was about to tell her to return to the boat when the girl in the field broke away, telling the women she had to go potty.

"Don't go far," one of the women yelled, "and don't make me come after you."

The girl found a spot not far from me and squatted. I pointed for Wendy to stay and approached the girl as if I was stalking a squirrel. By the time she'd finished, I stood behind her.

I pointed my crossbow at her head. "Don't make a sound and I won't hurt you. Are they family?"

The girl shook her head. Mud covered her light hair to where it was hard to tell its natural color. Mud also caked her face. "They'll come for me if I don't go."

"A few questions, then you can leave," I said. "Have you met other girls? Colleen Shen, Jasmine Morton, Aimee Morton?"

She shook her head. "I see lots of girls, but I don't get names. They sold most to Antiquities agents. They kept me to work."

"Come with us."

"I have to go, please. They'll kill my sister."

"Maybe we could help her escape," I said.

"Let me go."

"Ask your bounty hunters if they have information on Colleen Shen, or Jasmine or Aimee Morton. If they do, tell them I'll barter for them in an hour by that tree." I pointed farther into the woods. "Go."

As soon as she faced the field and her bounty hunters, I hurried back to Wendy.

"You know she'll turn you in," she said.

I hurried to a ledge where I could watch anyone approaching the tree.

TWENTY-FIVE

I sat on the ledge with my crossbow at the ready. The muddy girl talked to the two women. Wendy sat next to me, nervous, yet unwilling to leave my side.

"You should wait by the boat," I said.

"You're my best friend in the entire world."

"I'm your only friend."

Her shoulders sagged. "I love you, Regina. You're brave and smart and strong. I don't have much to offer."

"Don't say that." I lifted her chin. "I love you as a friend, my only friend. I don't want you to get hurt because of me."

"I'm not like you. I can't make it on my own. I want to be the best partner so you'll want me."

"I do want you, as my friend, my best friend." I squeezed her hand and returned my attention to the muddy girl.

One of the women smacked the girl's face. Then both women dropped their shovels and dragged the girl across the field to a group of two women and two girls my age. They talked, and then the three left to talk to a third group closer to the Wall.

"Do you think they'll know where your sister is?" Wendy asked.

"I hope so." Part of me, deep in my heart, believed that if I found Colleen, Mom would come for me. Finding my sister would make me worthy.

The two women and the girl headed toward their dig site, passed it, and went to the tree I'd indicated. One woman held the girl's hand, too tight judging by how the girl winced.

The other woman looked around. "You can come out. I've asked around. I have something you want."

Wendy held tight to my hand. I pulled away and moved down from the ledge.

"We have your sister and your sister's friends," the woman said.

My breath caught. My eyes watered. I stumbled. Hands caught me. An arm wrapped around my waist and a hand covered my mouth. I expected Wendy to cry out. I struggled to get her to let go, but the grip was too strong. Someone pulled me back to the ledge.

"Look at the field." It was a familiar gravelly voice.

Fran!

"Come on, little girl," the woman said. "It's safe. Let us take you to family."

I couldn't see the other two groups of bounty hunters anywhere in the field. Then I spotted someone uphill to my left.

Fran helped me up onto the ledge. "Are you stupid? It's a trap."

Wendy grabbed hold of my arm and squeezed.

"I have to find Colleen," I said.

"They can't help you, and they wouldn't anyhow," Fran said. "Let's go." She led the way uphill.

This felt like my last chance to find Colleen, but Fran was right. Bounties wouldn't help a Marginal like me. With barely a limp, Fran led the way beyond the ledge and down toward the channel. After we crossed the pebbled path, I spotted a third group of bounty hunters moving up that way. Three women and a weary girl left the path and climbed up behind the ledge.

We reached my boat among tall cattails. My older log-boat floated nearby. We ducked behind bushes and waited until we couldn't see the bounty hunters through the woods. Then Fran climbed into my old boat.

"How did you find us?" I asked.

"No one else takes this care making a log-boat. I followed you upstream after you escaped that patrol boat. They've dropped your name and image up and down the coast. You've become famous just by staying hidden."

I shrugged. "I need to find my family."

"Let's move before they hunt the shoreline."

Fran grabbed Wendy's left arm and lifted her canvas sleeve. "You're still wearing your implant?" She ripped Wendy's bandage off and stared at her arm. The wound had healed weeks ago after Mo-Mere removed the chip.

"I only wear it when I'm away from the island. Mo-Mere said."

"Patrols can track us. Is that what you want?"

Wendy shook her head.

Fran grabbed a stick to wedge the chip into. I stopped her. "Wendy can shield her chip."

"I don't like this."

"Sometimes it's helpful."

Fran handed me the chip. I took the aluminum shield from Wendy and covered the tracking device before I put it inside the bandage and taped it to her arm.

Keeping close to shore, Wendy and I followed Fran down the channel, away from the Wall. We stopped at times while Fran checked for traffic, and then we moved beyond a jetty devoid of vegetative cover and sneaked among the rush and cattails farther down.

We stopped at a cross-channel crowded with patrol and bounty boats, and tucked ourselves into a quiet cove where alligators once ruled.

"Thanks," I said to Fran. "But this doesn't help me find—"

"You won't find Colleen or your friends," she whispered.

"How do you know?"

"Becoming a celebrity has advantages. Everyone in the Richmond Swamps knows your story."

"From you?" I asked.

"I might have embellished a bit. It all started with them showing your picture like you were some notorious criminal. The harder they look, the more people add to your tale."

"What does that tell us about Colleen?"

"Bounty hunters talk," Fran said, "and word has gotten around."

"Tell me."

"They sold your sister and friends to the Department of Antiquities, which transported them over the Wall."

"What'll happen to them? How do I find them?"

"You can't, not without letting them capture you. Even that won't help. The Federation separates friends and family so they pose less of a threat. What intrigued me was their interest in Colleen."

"Why?"

"Her blood," Fran said, "her DNA. Don't ask. I don't pretend to understand that bio-junk."

My chest tightened. All along I'd hoped beyond reason that I could find her. "I failed her."

"No." Fran kept her voice low. "You and Colleen must have something the Antiquities creeps want. Keeping you away from them is our little victory. Don't you see?"

"What are you talking about?"

"For the first time, Marginals have something to care about. You."

"I didn't ask for that," I said.

"Yet for weeks, patrols and bounty hunters have turned this place upside down and here you are, still free."

"Not for long if we can't cross this channel," I said.

* * *

In all her years on Antiquities patrols, Inspector Demarco couldn't recall so much chatter on all communications channels at once. The moment the first bounty hunter called in suspicions that they'd spotted Regina by the Wall looking for family, the inspector pulled every agent into sector six. The reward also brought every bounty hunter for fifty miles and dozens of bounty wannabes, scavengers, and desperate locals looking for favors.

Colleen Shen was in custody, providing all the samples they could draw from the twelve-year-old. The problem was that her samples were fragile, not as strong or viable as Regina's blood indicated. This baffled the governor's best scientists. Perhaps the Antarctic labs could help, but Demarco was not going to jump into that political firestorm. She hadn't sacrificed so much to commit suicide by angering the governor.

"We have reports of the girl up north," one agent called in.

"No, she moved south, into sector seven," another agent said.

Demarco didn't know what to make of this confusion. "How hard can it be to find one fifteen-year-old girl with no family or connections?"

"It's a swamp," someone said over the Mesh-link.

"Who was that so I can fire you?" Demarco said. No reply. "I'm doubling the reward for Regina Shen. I want her alive. She's worth nothing dead or dying."

Every time Demarco upped the reward, more people joined the hunt.

More calls poured in that Regina was somewhere else. Demarco had gotten reports from as far away as sunken NYC and Charleston, which had survived rising seas better than most places.

"The girl's here, in sector six," Demarco said. "It's what she knows, where she's most comfortable. She doesn't have wings. She isn't a fish. The only way she travels is on foot or by boat. If it moves, find it."

TWENTY-SIX

The afternoon wore on. The scorching sun bore down on us. The channels grew crowded with patrol boats, bounty boats, and scavengers offering their services to the Department of Antiquities. Sky-skimmer drones buzzed up and down the channel and the cross-channel. A patrol boat with its gray Antiquities pendant anchored across the channel intersection from us, where it could watch traffic in four directions. Coarse-face Demarco stood at the rail.

Despite the heat, Wendy slumped under the brown-gray wrap in the bow of my log-boat. "We should have stayed home."

Fran frowned.

"I can't undo the past," I said. "We need a way across this channel and farther west."

"They'll troll out there as well," Fran said.

"Then let's go overland to the next channel."

Fran shook her head. "They have motion sensors. I told you. These bitches want you. I've counted five patrol boats, seventeen bounties, and a dozen scavengers."

"Some passed more than once," I said, recalling the registration numbers of each boat. "There have been only three patrol boats and five bounties."

"I'm sure there are more on other channels, and they're trained to track movement. We're safer staying put."

"How do we leave before temperatures drop and they spot us on infrared?"

"How have you stayed free this long?" Fran whispered. "On second thought, it's best I don't know."

"If we have to wait, let's fish." I pulled out some line and dug in the soil nearby for a juicy worm. The wiggly critter looked good enough to eat, but I snagged it on my hook. Pushing aside nearby cattails, I dropped the line and pulled out my net.

Wendy did the same, though her hands shook while she hooked her worm.

"We need water," I said, helping her. "Otherwise, we can't survive this heat, and I won't drink channel water."

Fran tossed me a jug. "Make that last." She dropped a line and slid lower in her boat.

A big bounty boat chugged along the cross channel. I pulled my brown wrap over me and dropped as low as I could. The boat turned and hugged the shore just beyond the cattails. The boat was new, one whose registration numbers I hadn't seen before.

Wendy covered herself while Fran scooted her boat behind thicker bushes. The bounty boat moved up the channel, turned around, and anchored close to shore west of us. Now boats blocked us in both directions.

Through cattails, I spotted two girls chained to the port side of the bounty boat, facing the channel. A woman with a sun visor and weary expression stood at the bow rail. Another woman joined her, with a ruddy face I could never forget: Bounty-killer. I strained for a closer look.

Wendy pulled me down. "What are you doing? They'll see you."

I shook so hard it took a moment to realize my fishing line was tugging. "That's the woman who killed Aunt Vera."

"Are you sure?"

Fran paddled closer as I reeled in my line. "You know that froggie?"

"She took my sister and killed a woman who was helping us."

Fran's line caught. By the time I pulled mine in, Wendy was reeling in hers. I scooped my net and pulled up a smallmouth bass, with a small body, too. Fran caught another. When Wendy reeled her line in, I scooped the net and pulled up two clams. Clams could be good.

I tugged the barbed hook out of the clams. The hook still had the worm. It must have hit bottom and snagged the shells. Then I studied the clams' coloring, recalling dozens of images Mo-Mere had shown us. "Poisonous. They contain dinoflagellates such as saxitoxin."

"Dino…sax. You sure?" Fran asked. "I mean, they look good."

"So do poisonous mushrooms. This neurotoxin causes paralysis so you can't breathe."

Wendy's face held the look of defeat.

"It's okay," I said. "It happens." I dropped the clams.

Fran caught them. "No so fast. I have an idea." She put the clams in her boat and turned to Wendy. "Drop your line exactly as before."

"What are you thinking?" I whispered.

Fran pointed toward the bounty boat.

"You can't be serious."

"They killed your friend. They took your sister."

"With all these other boats?" I asked.

"I'm just saying. Let's have options."

I skinned my bass, cut it open with my knife to remove the bones, and handed half to Wendy.

She refused. "You take it."

"You need your strength."

She held out shaking hands to accept the bass and stuffed the little critter into her mouth. Then she rinsed her hands, checked her worm, and dropped the line.

I savored my fish, letting the oils work their way across my tongue before it slid down my throat. Peering through cattails at the bounty boat, I was tempted to notch an arrow and take aim at Bounty-killer. The only other person I'd shot was the froggie who was with her.

Fran cast her line near Wendy while I caught another bass. I offered half to Wendy. She handed it to Fran, who practically inhaled the flesh. Wendy was being generous. She needed us in order to survive.

I found another worm, cast my line, and watched the bounty boat. The sun descended toward the west. I imagined Chinese dragons dancing over the Great Barrier Wall as the sky turned crimson. We could be the Mongols who breached the Great Wall of China, not by climbing over, breaking through, or digging under. They bribed a guard. Was that how Mo-Mere planned to get me into a Federation university? My skin glistened with sweat, but soon it would cool off and we would be more visible in infrared.

Something about the nearby bounty and Antiquities boats disturbed me. They were too close. Through cattails, I studied the two girls chained in the hot sun to the rail of the bounty boat. They could be twins. Nearby, the bounty hunters shifted positions.

Bounty-killer wore a muddy, short-sleeved top instead of the thin, black froggie outfit they used at night. She spent most of her time under cover of the helm, but stepped out to scan the channel. The woman with a weary, leathery face used binoculars to scan the shore on either side. Wearing a top similar to Bounty-killer's, Leather-face offered the girls water. I thought of other girls who'd died chained to their wreck.

A younger woman with translucent skin wore the same brown top. She stood next to Leather-face, holding a rifle. No, a tranquilizer gun, similar to what Coarse-face had used on me. I rubbed my arm. The lump and the wound were gone, but not the feeling of helplessness.

If Fran was right, and all this attention was on me, then my trip to the Wall had alerted them. It had been foolish. Yet staying on Mo-Mere's island, waiting without word, wasn't acceptable. I had to do something.

By the time the sun set over the trees to our west, I'd caught one more catfish. After skinning, I ate half and forced Wendy to eat the rest. Between them, she and Fran had pulled up two more clams, which I confirmed as the same poisonous species.

Fran climbed into the water and dove down. I couldn't imagine what we could do with four clams or even ten times that. What was she thinking? Throw them at the bounty hunters? We were wasting time.

In twilight, the patrol boat floated with full view of the channel intersection. Temperatures were dropping. Soon we would light up their infrared.

TWENTY-SEVEN

Fran surfaced, dropped a handful of clams into her boat, and prepared to dive again.

"Fran," I whispered. "We have to go before they see us on infrared."

She looked at the darkening sky and climbed into her log-boat. "Then it's time."

"We could swim under water," I said, holding up my breathing gear.

"I don't have gear, and unless you have tanks, we won't get far before we have to surface."

"Then what?"

Fran pointed to the bounty boat and handed me the last of the clams. "Are you certain they're poisonous?"

In dim light from the bounty boat I studied the shell color and nodded.

"Then follow my lead. Let's grab ourselves a bounty boat." Fran gathered the clams in a small canvas bag and climbed ashore.

I followed. "This is crazy. We can't sneak on board and overpower them."

"You're not seeing it," Fran said. "I'll draw the women to the bow. Then you and Wendy sneak onto the stern." She held up the gun she'd taken and checked the chamber. "Five bullets. We'll have to make it work."

"Gunshots will bring patrols." I gathered my crossbow and arrows.

Fran crouched low and crawled along the bushes between the pebbled path and the channel. Wendy shook her head but followed. When we were even with the bounty boat, we stopped and looked up from behind cattails. The boat looked to be fifty feet long and bulky enough to carry captured cargo.

I took Wendy farther along through the bushes until we were below the stern. Fran stepped out onto a narrow path, making far too much noise. She cursed and bent over.

When she stood up, a voice called from the boat. "Halt there. Show yourself."

Bounty-killer stood at the rail, her tranquilizer rifle aimed at Fran. A floodlight lit the area. I hoped this had been Fran's plan. I notched an arrow and aimed at the killer, but she was too far away for me to be sure of a hit. Besides, firing on her would draw gunfire from the others.

With a tranquilizer rifle over her shoulder, Leather-face dropped a ladder over the side and climbed down, along with the pale-skinned woman.

The younger woman approached Fran. "What are you doing?"

"Collecting clams." She dropped a couple and bent over to pick them up.

I was close enough to shoot Leather-face, but I hesitated. Bounty-killer watched from above, and the younger woman had a rifle. If I ran, the killer on the boat could hit me, and if she didn't, she could alert everyone to come after me.

Fran cradled the clams in her arms. "Please don't take these. They're all I have to barter."

"That's far too much for one girl," the younger woman said. "Give them here." She held out her hand.

"Please, ma'am. I'll barter some for my life." She held out a few clams.

Leather-face grabbed Fran's arm. I knew Fran didn't like being touched, yet she restrained herself, even hanging her head.

"I have a better idea," Leather-face said. "Why don't you come prepare them for us?"

"My mom needs me to bring her food," Fran said.

Leather-face grabbed the canvas bag. A few clams hit the pebbled path as she handed the bag to the younger woman. "I haven't had good clams in ages." She shoved Fran toward the boat.

The younger woman picked up fallen clams. Leather-face

pushed Fran to climb the ladder. Bounty-killer trained her rifle at Fran and scanned the clearing. Leather-face climbed next, followed by the younger woman with the bag of clams. Bounty-killer moved aside as Fran pulled herself into the boat. The other women disappeared below deck with Fran. Bounty-killer remained next to the ladder, shining her light along the path. Draped in our brown wraps despite the heat, Wendy and I hung low to the ground as the floodlight panned over us.

* * *

Bounty-killer turned off the floodlight and returned to the helm. I moved closer to the boat. I didn't like the ladder and couldn't see over the side, so I couldn't tell whether anyone else was waiting.

"Don't do this," Wendy whispered. "I know you care about Fran, but it's too dangerous."

"So is waiting. Temperatures are dropping. Soon, there won't be anywhere to hide. Stay here and keep an eye on me. I'll let you know when to come and whether to use the ladder or climb the back."

I had to pry loose of her grip. "I shouldn't have gotten you mixed up in this," I said, "but I need you."

Wendy forced a smile. It didn't soften her worried eyes.

A bounty boat passed up the channel, shining bright lights along the shore. I ducked behind cattails until it was gone, and then I jogged to the stern. An aluminum ladder ran from the upper railing down to a platform at the back for diving or fishing.

I climbed to the top and peeked over the side. It was dark except for lights in the canopied helm and below deck. I climbed over and decided this ladder was less visible. I motioned for Wendy. Soon, her head poked over the top.

"Anything goes bad, you jump and go," I whispered as I helped her over the side.

Wendy squeezed my hand but didn't cling.

I led the way along the starboard side until we saw the chained girls at the port railing. One of the girls looked my way. Her eyes narrowed. I put my finger to my lips and she nodded.

When another boat motored down the channel, with lights blazing, I hit the deck, pulling Wendy with me. I notched an arrow and waited until the boat passed.

Lights brightened the bow. Leather-face returned with a pan.

"You want one?" She held the pan under the nose of one of the girls.

The girl glanced my way. I shook my head.

"I'm allergic to clams," the girl said. She gripped her sister's hand.

"So am I," the twin said.

"Too bad," Leather-face said. "Tastiest clams I've had." She tossed clam meat into her mouth and offered the tray to Bounty-killer.

The younger bounty hunter pushed Fran up on deck and chained her to the railing next to the two girls. That wasn't good. I had no idea how to unlock or remove the chains from the railing. But the tubular aluminum screwed into the side of the boat. That gave me an idea.

I pointed to my eyes and motioned for Wendy to keep watch while I loosened the railing. Then I crossed to the port side, down from the girls, and removed my knife and its screwdriver accessory.

Fran glanced my way and turned to the bounty hunters. "How can you do this to your own people?"

"Girl's got to make a living," the younger woman said with a mouthful of clam. "No one delivers like we do, so don't get ideas about escaping."

I felt Wendy at my back instead of across the boat where I'd left her. I was careful not to drop screws on the deck or let them splash into the water. One of the twins watched. They were thin, Colleen's age or younger.

"Don't you care about all the lives you ruin?" Fran asked.

"Ruined!" Leather-face said. "Look around. This isn't a life. It's a death sentence. We're doing these girls a favor by getting them into the Federation."

"As slaves?"

"At least they'll eat on a regular basis." Leather-face popped another clam into her mouth. "Though they don't get clams like this in the Federation."

"We collected five girls during the storm in spite of losing our ship," the younger woman said. Her voice sounded hoarse. She drank from a mug.

Being with these froggies brought back the horror of Aunt Vera's death and Colleen's capture. If I'd rescued her, I could have spared her from being sent away, but then she'd have been stuck with my fate.

While Fran and the froggies talked, I wondered whether I was wrong about the clams. Were we doing all this for nothing? I removed another screw and dropped it into my pocket along with a half-dozen others.

TWENTY-EIGHT

I nudged Wendy down behind the helm's back wall and kept working.

"We got a good price for one," Leather-face said. "You sure you haven't seen her sister?" She held out a Mesh-reader. "She's worth a fortune, like citizenship and a big house in the Federation."

Fran stared at the deck. "I take care of my mom."

"We could use a strong one like you." Leather-face squeezed Fran's biceps and checked her teeth.

"We're not taking more crew," Bounty-killer said. "Don't need to with those two." She pointed to the sisters chained to the railing.

"Where did they take the girls you turned over?" Fran asked.

"You mean: where will they take you?" Leather-face asked. "Strong ones go to the mines or farm work. Those sweet things," she pointed to the twins, "will get household work or child care for some Elite family."

"What about special ones like the girl you're looking for?"

"Enough questions," Bounty-killer said. "Don't know and don't care."

I put another screw into my pocket and held the railing to keep it from rattling as I worked. It was hard to concentrate, knowing these slavers took Colleen and sent her off to slave labor, or worse, a lab. And they didn't care.

Wendy poked my arm and pointed to the younger woman. She sat on a bench across from Fran, holding her stomach. Her head tilted back as she gasped for air. I unfastened another screw. It dropped to the deck with a ping. The aluminum pipe of the railing came loose within the rail mounts. I pulled, but it jammed.

Leather-face dropped to her knees, gasping for air. She let out a ghastly groan and clutched her throat. She dug her fingers into her neck and collapsed onto the deck. I checked my notched arrow and the aluminum rail that wouldn't pull free.

"What the ..." Bounty-killer spat out clam meat and grabbed the tray.

I pulled as hard as I could on the aluminum tube. It slid down about a foot before it caught on the chains holding Fran.

Bounty-killer shoved the pan of clam meat into Fran's face. "What the hell is this? What have you done?"

Fran slid her chains free from the rail. I aimed my crossbow at Bounty-killer's head and braced my body against the side of the boat to steady myself. Fran dropped her arms, grabbed her knife, and swung the blade across Bounty-killer's neck. It happened so fast, I didn't have time to shoot. Bounty-killer slumped to the deck. I hurried to Fran's side.

Bounty-killer clutched her throat and grabbed at her belt for her pistol. Fran got to it first. "This is for betraying your own people." Fran kicked the gun away and pulled the woman's head back, widening the cut. I stood beside Bounty-killer as blood spurted into the helm. Her eyes looked terrified, then bewildered as they focused on me, the reason she was here. My face would be the last image she would see. She let out a grisly groan, gurgling blood as Aunt Vera had.

Fran turned to me. "Take off their uniforms."

I looked at Wendy. "Help the girls." I knelt next to the younger froggie. Her pale face turned blue. Her eyes turned my way, pleading. They registered recognition. Guilt swept over me despite what she'd have done to us. I brushed that aside.

While she struggled to breathe, I pulled off her boots, trousers, and top. She didn't look so threatening in torn underwear. Her eyes fixed on me, but she no longer had a pulse. I went to Leather-face and removed the clothes from her lifeless body.

Fran turned off the bow lights, leaving only helm lights to illuminate the deck. She unlocked the chains from her wrists and handed the keys to Wendy. Then she dug out tracking chips from Leather-face and the other women.

"What's going on?" I asked.

"Help me dump these two over the side."

I didn't like this. I'd messed up by approaching bounty hunters by the Wall. I wanted to get home to Mo-Mere, who knew how to fix things. But we were still trapped. While Wendy sat with the twins, I lifted Leather-face's legs and dragged her to the starboard side.

Fran lifted the bounty-hunter's upper body over the railing and let it dangle over the narrow stretch of water between the boat and shore. As the body slid over the side, Fran grabbed hold of the legs. Together we eased the body toward the water. It landed with more of a plop than a splash.

We both knelt next to the rail and looked around to see if anyone had noticed. I wiped sweat from my face and helped Fran with the younger bounty hunter. We carried her to the stern so she didn't land on her friend, and lifted her over the side. Then Fran wrapped brown cloth around Bounty-killer's blood-soaked neck as a scarf and dragged her into the helm, propping the woman by the controls.

Wendy and I mopped up blood from the deck with some bounty flags and dumped the bloody rags on top of the bodies. Then Wendy took me to the girls.

"Kara and Carmen Ross," Wendy said. "They're twins."

Up close, they looked to be Colleen's age.

"Thank you so much," Kara said in a soft, polite voice, "but when they come back."

"You won't see them again," I said. "Do you have family?"

Both girls shook their heads, like watching a mirror image.

"Do you have a home to go to?"

Same reaction.

"Then you have a choice," I said. "We can set you on shore and you can pretend none of this happened."

"Can we go with you?" Kara asked. "You're the one they're after, aren't you?"

"Why would you say that?"

"They show your picture to everyone. They took your sister and sold her to the Antiquities woman with the pebbly face." *Coarse-face.*

"What about the two girls who were with my sister?"

Kara shrugged. "That pebbly-faced agent took all three, and two others. These froggies wanted us as slaves. The agent tested our blood and told the bounties keep us until she was ready to ship us over the wall." She rubbed her shoulder where Coarse-face had given her a tracking implant.

Carmen spoke up. "I wish we could be brave like you."

I didn't feel brave, just foolish. It made me wonder if that was all bravery was: doing what you had to after you'd made a dumb mistake.

"We need to put them ashore," Fran said.

I stood between Fran and the twins. "They're coming with us."

"They'll only complicate things, especially if we get caught."

"Then don't get caught."

Fran shook her head. "Whatever. Can you haul your boats up so we can get going?"

I suspected Fran wanted us off so she could leave without us. Nevertheless, I was not going to lose both log-boats.

* * *

I led Wendy and the girls down the starboard ladder and through the bushes in the dark. We stopped now and then to listen, though not for long. I wanted this done before patrol boats spotted us.

When we reached the log-boats, the sound of movement came from up ahead. I pulled Kara beside me as Wendy did with Carmen. Moonlight reflected in Kara's wide eyes looking up at me.

I prepared my crossbow, strained to see, and wished I'd brought the bounty-hunters' infrared binoculars. I could barely see the helm and couldn't see Fran. In the dark, I couldn't tell if the ladder was still there.

Three figures in black froggie gear crept up the path. They glanced at the boat and kept moving. Another bounty boat motored up the channel toward the Wall at about the pace of the froggies on land.

After it was quiet, I turned and looked across the channel. The patrol boat remained diagonally across the intersection with only a dim helm light. *Infrared?*

"We have to move," I whispered. I untied my log-boat and pulled it out of the water. "Stay low and listen."

Wendy took the front while one of the twins took the back. By moonlight, the other twin stared up at me as if I could pull off some miracle. I untied Fran's boat and stopped to listen. Wendy and one twin moved through the brush, making too much noise.

Grabbing the front of the second log, I followed. When Wendy stopped, so did I, listening for froggies. When we got the log-boats below the ladder, we stopped. Lights shone along the pebbly path. I tucked the twins, one beneath each boat, while Wendy and I hid behind.

"Your scanner must be on the fritz again," a voice said from the path.

"I'm certain there were two or three images, maybe four," a higher-pitched voice said.

"Where did they go?"

"Wait until the temps drop. They'll light up like fireworks and you'll see the scared rabbits run."

"Hey, some logs."

"Leave them," the first woman said.

Voices diminished as they headed down toward where the log-boats had been. I waited until I couldn't hear them, and lifted one of my boats. "Can you push from the bottom while I climb?" I asked one of the twins.

Her nod was barely visible in the dark.

Holding the mooring rope, I climbed. Wendy helped push until I pulled the log up, over, and into the bigger boat. She climbed with the second log's rope while the twins pushed. I helped her get the log over the side, and the twins followed. We pulled up the ladder, left the log-boats along the stern rail, and joined Fran at the helm.

"Thanks for waiting," I said.

"That hurts," Fran said. She wore a brown bounty hunter outfit with no bloodstains. "You really think I'd leave a Marginal hero?"

"Stop it."

"At least we have transport." She fired up the engines.

"You're nuts. That patrol won't let us pass."

"It beats staying."

I wasn't so sure. Coarse-face's infrared could scan and see six on board, instead of the five they had earlier. If she boarded, we were doomed.

Propped up next to Fran by the helm was Bounty-killer, draped in a brown cloak that covered bloodstains and the cut neck. The froggie looked ready to say something, though her face had turned a pale shade of gray. I hated the killing and death, despite how ever-present it was in the swamps. Yet I couldn't help thinking this one deserved it for killing Aunt Vera for no other reason than protecting her girls.

Fran shook me. "Hey, are you with us? She's dead. Your Aunt Vera has justice."

This woman's death didn't bring Vera back.

"Snap out of it."

I pushed Fran away. "I'm fine. I wanted her dead, but it doesn't make things right."

"Maybe not, but we have to get out of here. You and Wendy put on this gear." Fran handed me one of the bounty outfits. "We'll drop the girls off at the first island."

"No, please," Kara said. "Froggies will only punish us more. Take us with you."

"Regina," Fran said, "you've been lucky so far. More mouths to feed and more faces to see won't help."

"I'm taking them to Mo-Mere." I pulled the brown bounty pants over my green canvas. "She'll know what to do."

"You barely have enough to survive on."

"They have nowhere else to go. Froggies will grab them if we don't help."

Rolling her eyes, Fran pushed a button to raise the anchor. She opened a tin of tar-smudge and applied it to her face. Then she applied some to mine. "You and Wendy take turns at the bow. Make sure to salute patrols properly. Lower your voice as if you've got a hacking cough."

I didn't like taking orders from Fran. I couldn't be sure what she was up to, though I didn't see a better plan. Wendy and I practiced saluting, with Fran giving tips. When we finished, we had the twins stand by the rail while Fran pulled the boat out into the channel.

I took first watch with the binoculars, scanning the channel and the patrol boat ahead of us.

TWENTY-NINE

While we cruised toward the intersection, I looked forward and along the shore, trying not to stare at the patrol boat across the way. Coarse-face stood at the bow with binoculars, scanning our boat and us.

With the binoculars Fran had given me, I pretended to scan the cross-channel and nearby lands. Temperatures were dropping. My infrared showed the three froggies along the shore. Their boat came into view, with two other bounty hunters on board and a girl chained to the rail.

Wendy sat on the deck, out of sight, holding my armed crossbow and one of the tranquilizer guns. She peered over the edge beneath the railing. Pretending to be chained, the twins stood by the rail, which Fran had pushed back into place. It rattled as the boat rocked forward across calm waters. Fran stood by the helm with the dead woman. No matter how hard I tried, I couldn't justify killing Bounty-killer, even knowing that if we'd let her live, she would have killed Fran and Wendy and turned me in. None of that mattered. I couldn't change what we'd done.

On the Antiquities boat, infrared showed eight ghosted images: Coarse-face at the bow, two at the helm, and five below deck. My guess was that four of those were girls chained in a tiny room. My heart raced, skipped, and raced some more as I thought of Colleen and Vera's girls. Coarse-face wouldn't have held them. She would have sent them away weeks ago. But they had to have been terrified.

"You'll do fine," Wendy said. "You have to."

"Thanks for the pressure. Now hush."

The radio crackled near our helm. Across the way, Coarse-face talked into a tiny handheld unit. "What's your status? Did you see something?"

"It's crowded," Fran said in a gravelly voice. "Other bounties have this covered."

"You think she moved?"

"Not sure, but we should spread out."

Fran had adopted Bounty-killer's voice. Was it close enough? I tried not to stare as Coarse-face fixed her binoculars on us. Before we'd boarded, this boat had five: three froggies and the twins. Fran, Wendy, and I were dressed as bounty hunters. But the dead woman made six. I didn't dare turn to check her image in infrared. It gave me chills to be on a ghost ship.

I motioned for Wendy to stand. She moved behind the twins so they hid her face. The lights of the patrol boat blinded me as we pulled near. When they panned away, I picked up a tranquilizer gun, slipped it behind me, and saluted. Wendy also saluted. I glanced into the helm. Dead Bounty-killer spooked me by saluting. Fran must have been holding up the arm from behind.

I returned my attention to the patrol boat. Through binoculars, I studied a pockmarked face with coarse cheeks, hard-edged chin, and no eyes visible behind spyglasses. I spotted two heat signatures in the helm and, by helm-light, identified them as the two who were with Coarse-face when she'd tagged Colleen and me. I turned away; I hated the inspector more than Bounty-killer. She paid bounty hunters to take Colleen and had all these people hunting for me.

"No additional passengers, I see," Coarse-face said over the radio's static. "Not a profitable evening. Where are you heading?"

"Following a hunch," Fran said. I expected her to break out laughing.

"Call in anything you find. I'll give you credit. Don't play hero."

The patrol boat pulled away and returned to its position across from us. We puttered east. My hands shook on the tranquilizer gun. Wendy collapsed onto a bench by the rail. The twins stared at me in awe, as if I'd done something. Fran was at the helm with the dead woman propped to the side. Now I understood why Fran hadn't dumped Bounty-killer with the others. The familiar face had helped us get past Coarse-face.

I scanned ahead and to the sides in infrared. Small bands roamed the shores. On a night like this, people had to be pretty desperate to move about. We passed several bounty boats on our way to the next crossing, where another patrol boat blocked our path.

"We've got company," I said. "We need to stop." Though Coarse-face could motor up behind, and we'd be surrounded.

Keeping binoculars at my eyes, I saluted into the dark. Wendy pulled the twins to their feet and copied my salute. I counted a dozen images on this patrol boat. With temperatures dropping, the images were crisper.

Four figures stood along the bow rail. Another four clustered in a small space below deck. One was at the helm, two wandered below. A floodlight blinded me. I clicked off infrared and saluted.

Our boat slowed but didn't stop. I feared Fran might ram the patrol, which would bring everyone down on us. Three agents in gray stood on the patrol boat's bow with tranquilizer guns while their floodlight panned us.

"What's going on?" Wendy asked.

"Stay calm." I lowered my arm and saluted again, in case they hadn't seen me.

Every instinct told me to drop and prepare to shoot, the Marginal response to any threat. But if we were to convince the patrol we were bounty hunters, I had to remain where they could see me and pretend I was a froggie.

The radio crackled. "Why are you out of position?" I couldn't place the voice, except it lacked any hint of Marginal accent: a Federation agent.

"Too crowded," Fran said. "We're checking with our partners." Fran slowed.

The patrol boat continued to block us from heading east. Fran turned south down the cross channel. When we made it to the next intersection, another patrol boat allowed us to head east. We moved from one intersection to another until we were out at sea. After we hadn't spotted a single boat in over an hour, Fran headed north.

I left Wendy at the bow as watch and went inside to talk to Fran. "You know they have tracking devices on this boat."

She nodded. "Leave that to me. I'll drop you upstream from

Mo-Mere's island. You'll have both logs for the four of you. Be careful." Fran looked exhausted, though not as bad as Bounty-killer, slumped against the wall. Flies buzzed her head.

"What about you?" I asked.

"I'll sort this out. You just stay alive and free. By the way, I think you have two adoring fans."

"I don't want that."

"Deal with it," Fran said. "Get the logs ready to drop overboard."

"Why don't you come with us?" I asked.

"In case you haven't noticed, I don't play well with others. Go live up to your legend."

* * *

I pinched the skin of Kara's left arm. She stared up at me with an innocence that tore at my heart. I closed my eyes, steeled my nerve, and focused on the tracking chip. I dug a small incision below the swelling. Blood pooled and slid down her arm. She grabbed hold of her sister yet held her gaze on me.

There was far too much blood. I couldn't recall how much I'd bled. The sea had washed it away. I dug the blade beneath the chip and slid it out. Wendy bandaged the wound with a tear of cloth.

"Keep this in case you need it," I said, "but we'll shield it so patrols can't locate you. Do you understand?"

Kara nodded and kissed my cheek. Carmen traded places and held up her arm. I wished it was easier the second time, but I found it hard to cut her soft flesh. After Wendy bandaged Carmen's arm, she helped me wrap both chips in aluminum shielding for later.

Fran joined us. "It's time."

She helped Wendy and me lower the log-boats into the water, trailing behind the bounty boat. I hugged Fran and climbed into the newer boat with Kara, the infrared binoculars, my crossbow, and a tranquilizer gun. Wendy and Carmen climbed into the other boat, which we linked like a catamaran. We untied the mooring ropes from the bounty boat and watched Fran motor north.

Using infrared binoculars, I spotted a lone figure on the island ahead of us. It gave me no comfort that patrols and bounty boats could do the same. It would make hiding the twins difficult. Fran was right, but I couldn't send them away.

Wendy paddled hard to keep up with me. The twins pitched in. When we reached the cove on the north shore, I saw Mo-Mere's motorboat and her skiff under the moonlight. We paddled to a smaller cove on the east side, where we tied up the boats.

It reminded me of other times I'd approached islands at night. At least now it wasn't pouring rain with storm surges. With a stick, I poked the narrow trail up to the clearing. At the top of the hill, I used the binoculars yet couldn't see anyone inside either cabin. A gun cocked.

"Mo-Mere?"

She shined a light in my face and then at the others. Anger in her face shifted to surprise. "Heavens be. Where have you been? And look at these cuties?" She approached the twins.

"I'm sorry, Mo-Mere. I went against your rules again. I had to learn more about Colleen."

"And your mom."

Nodding, I introduced the twins to Mo-Mere.

"I know who they are." She slung her rifle over her shoulder and pinched the twins' cheeks. "These smart little urchins would have been in Colleen's class, except their mother couldn't pay." She gave them a hug. "I'm sorry about your mother and about not being able to teach you. I know it makes no sense, but I could either teach, fish, or barter, but not all three."

The twins shrugged. "We have nothing to barter," Kara said. "But we promise to do as you say and work hard."

"You're welcome to stay. Let's get you inside."

I walked with Mo-Mere. "Fran saved us. She was brilliant getting past the patrols."

"Strange one, she is," Mo-Mere said. "Clever, but no patience for schooling."

"I'm sorry I disobeyed. I feel useless stuck on this island."

"I know, dear. I've been worried sick about you all day."

"You're not angry?" I said.

"Very." She grabbed hold of me with one arm and Wendy with the other. "You two are my only children. Not only did you put yourself in danger, you put Wendy at risk."

"I tried to talk her out of it," Wendy said.

"I'm sure you did. Did you learn anything useful?"

"Fran killed the bounty hunters who killed Aunt Vera and took Colleen," I said.

Mo-Mere opened the cabin door. "Did that make things better?"

I shook my head. "But their boat helped us escape. They confirmed they turned all three girls over to Inspector Demarco."

"I see." Mo-Mere pushed the others inside and held me back. "Maybe if I'd taken you with me the day of the storm I could have saved you all this pain."

"I don't blame you, Mo-Mere. Mom should have been there with us."

"Ah, your mother." She closed the door, leaving just the two of us on the porch. "I asked around. Your mother is not working with Antiquities. On the contrary, she was trying to understand why they tagged you and your sister on the day before the storm, and why they took such interest in her daughters."

"And?"

"As I suspected. Federation fertility clinics are failing. If they don't find a solution soon, we'll experience another population collapse, and possible extinction."

"What does that have to do with me?" I asked.

"They're convinced your genes could reverse this decline. Remember how they took your blood? Evidently, the results were unusual."

"Is that why you keep telling me I'm special? I don't like feeling special."

She pinched my cheek. "You're quite special. Only you can decide how to use that."

"Are you sure you're not my donor mother?"

"Heavens no, dear. Though I wouldn't mind. I couldn't have children."

"Did you know her?" I asked.

Mo-Mere shook her head. "That was long ago."

"But you and Mom were friends."

"We went our separate ways after we came to the swamps," Mo-Mere said. "She found me when you were ready for school, and we never talked about the years in between."

"I can't believe my real mom would leave me. That's all."

"Your mother loves you very much. After she heard you were with me, she spent all her energies looking for Colleen. You'd want her to do that, wouldn't you?"

"I guess." Tears streamed down my cheeks. "I want my mom."

Mo-Mere held me and let me lose myself in her comfort. Then she took me to the edge of the porch and gazed up at the half moon. "We'll have to scrounge harder for food and clothing, but we'll make do."

Guilt. I'd added burdens on her while she tried to help me stay safe. Already, I thought of the twins as my sisters, though they couldn't replace Colleen. But more bodies meant more heat signatures for patrols and bounty hunters to find.

* * *

I didn't mind sharing my room with Wendy, since Mo-Mere didn't want to send the twins to the other cabin. I did mind that Wendy wanted to talk while I could barely stay awake.

"Thanks for taking me," she said. "I mean I was scared, but you're so brave."

My eyes rolled. Fran had done the hard work, the dirty work. It made me realize she'd done it to spare me from having to kill that horrid bounty woman. "Get some sleep." My cheeks were still moist. I was home, yet I didn't feel safe. "In the morning, I'll talk to Mo-Mere about salvage ideas. You can come."

"Remember, I don't swim well. I'll do anything else."

Mo-Mere must have matched us up so I could help Wendy become stronger and Wendy could teach me how to work with others. But the one who could really help, Fran, wanted to be alone. It was all too confusing.

"What are your salvage ideas?" Wendy asked.

"In the morning."

While she talked, my soul sank beneath my pillow. The face of Bounty-killer haunted me. She'd coldly killed Aunt Vera. Fran hadn't flinched while cutting the bounty hunter's neck. I didn't want to be that way. Yet I was glad the killer was gone. She could no longer hurt my friends. That satisfaction brought with it guilt: *thou shalt not kill.*

The room fell silent. I couldn't see Wendy in the dark. She was probably pouting. She had me all to herself. She'd shared her fears and her need to be with me, and I hadn't responded the way she wanted. My throat choked up. Those I cared about got hurt. If I didn't let myself care for Wendy, she'd be safe. That had to be Fran's answer to the swamps as well.

In my mind, I retraced what had happened since Inspector Coarse-face injected her implant into me. I didn't want to relive all this, but the story needed remembering. It played moment by moment in my dreams, forcing me to relive the horrors in panoramic detail. Yet here I was with Mo-Mere and Wendy. I'd rescued the twins, and that filled me with happiness.

Then my world crashed in on me like the storm that shoved me out to sea. Darkness spread like tar, blotting out even starlight.

Mo-Mere burst into the room. "Patrol boat," she said. "No time for the fireplace. Slide across the floor. Keep low and still."

THIRTY

"Where's Wendy?" I asked. I crawled across the wood floor behind Mo-Mere, unable to feel my friend's presence.

"She's getting the twins." Mo-Mere led me into the kitchen corner and pushed aside the cooking stove.

In pitch darkness, I helped Mo-Mere lift a heavy steel panel. Stale air greeted us.

"I hadn't planned to use this yet," Mo-Mere said. "It's shallow and needs cleaning, but I gave it infrared shielding."

I climbed down four feet and she handed me a flashlight. I knelt, shining the light around a dusty cellar with concrete floor, walls and ceiling under part of the living area. Wendy shepherded the twins to the opening, and they crawled down beside me.

Mo-Mere handed down a heavy package. "Here's some food and water. Make it last. Not a sound."

She handed down my clothes and the few items I hadn't left in my log-boat. I prayed the patrols didn't find the boat with the tranquilizer gun. I should have hidden that elsewhere, but it was dark. Mo-Mere and Wendy dropped the panel into place and moved the stove over the hole.

We were trapped. If anything happened to them, we couldn't open the panel. My fear reflected in the twin's faces as they sat, watching me. *I don't have answers,* I wanted to say.

I smiled. "Everything will be fine."

"They're coming for us, aren't they?" Kara asked.

"Mo-Mere is clever. We need to stay quiet and turn out the light. Find a comfortable place."

"Where will you be?"

I panned the light over the gray boundary of our prison and picked a spot against a wall near the panel. When I turned out the light, the girls scrambled next to me, one on each side. They were so close I felt their jaws quiver. I'd rescued them from becoming bounty slaves. Now they expected me to save them again.

Reading about life in other places made me realize how much our swamps had shaped us. No matter how frightened we were, we had to hide it. We were only worth what we could provide to others, and a frightened child wasn't worth much. Yet Mo-Mere wasn't that way. Yes, as a teacher she could only accept those who paid so she could concentrate on teaching. But I'd had little to offer while stuck on her island for weeks and she never asked.

I hugged the girls. When I let go, they curled up next to me. In the dark, I could imagine them as Colleen.

Above us, someone pounded at the cabin door. The twins jumped and clung to me.

"Just a minute," Mo-Mere said from above.

The cabin door opened with a squeal. "Inspector Demarco," Mo-Mere said. "What brings you out in the middle of the night?" Mo-Mere made it sound as if she'd just gotten out of bed.

"Can I come in?" Coarse-face asked, a rhetorical question, for sure. The inspector could go wherever she pleased.

The floorboards squeaked, but less than I expected. Sensing the twins holding their breath, I leaned to each of their ears and whispered. "Breathe slowly." I felt them nod.

I imagined Mo-Mere lighting oil lamps. "I'll make some tea," she said.

"This isn't a social visit," Coarse-face said. "I believe you might be harboring persons of interest."

"It's just me and Wendy."

"Mo-Mere, everything okay?" Wendy asked.

"Yes, dear. Come sit next to me."

"We tracked Wendy near the Wall," Coarse-face said.

"We were looking for cloth and boots," Mo-Mere said.

"Then her signal disappeared until she was back on this island."

"I wouldn't know about that. Does anything interfere with the signal?"

"Never mind," Coarse-face said. "We tracked a bounty boat this way. We have reason to believe foul play."

"Pirates?" Mo-Mere asked. "We avoid them."

"The boat carried two girls, twins, and a crew of three. We found the boat scuttled at sea, abandoned. There was blood on the deck and no sign of the bounty hunters or their two charges. In case you're wondering, the blood's DNA matches the captain's."

I cringed at how Wendy might react and what the inspector might read into it. I held the twins tight and wondered if we could break out of the cellar. The problem was that I didn't know how thick the concrete was. And if I broke the infrared seal, Coarse-face could find me.

"What does that have to do with us?" Mo-Mere asked.

"Don't play games, Marisa. You have some fancy notion you help these girls by keeping them in this hellhole. You don't. Let me do my job. You and I aren't that different. We both want to help young Marginals. At least I find them steady homes that won't flood."

"I'm sure you think you help, but your caste system keeps them slaves. Whatever offspring they have will also be slaves."

"Enough evasions," Coarse-face said. "Where were you tonight?"

"When we couldn't find boots for Wendy, or cloth, we bartered for food and came home. We avoided the main channels, bounty boats, and scavengers. I have no idea what happened to your friends."

"They weren't my friends."

"If survivors ended up on this island," Mo-Mere said, "I haven't seen them. You're welcome to look."

"My agents are already searching the island," the inspector said. "If you're lying, we *will* take Wendy and deal with you."

"What can you tell me about these persons of interest, so I can watch for them?"

"Don't pretend you'd turn them in."

"What crimes have they committed?" Mo-Mere asked. "Or are they of some other interest?"

"We believe someone murdered the captain and crew. If the twin girls weren't involved, they could tell us who was. If they were involved, well ..."

The twins held tight. A Marginal would do most anything to

survive. Some even betrayed family. It finally sank in what I'd done. By rescuing the girls, I'd taken on the responsibility to keep them safe. I also risked them turning me in to save themselves. I couldn't have turned them away.

A floor squeak alerted me to movement above. "I've checked the house," a different voice said. "No sign of anyone but these two."

"Keep looking."

"What can you tell me about these twins?" Mo-Mere asked. "How old are they?"

Coarse-face described the girls nestled next to me and added, "The one who really interests us is a former student of yours, Regina Shen."

"What has she done?"

"I can't discuss that."

"Very hush-hush, then," Mo-Mere said. "What'll become of her if you catch her?"

"That's none of your concern."

"Is she dangerous?"

"She removed her tracking chip," Coarse-face said. "That comes with penalties, in case you helped."

"I haven't seen her in some time."

I loved Mo-Mere's use of double meaning.

"Neither have I," Wendy said.

"I see," Coarse-face said.

The front door squealed.

"What did you find?" Coarse-face demanded.

"No other infrared images, not even a bird," another agent said. *Don't look down.*

"We're not finished here," the inspector said. "If you find any of these girls, you'd best let me know."

"How would I do that without a communication device?" Mo-Mere asked.

"Elaine, give her yours," Coarse-face said.

"You didn't drink your tea," Mo-Mere said.

"Save it."

The door squealed. Then there was silence. I expected Mo-Mere to let us out, but she couldn't afford to give the inspector any reason to return.

"You two should get some sleep," I whispered. "We'll be here for a while."

I wanted them to move away so I could stretch out, but they remained, holding on to me. Closing my eyes, I saw Coarse-face grabbing these sweet sisters who had lost their family. The inspector might claim to help them by providing homes across the Wall, but from what I'd heard, they separated sisters, including twins. I couldn't let that happen.

I adjusted my position, stroked their hair, and held them. It was the least I could do while we waited to see what Inspector Demarco did next.

* * *

One problem with being in a dark, sealed room was having no idea of the passage of time. It could have been minutes or hours. I knew it wasn't days, because the girls slept in my arms. They'd have gotten hungry at some point. Though I was hungry and thirsty, I didn't want to wake them by getting into the supplies. My ears registered the settling of the house, the girls' breathing, rumbling in my stomach, and little else.

I imagined Coarse-face taking Mo-Mere and Wendy. My accursed imagination gave me several scenarios for the silence above us. All ended with the three of us locked in this cellar for the rest of our lives. I couldn't recall if I'd heard any evidence of Mo-Mere after the inspector left, *if* the inspector had left.

It was time to stop running and hiding. It was time to end the chief inspector's harassment. In the pit of my stomach, I felt the same way I had about Bounty-killer: she had to go. Yet I didn't hate enough to kill. I felt sorry for Coarse-face. She lacked the imagination to survive without hurting others.

As bad as it was being stuck on this island, this low-ceilinged room was far worse, particularly in the dark. But hunting for an exit would wake the girls and run down the batteries, and those salvaged items weren't very reliable.

The girls finally woke. I felt alert and imagined it had to be daytime. Yet my weariness told me I hadn't slept. I turned on the light so they could orient themselves.

They both looked up at me as they might have looked at their mother. "When can we leave?" Kara asked in the thinnest of whispers.

Putting my finger to my lips, I pointed upward.

"Can we eat?" she asked.

I opened Mo-Mere's package. Inside were three jugs of water. I handed one to each twin. "Go easy on this." I had the feeling all three had been for me.

They nodded.

I passed around hard biscuits and turned out the light. I waited and listened. Being with the twins made me feel closer to Mom, despite what she'd done. Forced to choose between helping one girl or the other, I don't think I could. If they weren't the same age, I probably would help the younger one. That didn't ease the pain of Mom abandoning us, but I began to understand how hard it could be.

There was scraping above us and then reflected sunlight. Mo-Mere's flashlight blinded me. "You girls okay?" she asked.

I squinted. "What happened?"

"Our friendly inspector placed sensors. I needed to *relocate* some of them."

"Is that pebbly-face woman gone?" Kara asked.

"Yes, dear. One of the agents spent the night. Wendy and I checked; it's safe to come out. We'll want to clean this space and put in provisions for tonight."

"I don't like creepy cellars." Kara squeezed my hand. "But it's nice to have a big sister."

Her coy smile was like Colleen's. I squeezed back.

While Wendy and the twins cleaned and provisioned the underground room, I took Mo-Mere outside into sunlight and fresh air. The warm breeze washed over me. "You know, if the inspector had taken you and Wendy, we couldn't have gotten out."

She nodded. "Any kind of escape hatch would weaken the infrared shields. I didn't have another option."

"Since the island is no longer safe, I want to salvage with you."

"And, my impatient one, I promised you could." Mo-Mere looked distracted.

"I mean today. I love you and your island, but it felt good to be out, despite the mess I got into."

"I love you, too, dear." She pinched my cheek.

"How did Wendy handle the inspector's questions?"

"She did great. You've been rubbing off on her in a good way."

"Do you think Fran got away?" I asked.

"I'm sure she did," Mo-Mere said. She scanned the waters beyond the trees. "Otherwise, Demarco would have said something."

I strained to see what she was looking for. There were no boats on the channel. "The inspector must have tracked the twins' implant chips to where Fran dropped us off. I should have removed them sooner."

Mo-Mere patted my shoulder. "You're not perfect, my dear. Learn from your mistakes, but don't dwell on them. Like you, many people removed their implants. Demarco sounded nervous last night. She's worried about a rebellion."

I laughed at the absurdity: Demarco, worried over twelve-year-old twins.

"I checked the girls before they went to bed," Mo-Mere said, "and replaced their bandages. You did a good job with only a knife. Herbal antibiotics should clean up any infection."

"I didn't want Demarco tracking them to you."

"Wise choice."

"What about Wendy?" I asked. "The inspector knew she'd been near the Wall."

"I took care of her implant before she went to bed. Demarco scanned her. Good thing she wasn't clever enough to remove the bandage and see we'd taped the chip to the underside."

"I messed up."

Mo-Mere smiled. "You brought me two new students. That's something."

"Now the inspector suspects you."

"Trust me, if Demarco had evidence that you and the twins were here, she would have taken us."

"Unless she left you as bait to catch me." My stomach tightened as I clutched the porch railing. "I feel so stupid. I knew Mom and Colleen were beyond reach, yet I couldn't help asking those bounty hunters. It was an obvious trap."

Mo-Mere squeezed my shoulder. "Don't be so hard on yourself. You're right to push yourself, but punishment won't help."

"But I've made such a mess."

"The best way to help your sister is to remain free. Plus, now a certain bounty hunter can't harm you or your sister."

"I guess." I stared at the untended garden. "I can't sit here on this island. I have to do something. I won't spend the rest of my life running from Demarco and hiding in a cellar like Anne Frank."

"She was in an attic."

"Same thing."

"Very well," Mo-Mere said. "We'll have to remain especially vigilant from now on, not only for you but for the twins. I have mixed feelings about them. I'm proud of you and I want to help them, but having them complicates things."

"I'm sorry."

"Don't be," Mo-Mere said. "It shows real growth that you're thinking beyond your own survival and that of your immediate family. You have a sharp mind, yet your heart is the most interesting part of you."

"You're my family now."

Mo-Mere hugged me. "I have a surprise for you."

"We'll do salvage today?"

"Don't be so impatient. This'll involve work."

"More skills you want me to learn." I sighed.

"Think DaVinci. You have a problem. He has a solution."

"A flying machine?"

"Too visible," Mo-Mere said.

I shook my head. "Then what?"

"A submarine."

"You found one?"

"I found parts that reminded me of DaVinci's drawings," Mo-Mere said. "It'll take some assembly. While it won't work like a Federation sub, it'll move underwater, and we can attach breathing bladders so you can stay under longer."

THIRTY-ONE

Wendy and the twins finished putting blankets, thin mattresses, lights, water, and dried food in the cellar. Then Mo-Mere sealed the opening and we went down to the cove where she moored her boats. With bounty hunter binoculars, I scanned the horizon in regular light and infrared, which grew fuzzy in the heat of another steamy day. To the north, local boats and scavengers were out on the channel, but no visible patrols or bounty boats.

Because she didn't like to swim or dive, Wendy stayed on shore with binoculars and the skiff's mooring rope.

"At any sign of danger, pull the skiff in," Mo-Mere said. "And hide the binoculars."

She provided the twins with goggles and synthetic rubber breathing bladders like mine. Then the four of us dove under the motorboat and around a rock jetty to a stash of salvaged and bartered items. I couldn't make out a submarine anywhere until she took me inside a tube salvaged from a huge chimney stack. Then the image crystallized. The cylinder was big enough around so I could swim through, and twice my length. I could imagine two people inside, though we'd also need room for breathing bladders so we could salvage.

And bladders Mo-Mere had, dozens of balloons clustered beneath a large plastic sheet. With these we could spend an hour on the bottom. Mo-Mere swapped breathing bladders and handed me one of her new ones. I attached mine to my belt and inhaled. The odor was rubbery.

For a nose cone, she'd salvaged a partly-corroded industrial aluminum funnel. With a hand drill and saw, we cut out the corroded parts to act as crude windows. Then we inserted a large, clear plastic funnel inside the aluminum one and bolted both to the aluminum cylinder. Using salvaged strips of aluminum in various shapes, we formed tail fins to close off the back and added a rusty inboard electric motor and propeller.

I surfaced with Mo-Mere to refill my breathing bladders. "This is amazing. We could go deep with this."

"I thought you'd like it. There are sunken treasures Inspector Demarco has hunted for years. I believe I know where they are. If so, we could preserve part for ourselves before they destroy the rest."

"You wouldn't turn treasures over to Demarco."

"It's all about barter," Mo-Mere said.

"What?"

"Our freedom. Now let's go. We have work to do."

While the twins watched Wendy for any signal, Mo-Mere and I dived to make repairs. I drilled holes for bolts to attach the nose. It wouldn't be watertight, but it didn't have to be. We closed off the front and cut a window on top of the main cylinder.

As the twins filled breathing bladders, we sealed air into plastic cylinders to use for lift or spare oxygen in an emergency. By the time we'd filled the last of the air tanks, Kara pointed to our skiff moving toward shore. Mo-Mere motioned for us to dive and then headed for shore.

The twins and I huddled near the sub as a boat pulled into the cove. From the newness of the gray hull, it had to be a patrol, probably Coarse-face.

I nudged the twins into the sub and grabbed the last piece: a pedal-gear, like those used to pump water into purification tanks. Using a hand drill, I punched holes in the aluminum tube and anchored the pedal-gear with bolts to the sub's frame. It made the sub heavier, but if batteries failed, this was the only power to the propeller. I pulled the tail section into place and tightened latches that fastened the propeller to the pedal-gear. Then I switched breathing bladders and climbed into the harness.

Outside, the murky waters of the channel washed by. I pedaled. The propeller spun, but we didn't move. Kara motioned toward the rocks. We were stuck. Then it hit me; Mo-Mere would have anchored the cylinder so it didn't wash away.

I released the tail section so Kara could swim out. She checked around the cylinder and moved some rocks. We floated free, but I had no control with the propeller detached. She swam in and helped me secure the tail section.

Back in the harness, I pumped at the pedal-gear. At first the sub didn't move. Then it pushed against the current. Using wires to adjust the tail fins, I turned and headed across the channel. It felt as if we were flying. Maybe that was why DaVinci enjoyed drawing submarines and flying machines.

We hovered below the surface as small fish swam by, and eased our way through cloudy water. The cove faded behind us. Unable to see boats on the channel, I wished Mo-Mere had salvaged something to use as a periscope.

I was surprised that my weak leg gave as much as my good one to the pedal-gear. Though it had been weeks, the leg still got twinges of pain. At least the muscles worked.

We approached submerged bushes and a cleft behind rocks. Using the fins, I pushed closer to the surface and found a place to rest the sub. I motioned for Carmen to remain inside while Kara refilled breathing bladders. I surfaced with binoculars and looked through waterlogged bushes toward Mo-Mere and the patrol boat.

Three agents walked the island while Coarse-face talked with Mo-Mere. I climbed onto shore, looked for alligators, and scanned the channel. A bounty boat scooted west toward the Wall. A scavenger boat headed out toward recently swamped homes.

On Mo-Mere's island, agents searched from one end to the other and through the cabins. They would not leave us alone. If I didn't do something, Coarse-face would not only take me but also punish Mo-Mere, Wendy, and the twins.

* * *

The agents returned to the patrol boat and headed west. Kara and I refilled breathing bladders and waited for Mo-Mere to dive and look for us.

Rather than dive, Mo-Mere took Wendy to the cabin. I scanned the island for clues and didn't see other agents, though they could have placed sensors. I might never be able to return to the island, my home. My chest ached. It was like losing Mom and Colleen all over again. Would I ever see Wendy or Mo-Mere again? At least the agents hadn't taken them. Yet.

Mo-Mere returned to the cove with Wendy, bringing one of my log-boats. They attached my log, climbed into the motorboat, and headed east, out to sea. I nudged Kara ahead of me and climbed into the sub. After we secured the tail section, I pedaled. The sub moved too slowly to keep up with a motorboat.

The two-person sub was cramped with three of us. I made the twins crawl behind me on either side so I could see forward. They had to be careful not to get caught in the gears. We weren't moving fast enough, but I couldn't risk surfacing where the patrol could see us. Then I remembered the battery system, if it would actually work under water without electrocuting us.

I pushed the starter. Nothing happened. I pedaled hard, my legs feeling the strain. We veered away from submerged rocks into the channel. I pushed again. This time the electric motor kicked in, shoving me backward as the sub lurched forward.

We surfaced like angry carp. Mo-Mere's boat floated ahead of us, not moving as fast as I'd expected. When we got close, I slowed the motor so we didn't crash. Kara and Carmen sucked on their breathing bladders, watching me, as if this was the most marvelous magic they'd ever seen.

I switched breathing bladders and looked at the instruments Mo-Mere had mounted next to the nose cone. A gyro direction finder showed us heading northeast, toward sunken Richmond. Over the centuries, most of the city had been over-salvaged, picked clean so many times that all we usually found was trash from our predecessors. Now and then, salvagers discovered a new site. Others found out and picked that clean.

Mo-Mere's boat stopped. I dived to avoid hitting her propeller. I circled around and came to a stop behind her boat. A rope dropped beside the propeller.

Kara took over the pedal-gear while I squeezed behind her. With Carmen's help, I opened the tail section, swam out, and closed it. When I reached the front of the sub, I saw something new on the bottom of Mo-Mere's motorboat. She'd attached hooks to the hull at the bow and stern that matched loops on top of the sub cylinder.

I tugged at the rope, and it fell. I attached one end to the front of the sub, swam to the front of the motorboat, and motioned for Kara to pedal. I attached the other end of the rope to Mo-Mere's boat. A second rope appeared by the propeller. I used it to secure the back of the sub.

Surfacing, I removed my breathing tube and gulped air. "Is it safe?"

"Never." Mo-Mere winked and smiled.

"What happened?"

"Bring the twins and any breathing bladders that need filling."

I brought the twins, fastened the tail section to the sub, and climbed on board with nine breathing bladders. While Wendy and the twins refilled them, Mo-Mere took me to the helm and headed northwest.

"I thought you brought my log-boat," I said.

"We secured it beneath the rear platform in case you need it."

"How did you know we'd left?"

"You rode too close to the surface," Mo-Mere said. "You need to dive deeper."

"Oh." I watched Wendy teach the twins. "Why did the inspector return?"

"I suspect the North American governor or even the Federation Premier is pushing for your capture," Mo-Mere said. "They're desperate."

"It's nice to be wanted."

"Stop blaming your mom."

"How do we get them to stop?" I asked.

"That'll be tricky, if you're up to it."

I nodded. "I'm sorry for disobeying. I want to stay with you, but I feel like a prisoner."

"I'm not angry that you want to help. I'm concerned for your welfare. Demarco will keep surprising us until she finds something. She has her eyes on our little cove and on my movements. If I dive, she'll know."

"Won't she follow us here?" I asked.

"Count on it."

"Then what do we do?"

"There's one thing Inspector Demarco wants more than you," Mo-Mere said. "Power and the artifacts that can help her get it."

"We don't have any. Don't give her your precious books. I couldn't bear."

"I'd sacrifice them for you."

"Why?"

"Nothing has gotten our community as excited as your exploits. Every day you stay free gives these people hope."

I stared at her. None of that seemed real. The only thing that did was my new family. I glanced at Wendy and the twins. For them to have any future, I had to do something. "What artifacts can we offer?"

"There's a treasure I've been holding on to. It's rich with books, sculptures and so much more. I'll offer that in exchange for her leaving us alone."

"You know she won't."

"She might if she believes I could bring her more," Mo-Mere said.

"Do you have more?"

"No, but she won't know that for a while. Besides, she understands the concept of repaying a debt. She built her life on favors returned. She couldn't survive without them."

"You think that'll be enough?" I asked.

"It's all we have. It'll be very dangerous in a rickety untested sub. You'll have to dive alone. I can't go. You know Wendy can't dive. I've fitted the bottom of this boat with breathing tubes the twins can use when Demarco returns. That way she'll find only Wendy and me."

"I'll do it," I said.

THIRTY-TWO

Everyone's confidence in me was both a comfort and a burden. Hands trembling, I fastened the sub's tail section and climbed onto the pedal-gear. I'd lost friends to the depths. It happened in an instant. You ran out of oxygen, got the bends scrambling too quickly toward the surface, snagged some underground bit of rock or debris, or fell into an Antiquities trap intended to keep you from salvaging.

There was no turning back.

An underwater flashlight would be my only lighting of the depths. After the twins untied the mooring ropes, I started the electric motor, angled the fins, and dived. Sunlight faded behind me. If this treasure was secure, it was because most salvagers couldn't find it or couldn't dive this deep.

The sub took me deeper than I'd ever gone before. Darkness closed in like Mo-Mere's cellar. I reached the mucky bottom, where the sub's propeller stirred up sediment that masked everything. The debris settled, yet my flashlight barely illuminated the plain ahead. To counter the buoyancy of the breathing bladders, I angled the fins down and ran the prop to keep from surfacing until the sub settled down.

I climbed out and tied the tail section to a jut of rock. Then I anchored the front. I took two extra breathing bladders and tied a rock to my waist to keep from rising.

By thin flashlight beam through murky water, the seascape looked like other sunken sites, flat between two hills, covered with debris from above, and active with sea life. Large catfish swam close to the sea floor. Clams drifted back to the bottom, mingling with crabs and what might have been the start of coral, too dark to see. It was easy to miss that the flat stretch of ground beneath sediment was a concrete enclosure: dull, gray concrete, like the Barrier Wall, covered with sea critters returning the landscape to nature.

According to Mo-Mere, before the deluge, this concrete structure hid beneath dense forest landscape to make it look like part of the woods. Someone had gone to great effort to preserve this treasure and its location, which Mo-Mere had pieced together from gossip and documents we'd salvaged on prior dives.

A cleft of rock concealed an entrance covered in inches of muck. I used a rock to scrape the dirt away, revealing a rotary handle I had to force. It turned slowly at first and then came loose. When I swung the large metal door up, no water rushed into the void. No air bubbles escaped. Whatever the owner's intent, the door hadn't held back the flood. After pulling the door onto its back, I glanced at the sub to be sure I could find my way. Then I aimed my light into the void.

Mo-Mere had said to look for a vertical door with a code pad. She'd even given me a set of codes to decipher. I dropped into the open pit and found a plastic-encased pad next to a gray door. The electronic panel looked dead, and in the dim flash beam, I couldn't tell if it was wet. I tried the codes and the pad lit up. Letters and numbers scrambled across the screen, surprising me that the panel still worked after hundreds of years and beneath 200 feet of water.

The panel flashed red: Invalid access code. I looked around. The pit was a concrete cylinder barely my height. The only distinguishing features were the panel and the door. The floor was relatively clear of outside debris and no sea life except what I brought in. *So that's it?*

I climbed out and looked around. Closer to the surface, with sunlight seeping down, I might have been able to find clues nearby, but not with this thin light and all this sediment. If I'd wanted to leave a clue …

My light settled on the metal door. Inside had a rotary handle like the one outside in order to lock the entry. Attached nearby was a plastic-encased item I recognized immediately: a twin to the Chinese cipher puzzle Mo-Mere had given me. During my salvage attempts, I'd only found one other, damaged by the floods. This one appeared to be dry within its plastic covering, which was surprisingly flexible to the touch.

My fingers played the gates on the cipher until it reached a solution using Mo-Mere's code. That revealed a second set of numbers. When I entered those into the plastic-encased pad, the door cracked open. Again, no water rushed in. Maybe someone had already cleaned the place out.

I switched breathing bladders and swam into a large room lined with cabinets and shelves stacked floor to ceiling with plastic bins. By the looks of the rusted steel pillars, water had seeped in long ago. The shelves were in various stages of collapse. It made me wonder if the owner had died before she, or he, could secure these treasures from the seas. Precious sculptures and other artwork littered the floor, many cracked, faded or broken. Others looked as if they'd glided to the floor. Perhaps those shelves had collapsed after the room flooded. This represented the life's work of hundreds or thousands of artists. If the Department of Antiquities got their hands on these, they could be lost to future generations. I wondered how much we could hide in Mo-Mere's cellar, which also wasn't waterproof.

I swam through this room to another, lined with dozens of shelves of books, all preserved in plastic. Why, if the owners knew of the floods, didn't they take these treasures to higher ground? Maybe there was no safer place with the wars. Besides, Antiquities had grabbed any treasures that had been moved.

In the corner at the back were the packages Mo-Mere had mentioned, more carefully wrapped than the others. I tied them with nylon rope, removed the rock from my waist, and pulled three bundles behind me. I swam through the physical artifact room, through the double doors, and outside, turning off my light the moment I located the sub.

Upon reaching my underwater transport, I pulled the packages inside, traded breathing bladders, and returned to the library. I dragged two more book bundles to the sub, then gathered nine gold candleholder statues and took them outside. I secured the two doors, walked the statues across the clearing, and nestled them in a rock cave to protect them from storm surges. We would offer these to Demarco.

I freed the sub from the rocks, climbed in, and closed the tail section. Shining my flashlight at the largest plastic bundle, I saw that the cover looked like leather. Could this really be an original Gutenberg Bible? The other bundles contained the works of Shakespeare, Asimov, and others I'd only heard about.

If only I could return to protect the entire collection, but my oxygen was low, and it would be hard enough to surface with this weight. I pressed the start button. The motor didn't kick over. I pressed again. Nothing. I began to pedal. The propeller whooshed behind me, but the sub didn't move. I hit start again. This time the motor pushed the sub forward. I adjusted the fins to lift, but the sub rose much too slowly.

My mind raced over what to toss overboard. Doing that would require opening the tail, which risked damaging the sub and destroying any chance of using the propeller. Descending had been much easier. I was glad I hadn't put Wendy or the twins at risk.

I switched breathing bladders and adjusted the fins for maximum lift. I wondered how to find Mo-Mere if she'd drifted. Remembering the gyro-compass, I pulled it in front of me and directed the sub to retrace our steps. But I had no way to judge the current's effect on the sub or the boat above, and what if the motor died? I couldn't pedal fast enough or swim with the books. I'd tried that with Mo-Mere's treasures.

I looked up through one of the window. The sun shimmered on the surface. I spotted Mo-Mere's boat with the twins holding onto handles she'd placed on the boat's bottom. One of the girls pointed my way and waved.

Nearby was Coarse-face's patrol boat, with a new scrape down the starboard side. I wanted to ram her for hounding us, but the cobbled-together sub would do little damage to the patrol and would collapse, sending precious books to the depths.

The patrol boat pulled next to Mo-Mere. I lined up my approach, turned off the motor, and pedaled. The twins tied the mooring ropes to Mo-Mere's boat. Then I climbed out of the tail section and swam next to them. Through the breathing tubes came the rumble of voices from above.

"You misjudge me," Coarse-face said. "You can't buy me with artifacts. I'll locate Regina and the twins without you."

"I could save you time and effort," Mo-Mere said. "I'll do your dirty work."

"I'm taking Wendy. Then you'll come around. Bring me Regina Shen."

"I've told you. I have no idea where she is. You agreed to give me three more years with Wendy."

"Stop playing games," Coarse-face said. "Give me Regina and you can keep Wendy as long as you'd like."

"I can't give what I don't have."

"Don't make me arrest you."

They were my family, in danger because of me. If words could win, Mo-Mere would have found the right ones. It was my turn. Returning to the sub, I climbed inside and stumbled over the hand drill I'd used to assemble the sub.

After switching breathing bladders, I took the drill and some screws, and swam to the patrol boat. Holding onto the rudder, I forced a screw into the joint. Then I drilled into the engine compartment. Fiberglass peeled away, as if I were boring into an apple. When water rushed in, I swam toward the bow and drilled a second hole. It wouldn't be enough; the bilge pump could handle that. Fiberglass chips drifted like worms as I drilled more holes along the hull.

The motor revved, and the boat lurched forward.

THIRTY-THREE

I dodged the propeller and swam back to the sub. My breathing bladder was running low. By the time I reached the sub, the patrol boat was cutting a large arc around us, sinking lower in the water as it went. The boat listed forward and came to a full stop.

I surfaced at Mo-Mere's stern. Shots rang out from the patrol boat. Dot-dot. Dot-dot. Dot-dot.

"They have Wendy," Mo-Mere cried out.

"Take Carmen and go," I said. "I'll rescue Wendy."

"Regina?"

I dove, untied my log-boat from beneath the stern platform, and attached it to the top of the sub. I motioned for the twins to follow me. We each took a bundle of books from the sub and tied them to the bottom of Mo-Mere's boat. Then Kara and I climbed into the sub while Carmen released the ropes. I pedaled while trying to start the motor. The sub began sinking. Carmen climbed aboard Mo-Mere's boat and they motored away.

The patrol boat's bow dipped below water. They launched a sea-skimmer. It sank. I pressed start again. This time the sub's motor whirred. I approached the patrol boat as bodies hit the water. Only one wore green canvas: Wendy. Her face distorted by terror, my friend, who feared drowning, dogpaddled with her hands cuffed. Antiquities agents were too busy saving their own skins to worry about her.

Sinking below the surface, she scrambled to kick her way up. I pulled the sub and log-boat beneath her. Eyes wide with dread, she grabbed hold. I turned and headed for an island off to the west, surfacing now and then so she could breathe.

Beyond the tip of the island, I stopped and let the sub rest on a ledge. While Kara refilled breathing bladders, I swam to Wendy. She clutched the sides of the log-boat, shaking. When she saw me, she let go, pulled me up, and hugged me. "I thought I was going to … drown."

I held her tight. In the distance, the patrol boat disappeared below the surface. I wanted Coarse-face to die, though not by my hand.

"I have an idea," I said. "I need both of you to help."

Wendy shuddered. "If it doesn't involve diving."

"It does, but you can handle it. Watch what I do."

Trembling, Wendy nodded.

We refilled breathing bladders, and the three of us climbed into the sub. With Wendy wedged to my left and Kara to my right, I showed them both how to use the controls. When we approached where the patrol had been, bubbling pockets of air trailed the boat's descent. We followed.

A gray-uniformed body floated by. Below, the patrol boat hit bottom, tumbled sideways, and rolled to a stop right-side-up. It shuddered and settled into a crevice. I pulled up next to the boat.

Wendy took my place at the pedal-gear. I grabbed extra breathing bladders, crawled out, and swam into the patrol boat. I aimed my flashlight at it. The first body to greet me was a gray-coat holding a pistol, her leg pinned to the deck, and a bullet hole in her forehead. Nearby was a second armed gray-coat, also shot. Part of her skull was gone. Had Coarse-face shot her own agents? Was this a mutiny?

A third agent lay near the helm, a look of surprise on her face, along with two gunshot holes. I went below deck, expecting to see a cage with imprisoned girls. Thankfully, the cage was empty. I took a deep breath, realized I was wasting precious air, and held it.

There were no more bodies. The captain's quarters held electronic equipment, including a screen, weather monitors, and a Mesh-reader. I bundled them in a gray canvas bag and returned to the upper deck. The helm brimmed with expensive equipment allowed only to Antiquities agents. I pulled out what I could and added it all to my collection. Then I returned to the sub. That salvage could be worth a fortune in the right hands.

After I secured the electronics in the front of the sub, I remembered the artifacts nearby.

* * *

With limited visibility, it took a few moments to orient myself. From my many dives I'd developed a sixth sense of what I couldn't see, a mind-map that helped to locate sunken treasures.

Taking fresh breathing bladders, I swam toward the cave where I'd tucked the nine golden artifacts. I switched breathing bladders, walked the bulky objects to the patrol boat, and placed them in the captain's quarters. I took a tranquilizer gun and one of the gold statues, and returned to the sub, where I took the controls.

Wendy looked happy, yet worried. She pointed to the breathing bladders. We'd been down too long.

The motor struggled to move us off the bottom as it kicked up sediment all around. Earlier, I'd worried about surfacing too quickly and getting the bends. Now I feared we'd have to dump the electronics in order to make it.

We began to ascend. Our surroundings grew brighter until I saw the surface. There were no boats. Three gray uniforms floated above us, face down. I couldn't see faces well, but none looked like Coarse-face. I did the math. Five agents had scoured Mo-Mere's island. Three would have remained on the boat, so eight, maybe. There were three bodies with the boat, three here, and one sinking. That meant only the inspector had survived.

I turned the sub west as we rose and saw a lone figure swimming toward the nearest island. She might make it, too.

We motored to a spot between Coarse-face and the island. I kept the sub below and traded places with Wendy on the pedal-gear. With Kara's help, I climbed out and took the tranquilizer gun with me. Then I untied the ropes, freed the log-boat, and climbed in. The humid swamp air smelled sweet after hours of breathing through rubber tubes.

I checked the tranquilizer gun, loaded, and aimed it toward the inspector. Coarse-face swam in my direction with strong, determined strokes. She had a long way to go, but she was a Marginal, bred in these waters.

She surfaced for air, saw me, and stopped. "You?"

216

I made sure she saw the gun. "You used one of these on me and left me for the gators."

Coarse-face swam closer. "You aren't allowed to have weapons."

"And you aren't allowed to kidnap me, my friends, or my family." I maintained my distance.

"The Federation gives me authority."

"I don't. Now stop or I'll shoot."

Treading water, she took a deep breath. "You'd shoot a government agent? I don't think so."

"Are you willing to take the chance I'll miss?" I held up spare tranquilizer shells. "It's a horrible way to go, paralyzed and unable to protect yourself. Like leaving me for the gators."

"What do you want?"

"I want you and your friends to leave me alone. Leave those I care about alone. And return my sister, Colleen."

"I've already turned her over to the governor's staff," she said. "She's out of my control. If you're thinking of a bribe, Marisa already tried. I'm not interested. Surrender and make this easy on yourself."

"I'm holding the gun and you want *me* to surrender."

Coarse-face swam closer. "I'll see to it you get a good home in the Federation."

I paddled away. "You mean as a rat in one of your labs."

She looked stunned. "They only want some of your blood. Then I'll see you placed in a good home."

"You know how you can tell if an Antiquities agent is lying?" I said. "Words flow out of her mouth. I'm prepared to barter."

"I don't barter with criminals."

"Okay," I said. "How about this: You might want to salvage your patrol boat to hide evidence of murder and illegal artifact collection."

"What are you talking about?"

"You shot the ship's crew. The captain and two of the crew were pinned to the deck. Three float in the water, while one is sinking. You're the only survivor."

Treading water, Demarco lifted a pistol. "I'll shoot you, too, if I have to."

I pointed the tranquilizer gun at her head. "If you were going to shoot me, you would have done so already. I have a better idea. What if I salvage for you?"

"Salvage what?" Demarco gulped air.

"Your boat holds precious artifacts. If someone else discovers them, they're evidence of your motive for killing your crew."

Demarco's eyes narrowed. "Blackmail?"

"Insurance," I said. "If I salvage them for you, no one needs to know how you got them. In exchange, you'll leave me, Marisa Seville, and her students alone."

"The governor won't allow it."

"Then you'll have to be clever and stall her," I said. "If anyone interferes with my salvage or attempts to capture me, I'll trigger booby traps and destroy the entire collection. You'll get nothing."

"You're too sentimental to destroy them."

"At that point, I'd have nothing left to lose. Throw the gun over there." I pointed to deeper water, keeping my rifle aimed at her bobbing head.

She considered, and then tossed the gun. A bargain couldn't last, but maybe I could buy time.

"Okay," I said, "I'll throw you a rope. You climb in and paddle to the next island. Then you get out and call for help."

"With no communication device?"

"I'll provide one from your patrol boat. Every Sunday, I'll leave a package where I let you off. No one but you and I will ever know where your patrol boat is or what happened, unless you betray me. If you do, you'll never see another artifact. And I've got evidence that will show your boss what you've done."

Demarco swam to the log-boat. I pulled out my crossbow and notched an arrow. I held both bow and gun on the inspector.

"You know this is treason," she said.

"Only citizens can be accused of that. Now get in and paddle to that island or the deal is off."

She climbed into the log-boat.

I held up a gold statue of a woman in flowing gown, holding a flame over her head. It looked like the Statue of Liberty, except with a different face and a cylindrical opening on top of the head. They'd turned Liberty into a candleholder, some gaudy display of a pre-Collapse chieftain.

"What about this?" I asked. "At heart, you're a salvager, like me."

Her eyes widened until I thought they'd pop out of her head. I'd heard about poker faces. Hers would not have passed.

"Do we have a deal?" I asked.

Nodding, Demarco reached for the statue.

"Not until we reach shore. Otherwise, I'll toss this. Good luck finding the little bauble in the muck."

She took up the paddle and pulled us toward shore.

THIRTY-FOUR

I dropped Inspector Demarco in the island shallows with the golden statue. Then I headed west in the log-boat, which was soggy and slimy from dragging it to the depths, and from ferrying Coarse-face. Upon reaching the west end of the island, I saw the sub poorly hidden amid sunken vegetation. Wendy and Kara were refilling breathing bladders. I paddled to them.

Wendy hugged me so tightly I couldn't breathe. "I thought I'd drown. Those chains weighed so much." She sobbed. "You saved me again."

"We'll talk later. Do we have enough air to dive?"

She nodded.

I fastened the log-boat to the top of the sub, tucked Wendy and Kara inside with me, and dove into the middle of the channel. When it finally hit me what I'd done, I shook so hard I was glad for the exercise of pedaling. I couldn't be sure the inspector wouldn't send her patrols after me, along with bounty hunters, scavengers, and everyone else motivated by hunger. Yet she wouldn't dare send any divers into the area until she'd made sure no damning evidence remained.

I grabbed another breathing bladder. I didn't know where else to go, so we floated around Mo-Mere's island looking for patrols and froggies. We didn't see any. We reached the cove where we'd built the sub; the motorboat was next to the skiff. Not seeing any danger, I hid the sub in a cleft of rock south of my other log-boat.

I pulled electronic salvage from the sub while Wendy and Kara tied up the boat and sub to branches close to shore.

"I can't believe you got me to dive so deep." Wendy's eyes showed a mixture of excitement and fear. She trembled as she refilled the sub's breathing bladders.

"You're a cat with nine lives," Kara told me.

"Only one," I said, "and it won't be worth much if the inspector doesn't leave us alone."

We refilled the sub's air containers and carried the electronics up a narrow path toward the clearing around the cabins. I stopped, listened, and checked the path for traps. I scanned the sides of the island for boats and didn't see any. As a precaution, I notched an arrow into my crossbow with the safety on and slung it over my shoulder. I set down the electronic equipment, pulled the tranquilizer rifle forward, and headed across the clearing.

Carmen burst out of the main cabin, ran to us, and hugged me. "You're back! You made it." She let go and led her sister by the hand toward the cabin.

Mo-Mere stepped off the porch and joined us. She hugged me and then held me at arm's length. "You have grown up this summer." She clutched my hands. "I thought I'd lost you. Come on inside." Mo-Mere pulled me toward the cabin. "You're soaked. You'll wrinkle like an old woman."

I couldn't stop the tears. I'd been on adrenaline so long, fatigue took over. I melted into her.

Wendy followed the twins into the cabin to change. I held Mo-Mere back. "I did something so incredibly foolish."

"I know, dear."

"What do you mean, you know?"

"Shortwave radio. We rarely use it for fear patrols will home in on the signal, but it's been buzzing."

"About what?"

"About you, dear. It's not every day someone sinks an Antiquities patrol boat and confronts the chief inspector with one of her own tranquilizer guns."

I stared. "You saw that?"

She squeezed my hands. "I had friends watch with binoculars. You were quite brave today. Foolish, maybe, but clever."

"I don't think I accomplished anything." I stared at the puddle around my feet.

"We'll talk." She led me into my room. I clutched Colleen's

necklace and transferred it to a dry pair of canvas pants, which I put on along with other fresh clothing. As I changed, I told Mo-Mere all about diving, the patrol boat, and dead bodies.

"Demarco told me she turned down your offer," I said.

"It grabbed her attention, but the captain accused her of keeping artifacts instead of destroying them. Then there was shooting. Evidently, Demarco has enemies within Antiquities, though not the type who would be friendly toward us."

"I tried to make a deal with her," I said, "but we can't trust her."

"No, dear, but we can trust her greed."

I gave her a puzzled look. "How much do you know?"

A sly smile creased her face. "Would you like to see pictures?"

"Mo-Mere? Really?"

"We have images of Demarco taking a bribe," Mo-Mere said. "We can't see who she took it from, just another Marginal in green canvas, but the inspector's face is clear. When she gets online, she'll see these."

"So she'll leave us alone?"

"No, dear. The governor still insists they bring you in to help solve their fertility crisis. You have a unique gene mutation they can't duplicate in the lab. Even Colleen doesn't have it."

"But she's my sister," I said.

"Only identical twins have the same genes. Even then, epigenetics causes genes to express differently."

"You've known all along?"

"Only that you're a very special girl," Mo-Mere said. "I wasn't sure about the genes until Demarco confirmed it."

"Why did she kill all those agents and let us live?"

Mo-Mere laughed. "Always full of questions. Greed got the better of her. The captain and crew mutinied around the time you sank their boat. Demarco used the sinking to her advantage and killed them. By the way, sinking her ship saved us. The other agents might have arrested Demarco and taken Wendy and me. I can't thank you enough. How did you do it?"

"I used the drill from making the sub," I said. "Now what?"

"We wait. If anyone other than Demarco recovers her ship's recorder and finds out anything damaging about her, the governor could replace her with someone worse. Or the governor might force Demarco to turn us in. It also depends on how well we've tapped into her greed."

"What if we had the ship's recorder?"

"Regina, is that what you brought home?"

I nodded.

"It has a tracking device," she said. "We need to disable it."

* * *

I followed Mo-Mere to the clearing. She picked up the ship's recorder and used her belt-knife screwdriver to open the waterproof panel. She removed the battery and behind that, the tracking device. I took the little chip to the north side of the island, wedged it into a sliver of bark, and tossed it out into the channel. Then we gathered the rest of the electronics.

"You have Demarco's Mesh-reader, I see." Mo-Mere opened the device and activated it. "Doesn't look password protected, either. Let's secure this in the cellar of the other cabin. I can't believe you took these."

"Stupid, eh?"

"The ship's recorder tracking chip was a gamble, maybe, but this could be very useful to your education." She opened the door to the other cabin. It was the mirror image of the first, right down to the wood-burning stove.

"You've been a clever girl today," Mo-Mere said. She pushed the stove aside to reveal a metal pan, made to look like a safety cover protecting the wood floor from embers. Pulling aside the cover revealed a dark opening like the one the twins and I had hidden in. I climbed down. She handed me the books, electronics, and a flashlight. This cellar brimmed with dozens of packages like the books I'd brought. I wanted to fill her library with what I'd seen.

"We'll get you and the twins situated to sleep in the other cellar," Mo-Mere said. "Then we'll need your puzzle-solving skills to break into Demarco's files. They should be rather illuminating."

I climbed out of the cellar and helped her reset the panel and wood stove. "Demarco said she couldn't help me with Colleen."

"I know, dear. She claims to have turned your sister over to the governor's labs, probably to test blood, DNA, and tissue samples. She claimed your sister would be cared for, though I doubt Colleen will see daylight until they've taken what they can from her."

"Then they'll throw her away like so much garbage," I said.

"I don't think so. They'll keep her alive to mine her genes. As for your friends, Demarco confirmed she took Jasmine and Aimee to Elite farms as housemaids. It's better than the other options."

"Sounds like prison to me."

"Demarco claims she helps our girls by placing them in the best possible homes," Mo-Mere said, "before the coastline disappears altogether."

"Do you believe her?"

"She believes her clever rationalization."

"What about my mom?" I asked.

"From what I've pieced together, she did work part-time for Antiquities, under an assumed name."

"Why?" I asked.

"As a spy. It allowed her access to information to help you, Colleen, and her friends. I often wondered where she got some of her insights. She was the first to alert us to the severity of the storm. After all, patrol boats have the best weather trackers."

"She left us."

"Your mother knew how bad the storm would be," Mo-Mere said. "She knew I'd look for you and Colleen. She must have believed she could best help you both from the helm of a patrol boat."

"That doesn't forgive her not coming for us."

"She got word to me, buried in the recent radio chatter. After Vera's boat crashed, your mother put all her energies into helping Colleen, as I'd suspected. She knows you're as safe as can be here, and that contacting you would put you in danger. Colleen has no one."

"Mom's trying to get into the Federation to find her?"

"She used Demarco's connections to cross after the storm. That's why she can't come for you. If your mother were here, wouldn't you want her to help Colleen?"

"I suppose."

"No suppose about it. Don't judge her too harshly, and don't try to look for Colleen. That would compromise what your mother is doing."

"Can I talk to her?"

Mo-Mere shook her head, her eyes filled with sadness. "She

took on a new identity. If anyone connects her to you, she'll be trapped."

I fingered the turquoise necklace Mom had given Colleen and decided to wear it for them. Then I pulled out the bronze medallion with its strange symbols and squiggly lines.

"Where did you get that?" Mo-Mere lifted my hand for a better look.

"It was the only thing I could salvage from my home. Mom said it came from my donor mother. Is she the reason my genes are unique?"

"You'd better sit." She sat across from me at the kitchen table. "First, never let anyone see that medallion."

"What's going on? Why are you so upset?"

She wrapped my fingers around it. "I've seen this before. You don't want anyone to question you about it, especially now."

"Mo-Mere, you're scaring me. What's so special about these symbols?"

"What I'm about to tell you is sheer speculation," she said, "but it's an informed, educated guess. It explains a lot."

"What, Mo-Mere? Just say it."

"I don't think you have a donor mother."

"How's that possible?"

"I believe you have a donor father," she said.

"You mean those rumors …"

She opened my hand and pointed to a circle with an arrow. "That's the traditional symbol for men. A colony lived on a secluded island southeast of here. For a long time, Antiquities patrols killed males on sight, so we kept the colony hidden."

"That's where you learned about infrared shielding and all that?"

Mo-Mere nodded. "The Federation destroyed my ability to have children, or I would have."

"Had a child with one of them? What if it were a boy?"

"Boys were taken to the colony and raised there," Mo-Mere said. "The colony is gone. I've heard nothing in years, but your mother may have gone there to have you."

"And Colleen?"

"My guess is you have different donors. That's why your genes aren't the same."

"Why would you think I have a father?" I asked.

"That symbol. There was a man who gave such a memento to each woman he donated to. I believe the medallion came from him."

"I have half-sisters and maybe brothers?"

"Sisters, yes," Mo-Mere said. "Brothers, unlikely. Too hard to hide in the shrinking swamps. The Federation thought they could get by without men. Their EggFusion Fertilization process was successful for generations, but for some reason, the process is dying. Every attempt they've made to save it has failed."

"So they need males after all. Is there any way I could meet my father?"

"I doubt he's alive. If he is, I have no way to find him. You can't look, either. If you found him, you'd lead Demarco and others. Besides, it's only the speculation of an old woman. Even if I'm right, you might not find the right individual donor. Only a DNA test could prove that."

"And the Federation controls those," I said.

She nodded. "So you're stuck with me for the time being."

I hugged Mo-Mere. "I like having you as a mom, even if you aren't my biological one. I'll try to behave better if you'll let me be more helpful to earn my keep."

"You did today. Come on, we don't want the others worrying."

I took Mo-Mere's hand and followed her into the other cabin with Wendy and the twins. It felt good to be home.

* * *

Humiliation didn't begin to sum up how Demarco felt, dripping wet, on a rocky beach, calling for help. Nothing could be more humiliating than a fifteen-year-old Marginal swamp rat outsmarting you. It took one to know one. While she admired Regina, the inspector wished she had her tranquilizer gun while Regina paddled away. Demarco had been so close. She'd even pressed the flesh in a handshake to consummate the deal.

She'd considered trying to overpower the girl, but she couldn't because of the risk of exposure. She faced other threats from within the Department. Regina turning over evidence would fuel that fire and bring enemies willing to kill for Demarco's job.

The inspector clutched the gold statue, worth a year's pay or two, and remembered the promise of more. She made the call. The second humiliation was having Captain Jenner pick her up. "Don't ask," was all Demarco could manage before she put the other agents ashore and went to the captain's quarters.

She took a deep breath before facing the governor. The ancient face bloomed across the wall-screen with a scowl that sent puffs of caked powder drifting onto her shoulders like dandruff.

"I was about to write you off," the governor said, "and appoint a new chief inspector."

Demarco sucked in between her teeth. "A spot of trouble, Your Majesty. Pirates sank our boat, killing the crew. I barely survived."

"Yet here you are. Isn't the captain supposed to go down with the ship?"

"She did, Your Majesty. She gave her life for the cause." Demarco smiled, proud of her Marginal ability to endure.

"What news on my DNA subject? Do you have her?"

"I have something much more interesting, Your Majesty. I believe we could have a museum find superior to what fell out of the Smithsonian."

"I don't give a rat's rump about trinkets. Do you have the girl?"

"I believe there may be other girls who can provide the DNA we need."

"Then bring them."

"It's a delicate matter, Your Majesty. We might grab one girl now who could disappoint as Colleen has, or allow my plan to unfold to give us a dozen to ensure success and diversity."

The governor chewed on that. Her face contorted like an old relic scarred by time. "Don't screw this up. Your career and your life, depend on it."

Demarco nodded and bowed her head. *As does yours, it seems.* The inspector might have chosen differently if she'd had more to gain and less to lose by helping the governor. She kept that to herself.

PEOPLE

Colleen Shen: Regina Shen's twelve-year-old sister.

Fran: Marginal girl Regina meets as a result of the storm.

Gina Wilmette: Governor of North America and Grand Old Dame.

Joanne Demarco: Chief inspector of the Department of Antiquities. Born Marginal, she has high ambitions and Governor Wilmette's ear.

Mo-Mere (aka Marisa Seville): Regina's teacher and mentor. Born in the Federation, she was cast out as a Marginal many years earlier.

Regina Shen: Chinese/Hispanic Marginal girl living in the Richmond Swamps.

Wendy: Student with Regina under Mo-Mere.

Zola Shen: Regina's mom, born in the Federation and cast out as a Marginal.

TERMS

ACM: After Community Movement, beginning of calendar for the Federation.

Caste system:
- ➤ Grand Old Dames (GODs): Founders of the Community Movement, they now rule. They've been kept alive for 300+ years with expensive medical miracles.
- ➤ Elites: Serve Grand Old Dames as senior government and business leaders.
- ➤ Professionals: University educated, they serve Elites by providing professional services.
- ➤ Working Stiffs: Workers on farms and in factories and mines. They do physical labor.
- ➤ Marginals: Outcasts forced to live on the seaward side of Great Barrier Walls, in sinking swamps.

Community Movement: Restored civilization and created the World Federation with New Harmony and a caste system in which men have been extinct for centuries.

Department of Antiquities (DOA): Responsible for preserving official historical records and destroying opposing information and pre-Collapse artifacts for the World Federation.

Great Barrier Walls: Concrete walls built around all continents to hold back rising seas.

Great Collapse: Occurred 300 years earlier as a result of abrupt climate change, rising seas, and open warfare.

Mesh: Their controlled internet where all information is in the Mesh-cloud controlled by the Department of Antiquities.

New Harmony: Guiding principle that harmony is the most important value. Used to justify and perpetuate the caste system.

Sky-jumper: Vertical-take-off-and-landing aircraft used by DOA.

World Federation: Controls the world through continental governors.

ACKNOWLEDGMENTS

I want to thank all those people who inspired and helped me along this journey. I want to thank my wife, Sue, for her support. I am grateful to my writing groups for their input over the years: The Troubadours, The Barrington Writers Workshop, and the Algonquin Area Writers Group. I especially wish to thank my editors, Leah Carson and Laurie Laliberte, for their patience and diligence in helping to make this a better story.

OTHER STORIES BY LANCE ERLICK

THE REBEL WITHIN (Rebel Series book 1)
Annabelle Scott is out of step with her post-Second Civil War society. The government exiles, quarantines and forces males to fight to the death to train the military elite. It's the same regime that took her biological parents when she was three, an ache that won't go away. She can't burden her adoptive mother or beloved younger sister with her need to find her birth mother—or her attraction to Morgan, a handsome redheaded boy she spies at a local prison.

Pressured into enlisting in the elite military to capture escaped boys, Annabelle rebels by helping Morgan escape. Now she must survive training with gung-ho recruits while she continues to help Morgan and hunt for her imprisoned birth mother, all without destroying her relationship with her sister, endangering her mother, or landing in prison or exile.

THE REBEL TRAP (Rebel Series book 2)
Voices in Annabelle Scott's head aren't God or signs she's going mad—yet. Despite being a Mech Warrior recruit, she rebels against her female-dominated régime by not only refusing to kill Morgan, a handsome boy she's attracted to, but also helping him escape.

Annabelle's commander gives her auditory implants and contact cameras for an undercover assignment to investigate her corrupt police captain. Morgan hacks the implants to plead for her help in freeing his brother. As a pawn in a bigger game, she wants to help Morgan yet needs to discover the link between an attempted assassination of her adoptive mom, her police captain, and the geek institute that holds Morgan's brother. Can she do so without falling into a trap that could destroy her family and get her killed?

Written as a standalone story, *The Rebel Trap* follows Annabelle's adventures from *The Rebel Within*.

REBELS DIVIDED (Rebel Series book 3)

The first time Geo Shaw sees Annabelle Scott, they meet as enemies and she doesn't kill him, which mystifies them both. It's after the Second American Civil War with the nation divided into the all-female Federal Union and the warlord controlled Outland.

When the Outland warlord kidnaps Annabelle and her beloved sister, and then kills Geo's father, Annabelle and Geo are thrown together. Can they overcome mutual distrust and work together to rescue her sister and gain justice for his father's murder? And will their feelings for each other derail or further their goals?

Written as a standalone story, *Rebels Divided* is also part of the Rebel series, three years later.

MAIDEN VOYAGE (short story)

Security Chief Nina Rekovic reluctantly followed her lover to join the crew of the all-female Maiden's Ark, which left Earth five years earlier. Her job is to maintain the peace threatened by Returners who feel deceived and grumble against the autocratic captain who financed the voyage.

A distress signal says Earth is lost, stranding lunar and asteroid colonists. Someone sabotages the Ark's vital fertility lab, which is blamed on Returners. Rekovic gets cryptic messages that could be help or part of a trap. While treading a fine line between Returners she sympathizes with, the dictatorial captain who doesn't trust her, and her estranged lover who betrays her, can Rekovic solve the conspiracy before she's imprisoned or worse?

WATCHING YOU (short story)

At the intersection of pervasive networks and the Patriot Act, we have the ability and some say the obligation to know everything about everyone. Can privacy survive? Can the individual endure?

Harold is a second-class citizen and a low-level worker in a government surveillance system charged with reviewing "criminal activity." He has private thoughts about a woman he's forbidden from approaching. He will not be deterred.

ABOUT THE AUTHOR

Lance Erlick grew up in various parts of the United States and Europe. He took to stories as his anchor and was inspired by his father's engineering work on cutting-edge aerospace projects to look to the future. He writes science fiction, dystopian and young adult stories and likes to explore the future implications of social and technological trends. He is the author of *The Rebel Within*, *The Rebel Trap*, and *Rebels Divided*, three books in the Rebel series. In those stories, he explores the effects of a world that discriminates against males and the consequences of following conscience for those coming of age. He is also the author of *Regina Shen: Resilience*. This is the first novel in a new series that takes place after abrupt climate change has led to a Global Collapse and a new World Federation.

Find out more about the author and his work at LanceErlick.com. Go to that website to sign up to receive occasional email newsletters with links to free short stories, and updates on new releases and other writing developments.

Made in the USA
San Bernardino, CA
25 March 2015